GEM

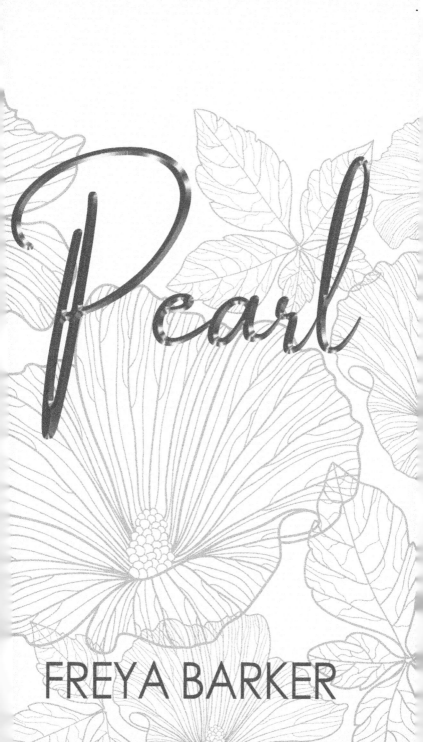

Pearl

FREYA BARKER

PEARL

ISBN: 9781988733852

Cover Design: Freya Barker
Editing: Karen Hrdlicka
Proofing: Joanne Thompson

GEM: a privately-funded organization operating independently in the search for—and the rescue and recovery of—missing and exploited children. Although, at times working in conjunction with law enforcement, GEM aims to ensure the victims receive justice... by whatever means necessary.

GEM Operator Pearl; layered, mysterious, a protector.
She masks as delicate, analyzes, and moves stealthily.

Hot on the trail of a young accomplice in a child exploitation ring, Pearl finds herself posing as a teenager to get close. Unfortunately, joining a group of kids on a wilderness quest means stepping out of her comfort zone and into uncertainty. But with the target in her sights her focus stays razor-sharp.

The last thing she needs is the dogged journalist who's been close on her heels catching up and rattling her cage. When he inserts himself into her investigation, she has no choice but to go along.

Thrown together in a mutual pursuit of justice, the negative energy between them sparks up in a new way.

PROLOGUE

"HI, JANEY. MY NAME IS SANDRA. I'M A SOCIAL worker with Child Protective Services."

I hear her voice but I don't want to turn around. I'm too embarrassed.

Stupid Billy Crocker and his big mouth. He's the reason the teacher brought me to see the school nurse, and now I'm in a heap of trouble. Even the principal got called in.

I should've worn my black sweatshirt, but it's been hot out for days and I was afraid I'd get laughed at. Hoping my back had scabbed over, I ended up putting on a T-shirt and kept my long hair loose.

That was a mistake.

Billy, who sits behind me in class, noticed blood on the back of my chair.

"Janey?" The nurse bends down in front of the bed I'm curled up on. "I'm going to show Sandra your back, okay?"

I squeeze my eyes closed when she reaches over me and pulls the sheet down. I'm mortified when I hear the other woman hiss between her teeth.

I've never looked at my back, but I've felt the ridges and scars my mother's switch left behind.

"Who did this to you, Janey?"

I PEEK OUT FROM UNDER THE SCRATCHY BLANKET AND look around the dark room.

It looks spooky, with only a little bit of moonlight coming in through the windows.

I share a bunk bed with Kate, another new girl here. She already picked the bottom bunk, so I took the top. I would've picked that one anyway, I feel safer up here.

We share the room with Rajani, who seems nice enough, even though I haven't said much to her. Or anyone else, really. There are five other girls who share the room next door, but they're all older and mostly ignore us.

The boys have a dorm room on the other side of the building and we're kept mostly separated, except at meal times.

It's only been four days since the social worker brought me here, but I already know I don't like it. Every day I have to meet with this woman for therapy. She's supposed to be a doctor, but she asks strange questions and makes me feel really uncomfortable.

There's also a guy—his name is Josh—and he runs

education and activity programs. Some of the kids seem afraid of him.

He gives me the creeps.

I'm pretty sure something weird is going on here.

ONE

PEARL

"You..."

Asshole. How the hell did he find me?

"Pearl, fancy meeting you here."

I'd like to wipe that arrogant smirk off his handsome face. What a waste of good looks.

"You're trespassing," I snap, pointing at the small sign indicating 'Private Beach.'

The beach house I'm staying at sits on a few acres of land with about two hundred yards of ocean frontage. GEM—the organization I work for—rented the place when the rest of my team joined me here on Grand Cayman a few weeks ago. The rental I had before only had one bedroom and was in George Town, near the airport. Nothing much to look at, unlike this house.

Sadly, I've spent most of my time here holed up inside, working. Raj, Kate, and Mitch—the rest of my team—headed back home yesterday, and I'm supposed to fly out in two days.

I stayed behind to follow up with the captain of a luxury yacht scheduled to be back sometime tomorrow from a two-week-long chartered trip around the Caribbean. The captain has eluded me for the two months I've been here—doing little more than dropping off a load of passengers and picking up the next before taking off again—but I plan to be at the dock when he shows up tomorrow. I'm not going to let him slip through my fingers again, but today, I'd promised myself a leisurely day on the beach.

Well, so much for that. There is no way I'll be relaxing with Lee Remington hovering over me.

The first time I met him was in a parking lot, and I gave him a bloody nose when my car door slammed in his face. That's by far my favorite memory of all the interactions we've had since then. The man just rubs me the wrong way.

Maybe it's because I suspect he's one of those guys who wouldn't hesitate to use the fact he's tall, dark, and good-looking to open doors for him. Or, perhaps, it's his job as a freelance journalist that doesn't sit well with me.

Another reporter who caught me in the parking lot outside the club I worked at in Cincinnati, many moons ago, had left a sour taste in my mouth. He claimed he was doing a story on an assault that had taken place behind the club a couple of days prior. I guess I'd still been a little naïve at the time and shared way too much with the guy. A few days later, a covert picture taken of me dancing inside the club was featured in a local newspaper, next to his article titled "Sex Trade in the City."

The bastard used my name as he blasted the industry. It cost me my fiancé, my job, and quite a few friends I'd made.

So yeah, I'm not a fan and I have a really long memory.

I huff when Lee wordlessly plops down in the sand beside me, looping his arms around his knees. I'm trying hard not to notice how he looks even better in cargo shorts and a well-washed Pink Floyd shirt than he does in jeans.

"I don't recall inviting you."

He turns his head and grins at me. His eyes are hidden behind the shades he's wearing, but I swear I can feel him scrutinizing me.

"I bumped into Mitch and your friends at the airport when I was getting in yesterday. They told me to check in on you."

"Bullshit," I grumble, wrapping my towel around me.

Although...I wouldn't exactly put it past either Kate or Raj to send him by to needle me. They know how I feel about the man.

"What are you doing in the Caymans anyway?"

"I'm not allowed to have a vacation?"

I roll my eyes at him. He's as likely to take a vacation as I am. There's a reason he's here.

He stretches his long legs, crossing them at the ankles, getting comfortable. His dark skin gleams in the sun, mocking my almost pasty complexion. I've barely caught any rays while here, having spent most of my time inside behind the computer.

"Sorry, not buying it."

I get up, tying my towel tightly around me as I gather up my things. The man makes me uncomfortable, and I've got better things to do than hang out on the beach with him.

"Where are you going?"

"Some of us have work to do."

I know I'm being snippy, but Remington brings it out in me. It doesn't deter him from jumping to his feet and following me back to the house.

"You're meeting with Robert Justice tomorrow," he states casually, stopping me in my tracks.

"How would you know that?" I ask suspiciously.

I'd be shocked if my teammates shared my hopes of intercepting the captain at the dock.

He shrugs, turning his eyes to the endless blue ocean.

"I'm here to talk to him and assume, since you're not on the flight with the rest of your team, you're hanging around for the same reason."

It shouldn't surprise me Remington is chasing down the same leads I am. The big difference is he's chasing a story for a byline, while we're chasing down criminals to make sure they receive justice. Not exactly the same objective. Although, I grudgingly admit his knowledge came in handy earlier this year when we managed to shut down a youth center in Lanark, Kentucky.

Several teenagers had gone missing and we uncovered what can only be described as a ring of sexual predators.

What had been a shock was finding Josh Kendrick at the helm. A man who was supposed to have died twenty years ago.

Oh, he was using an alias and his appearance had changed dramatically over the years, but Kate, who'd been at the center posing as Opal Berry—her cover name—recognized his voice immediately.

You'd think, after two decades, the sound of a voice would be hard to remember, but I don't think any of us would ever forget Kendrick's voice.

The man is dead now, his center shut down, and the sick perverts using his services are in jail and awaiting trial, but we have reason to believe this case was only the tip of the iceberg.

It's why I ended up in the Caymans, following a lead by the name of Jesper Olson. He'd gone missing from the center as well, however, we discovered later he was not a victim but rather part of the plot, acting as a decoy to lure the other kids.

Jesper ended up on the islands where I tracked him down. He was working on the *Distant Promise*, the yacht captained by Robert Justice, but sometime in the past few weeks the boy disappeared again.

I suspect he may have been dropped off somewhere during the yacht's previous cruise, which is why I need to talk to the captain.

Alone.

Lee

I watch her stomp off.

Although, with her small feet sinking into the fine beach sand, it doesn't really have the required effect.

As small as the woman is, I know better than to underestimate her. The one and only time I did, I ended up on my ass. That tiny package packs a big punch in more ways than one.

You'd think someone who weighs significantly less than what I bench press wouldn't be able to take down a man twice her size, but you'd be wrong. Pearl looks deceivingly young and innocent with those delicate features and funky, angled, bob haircut.

I don't bother following her, knowing I'd undoubtedly get the door to the beach house slammed in my face. She's prickly, to put it mildly, which is why I opt not to share how I ended up here. Given that it was Jacob, her boss, who asked me to come and, apparently, he didn't share that with her, I can only assume she wouldn't be happy.

He's touched base with me from time to time these past months, looking for the same answers I am. Recognizing the mutual benefit to sharing information, I've been keeping him abreast of any progress I've made and vice versa.

Even though I'm not sure what his motivations are, our objectives seem to run parallel: to bring down the three individuals responsible for atrocities that took place two decades ago. Including the murder of my mother, who'd been a housekeeper at Transition House—a youth home at the center of the depravities—and was killed for what she knew.

Transition House burned down, its management supposedly having perished in the fire, but I've always had my suspicions around that. With good reason, as it turned out. Josh Kendrick—once program manager for Transition House—appeared back in Lanark as the director of the new youth center.

The sick bastard wasn't back for long though. If he hadn't made the mistake of kidnapping the daughter of an FBI agent, he might've gotten away and started up shop elsewhere, but Opal—another GEM operator—took him out.

One down, two more to go.

I get to my feet and wipe the sand off my ass. I'm hungry and could go for some conch fritters. For a second, I wonder if I should ask Pearl along to try and break the ice, but I'm pretty sure that would be wasted energy.

I'll catch up with her tomorrow morning at the dock.

———

I CAN'T HEAR WHAT SHE MUMBLES UNDER HER breath when I saunter onto the dock, but I have no doubt it's far from complimentary.

Pearl's almost-black eyes regard me with disdain.

"You're going to be in the way."

I shrug. "Who knows? I could be useful. I understand you haven't had much luck so far."

Her scowl makes it clear she's not happy with the reminder.

"You think you can do better because you're a man?"

"Yes, I do," I tell her honestly.

It just so happens, in this case, being a man—a Black one at that—he is more likely to talk to me than he would to an Asian woman. Not because I think I'm superior, but Robert Justice might.

It's on my tongue to tell her Jacob Branch called me for that exact reason, but with the yacht coming around the end of the pier, this might not be the best time to get into that.

Pearl caught sight of it as well and spreads her stance, folding her arms over her chest as we wait for the ship to dock. I catch the older man eyeing her suspiciously as he orders his crew to fasten the lines.

The moment he sets foot on the dock, Pearl marches up to him, determined not to let him pass her by.

"Excuse me, Robert Justice?"

"*Wah gwaan,*" I interrupt, asking the man how he's doing as I brush by her and hold out my hand.

With his narrowed eyes still on Pearl, he accepts the shake.

"*Wah duh yuh want?*"

"*Lee Remington, mi ah journalist,*" I introduce myself. "*Mi a luk fah information, cyaah wi talk?*"

I can feel the steam coming off Pearl, but I ignore her as I follow Justice, who starts walking toward the small office building at the end of the dock.

"*Mi know nutten,*" he mutters, trying to cut me off.

"Eh bout Martin Duyvenvoorde he wuk fi yuh."

At the mention of his employee—the name Jesper Olson used here in the Caymans—he glares at me with guarded eyes.

"Nah nuh muh," he responds.

Maybe not anymore, but we know he went out on the previous cruise as part of the crew.

It takes a bit to get him to admit the kid debarked in Florida three weeks ago, but that's about as much as I can get out of him.

Last year, his yacht was chartered by a company by the name of Glan Development, but the moment I mention that name he blanches, shutting me down.

"Deh ask tuh bai questions a dangerous," he warns me before he shuts the door in my face.

He's obviously scared and I don't blame him.

Glan Development is a subsidiary of Glan Industries, which is part of an almost impenetrable network of shell companies I've tried to untangle.

Pure Caribbean is another one we found when following the flow of illegal funds. This company has a physical address here on Grand Cayman, but there's nothing but a run-down, empty warehouse. The moneys handed over by rich fuckers paying for the sexual exploitation of minors landed in Pure Caribbean's local bank account, where due to Cayman banking laws it is shielded.

These people are sick and ruthless. They have money, connections, and will do anything to protect those interests and their own asses. They wouldn't flinch at killing Robert Justice or anyone else for that matter.

"Of course you speak Patois," Pearl snarls when I turn to her.

"Jamaican born," I explain.

Portmore, Jamaica, to be more specific, although I did most of my growing up in Kentucky. My mother moved us there when I was only three but continued to speak Patois at home.

"What did he say?"

"The kid was dropped off on Key West. That's all he was willing to tell me."

"He's back in the U.S.?"

"So it seems."

She mutters a string of unladylike expletives before she turns on her heel and heads for the parking lot.

"Hey!" I call, jogging after her. "Wanna grab some lunch? I know a place—"

"I have to pack," she evades, already getting into her rental vehicle.

Of course she has an excuse ready.

Don't know why I even bother trying to be friendly, she obviously hates my guts.

TWO

PEARL

A foul odor hits me when I open the door to my apartment.

Dropping my bags, I rush to the kitchen to open the sliding door to my little patio and the window over the sink.

Gross.

I was so sure I'd gotten rid of any perishables before I left over two months ago. There's nothing in the sink and I remember taking out the garbage.

When I pull open the fridge the stench almost knocks me on my ass. What looks like a biological experiment exploded inside.

Dammit, they must've had a power outage, because what I assumed could survive for a while in the fridge, clearly hasn't.

The freezer compartment is even worse and I quickly shut the door again.

First, I need to get some airflow in here. I turn on the fan over the stove, open the sliding door, and head for the bedrooms and bathroom to open the windows there.

So much for getting laundry started and making a pot of coffee before hopping on my computer to pick up the trail on the Olson kid.

I had my return flight home changed to one going to Key West, where I spent the past few days tracking down Jesper. My first target had been the harbor where he must've gotten off the boat, flashing his picture at anyone working there or at any of the businesses around. After two days of pounding the pavement, I finally hit pay dirt at the Sunset Tiki Bar and Grill, where a waitress thought she recognized him from a few weeks ago. She remembered carding him when he asked for a beer.

He had a Cayman driver's license, which showed him to be twenty-three. Unfortunately, she couldn't recall the name on the license, but did point out his hair was dark, not blond like in the picture I showed her. Of course, he paid cash for his meal, which wasn't helpful.

The most useful piece of information I got from the girl was he'd asked about the nearest Greyhound station, and she directed him to the one right at the airport.

The attendant there wasn't much help. She was a stickler for rules and wasn't impressed with the private investigator's license Jacob has us all carry. She did mention the only way I'd be able to get access to their information or security camera feed was if I was law enforcement with a warrant.

Little does she know I don't need a warrant, I just need some time and my computer to access that information, so I hopped on the first flight home.

However, instead of settling into my task, I now have to dig up a pair of rubber gloves, a garbage bag, and a bottle of bleach to clean the damn fridge.

Vile.

I'm surprised the neighbors either beside me or upstairs haven't complained about the smell, which still lingers after an hour and a half of emptying and scrubbing the fridge.

Of course, just as I'm sitting down in my office with a cup of coffee, my first load of laundry in the washer, my damn phone rings.

"How are the Keys?" my friend, Kate, asks.

I sigh, and lean back in my chair.

"I'm sure they're wonderful, but I wouldn't know. I just got home."

"No luck?"

"I didn't say that." I take a fortifying sip of my coffee. "I have reason to believe Olson took a Greyhound bus from the airport in Key West, but the woman at the counter wasn't very forthcoming. He could be anywhere by now, so rather than waste time spinning my wheels there, I decided to come home. I've got everything I need here to do a little digging."

"You mean hacking," she scoffs.

"Potato, potahto," I fire back.

"Did you at least get a chance to enjoy the beach for a few days in the Caymans?"

It's my turn to scoff.

"Ha. You know I didn't."

"I guess Remington caught up with you?"

"Yeah. Thanks, by the way, for giving him the address."

"Hey, that wasn't us. He already knew where to find you."

"How?"

"I figured it was Jacob. He's the only other one who could've given it to him."

Jacob? Why the hell would he do that?

"That doesn't make sense."

"It may to Jacob. You know how he is."

I do. Our boss is a bit of an enigma.

None of us have ever met him in person. The man hides behind a voice and what I suspect is a fake identity. To this day, I haven't been able to put a face to the name, but his identity is tight. Lord knows I've tried to find a crack in his cover but without result.

"So...how did it go?" she presses.

"As expected, he was arrogant, inserted himself into my investigation, and basically took over. I blew him off when he wanted to sit down and pick my brain over lunch. He's a menace."

I still get riled up thinking about Lee Remington, which I do too much of as it is.

"I'm not sure you're reading his motivations correctly," Kate suggests carefully.

Why is everyone trying to make the animosity perco-
lating between Remington and me into something else?
It's ridiculous.

"Oh, I think I am. He'll do anything to prove himself
superior, I don't think he's ever gotten over the fact I
knocked him on his ass," I protest.

I ignore her sounds of disagreement and abruptly
change the subject. Enough about him.

"Were you calling with news?"

She chuckles softly, but thankfully gets down to
business.

"Yes, actually. Mitch and I are heading out to Huntington, West Virginia. A thirteen-year-old girl went
missing last week. Police have treated it like a runaway
since she's apparently run before, but according to the
parents—who   contacted   us   in   desperation—their
daughter was doing much better in recent months."

"Parents don't always have the insight they think they
do," I observe.

"True, but show me a child who'd willingly leave
behind the brand-new puppy the family just picked up
for her, the weekend before she disappeared."

Hmm. That does seem a bit of a stretch. Unless, of
course, the parents had something to do with her disappearance.

"You want me to do a little digging into the family?"

"Would you? I'll email over what details I have.
Names of friends, teachers, family members. See if
anything interesting pops up?"

Jesper Olson will have to wait, but his trail is already a

couple of weeks old anyway. Finding this girl is more urgent.

"What's her name?"

"Amelia Sherwood."

My computer beeps with an incoming email from Kate. I click on it, and the first thing that pops up is a picture of a pretty, young girl underneath the dyed black hair and dark eye makeup. Her attitude jumps off the image. Thirteen and scowling at the camera.

There's something nagging at the back of my mind.

"Sherwood...why does that name sound familiar?" I want to know.

"Remember that case in Huntington a few years ago of a soccer coach molesting girls on his team?"

He'd not only molested them; he'd filmed his actions and posted it on a website for pedophiles. The guy didn't last long in jail, he was shanked in the dining hall during a scuffle. Even the most hardened criminals have little tolerance for child abusers.

"Donald Sherwood. Yeah, now I remember. Any relation to our missing girl?"

"Her uncle."

"No shit? Wow. That must've been hard on the family."

"You're not kidding," Kate agrees. "Especially since Amelia was on his team."

I look at the image again, this time with a better understanding of the unhappy girl depicted.

"Don't tell me..."

"Oh yeah," she confirms my unfinished thought. "I think she may have been one of his victims."

Lee

On a normal day, it's only a two-hour drive to Huntington, but I've been on the road for almost four hours and I'm only now crossing state lines.

An accident on Interstate 64 just outside Grayson closed all eastbound lanes of the highway and all traffic was diverted onto county roads, causing congestion there.

I wouldn't have known about the missing girl if Mark Bailey, an editor at the *Charleston Gazette,* hadn't called me. The *Gazette* was one of the newspapers that bought the story I wrote on Donald Sherwood a couple of years ago. I'd attended that trial from opening statements through to the verdict.

While I was doing background research, I discovered Sherwood's own niece had been on the soccer team. I had contact with the parents a few times but at their request, kept theirs and their daughter's name out of my article.

Even though they never admitted it, I wondered if the girl had been one of Sherwood's victims as well. I remember her, a little thing with long blond hair and a weary look in her eyes I felt was out of place for a girl her age.

Now, years later, that girl is missing, and Mark wanted to know, since I'd dealt with her parents before, if I'd be interested in checking out her disappearance.

He was able to send me a copy of the police report, made eight days ago, when Amelia went missing. The picture supplied of the thirteen-year-old threw me for a minute. She'd changed her appearance drastically, which shouldn't really be that surprising. She's not the only sexual abuse victim to reinvent herself.

I turn into the Ritter Park neighborhood with its familiar cobblestone roads. The address listed on the police report hasn't changed over the past few years. I pull my Highlander up to the curb in front of the vaguely familiar, older, two-story house.

The Sherwoods still live only two blocks from the seventy-five-acre municipal park. Wouldn't be too hard to get lost in if you wanted to.

"Lee?"

Derek Sherwood is clearly confused to find me on his doorstep. I'm a little taken aback he seems to not only recognize me but still remembers my name. It's not like we've kept in touch over the years.

He grabs my hand and shakes it hard.

"I heard about Amelia."

His expression immediately falls and I notice the strain on his face. He looks like he hasn't slept in a week, which doesn't surprise me.

"Come in." He steps aside and waves me through. "Maggie has taken a sedative and is taking a nap," he says as he leads me into an uncharacteristically messy living room.

The last time I was here, I recall the house being meticulous.

"I'm sorry for the mess," Derek mutters, clearing a blanket and some random items of clothing to make room for me on the couch. "Can I get you a coffee? Something else to drink?"

"No thanks, I'm fine. I'm sure you've been over this a hundred times already, but could you tell me what happened? I'd like to help if I can."

Sighing deeply, he takes a seat on the edge of a recliner, dropping his head in his hands.

"Maggie had already left for work and I was getting ready to head out. Amelia wasn't up yet. She'd started having a hard time getting out of bed in the mornings."

"Not unusual for a teenager," I offer.

He glances up at me.

"No, I guess not. Anyway," he continues. "I knocked on her bedroom door, didn't get an answer, so I went inside. She wasn't there. I noticed her bed was made, which seemed odd."

"That her bed was made?" I prompt him when his eyes drift over my shoulder, likely reliving those moments in his mind.

He nods. "Yeah. Amelia never makes her bed; Maggie usually does when she comes home around noon for lunch. It's an ongoing argument between them," he explains. "Anyway, her backpack—the one she takes to school every day—was gone."

"So you figured she may have left early?"

The eyes he fixes on me are pained as he shakes his head.

"See that's just it, her books were piled up on her desk and the school bus wouldn't be there for another fifteen minutes. I knew something was off so I called Maggie, and she said she hadn't seen her or been in her room that morning. I searched all around the house and then I walked to her bus stop and asked a few kids who were waiting there if they'd seen her. By the time I got back, Maggie was already pulling into the driveway."

He gets to his feet and starts moving around the room, pacing.

"When did you decide to call the police?" I ask gently.

"A few hours later. Maggie searched her room and noticed some things gone; a few clothes, a couple of toiletries, a picture of our old dog, Buddy—he died last year—her diary, and a small jewelry box my mom gave her for her ninth birthday."

"Sounds like those things were meaningful to her," I observe, and he nods in confirmation.

It would seem the girl packed her own things. So far it appears Amelia left under her own volition.

"I know what you're thinking," Sherwood comments. "Which is the same thing the police thought; that she'd run off. But Amelia left behind her phone and her iPad. She never went anywhere without her phone, and her iPad had become her lifeline these past months."

"She left them?"

"Yeah. Maggie checked to see who she might've talked to last, but all her data was removed from both the phone and the iPad. It looks like she did a factory reset on both."

Now that is interesting. The only reason I can think of for her to reset her electronics is to erase information she didn't want her parents to see, but wouldn't it have been easier just to take them with her?

"Is Amelia that tech savvy?" I inquire.

"I wouldn't have thought so. I mean, she's fast enough with her thumbs but any time she wanted a setting changed or a new set of earbuds added to connected devices, she'd ask me."

So maybe someone else did it, or walked the girl through it.

"I assume the police took the devices?"

These days law enforcement have different tools at their disposal to retrieve deleted files from electronics, even after a hard reset.

"No, they didn't, actually. The officer who showed up to take our report seemed convinced she'd turn up in a day or two. Only the last few days have they started taking things a bit more seriously. Probably after I called in a private organization to help me look for her."

"What organization is that?" I ask, already suspecting the answer.

"GEM. They search for missing kids," he confirms.

"I've heard of them."

"I handed over the iPad and the phone to them, just

the other day. They said they'd bring someone in who may be able to recover the data."

That would be Pearl Han, GEM's computer whiz.

A jolt of anticipation hits me at the thought of seeing her again.

THREE

Pearl

The parking lot of the TownePlace Suites is busy.

I do a few loops before I find a spot I like with enough room on either side, and back in. I don't want some idiot scratching my pretty, black-cherry paint with their door again, I just had my Chevy detailed.

The hotel Kate and Mitch are staying at isn't exactly top-of-the-line, but I can see why they picked it. It's on the outskirts of town, has easy access to the main road—both in and out of town—and is only a couple of miles from the Ritter Park area where the girl went missing.

I'd finally been able to tap into the security feed from the Greyhound bus station in Key West. Then I spent many hours scouring the video until I caught sight of a skinny, tall guy with the hood of his sweatshirt covering his head stepping up to the ticket counter.

Even early May in the Keys is too hot for a hoodie, so

he got my attention. A quick glimpse of his face when he turned around was enough to confirm it was Jesper Olson. The time stamp made it easier to check the feed from the other cameras, and I caught him getting onto the bus to Miami.

Unfortunately, that's where the trail ends. I watched him getting off at the bus station at the Miami airport and disappear in the crowd.

It's not sitting well with me that a now nineteen-year-old kid has me running around in circles. Which is why it was perfect timing when I got the call to join Kate and Mitch in Huntington. Maybe the change of scenery is what I need to clear my palate.

I grab my bags and head into the lobby, stopping at the front desk to check in to the room that connects to the suite the others are in.

My stomach starts growling when I drop my toiletries on the bathroom counter. I wanted to get here before dark and hoped there was a half-decent restaurant in the hotel, but apparently not. All they have are a few shelves of snack foods and a cooler with drinks in the lobby.

I did notice the Bob Evans just down the road, but couldn't bring myself to stop there for dinner. Let's just hope I can get Uber Eats or Grubhub delivery here.

A soft knock sounds from the other side of the connecting door and I quickly unlock it. Kate is standing on the threshold surrounded by the smell of melted cheese. My stomach responds immediately.

"You have food?"

She grins. "Gourmet pizza from this place called the Fox's Pizza Den. Mitch just picked it up."

She steps aside and waves me through. Mitch is standing by the table over a giant pizza box, loading a piece on a paper plate. The thick strands of cheese have my mouth watering.

I try to eat healthy but pizza is my Achilles' heel. I haven't encountered a pizza I could resist yet. I aim for the big box and grab a paper plate, bumping Mitch aside.

"Leave some for the rest of us," Kate requests as I load the third piece on my plate.

"Hungry," I mumble around my first bite of greasy goodness.

"Apparently," she complains. "And might I point out again how ridiculously unfair it is you can eat your weight in pizza without any consequences, yet all I have to do is take in the aroma and it goes straight to my ass."

"I happen to like your ass," Mitch comments from the couch.

"Oh, I know, honey. That's because—" Kate starts before I cut her off.

"Please, spare me. You'll just ruin my appetite," I protest with my hand up, palm out.

It doesn't stop Mitch from shooting a lascivious look at Kate.

Oh, *yuck*.

Don't get me wrong, I love Kate—and Mitch starting to grow on me—but I've had to live with these two lovebirds for a few weeks in the Caymans. I've intercepted googly eyes and witnessed PDAs more than I care to in my lifetime.

I take a seat on the desk chair in the sitting area and focus on my food.

"Mitch got you a Dr. Pepper," Kate announces, sliding a can in front of me.

My other guilty indulgence.

Okay, I guess Mitch is deserving of a spot on my list of favorite people.

"Thanks." I salute him with my can. "While we eat, want to get me up to speed?"

"Sure. Did Raj and Jacob brief you on the basics?" At my affirming nod he continues, "Unfortunately, we don't have a lot to add, other than local police really dropped the ball on this one. They dismissed the parents' concern and brushed it off as a runaway case. They didn't even bother taking her phone and iPad, which is how we ended up with them."

"We've been playing catch-up so far," Kate takes over. "The parents provided us with a list of Amelia's friends—a sadly short one, I might add—and we've been in touch with them. We've also been to her school, talked to her teachers and the school counselor. She concurred with the parents that in the past month or two Amelia had been picking up her grades and staying out of trouble."

"What caused the change?" I ask.

"The parents think it may have been the group trip during spring break they signed her up for," Mitch answers. "Some kind of character-building, wilderness quest recommended to them. Five days and nights at

Holly River State Park. Some Outward Bound type program for kids. It was run by an organization called Evolution Quest."

"Evolution Quest? Never heard of it," I note.

"I've come across the name during my time with CARD," Mitch shares. "They have an office in Charleston."

A few months ago, Mitch was still part of a Child Abduction Rapid Deployment team for the FBI's Violent Crimes Against Children unit. After his own daughter was abducted and subsequently rescued, he's handed in his badge and joined forces with GEM.

"Mitch says they put on these trips all over the country," Kate fills me in. "All geared toward kids who are struggling for one reason or another. It's supposed to boost confidence, teaches basic survival skills, problem-solving, teamwork, that kind of thing. Anyway, according to her parents—and it was confirmed by the school—Amelia seemed to have turned a corner after that, which is why they didn't believe she'd suddenly run off."

"We didn't get much else," Mitch observes. "Her two friends weren't really able to contribute much, other than Amelia hadn't really hung out much with them outside of school."

"All right, then let's see if we can get anything off her electronics."

I shove the last bite of my pizza in my mouth, wipe my hands on a napkin, and drop it and the paper plate in the trash can. Then I head through the connecting door and fetch my computer bag. Shoving aside the pizza box,

I set up my laptop and extra screen on the dining table and notice I left a cord in the Chevy.

"Shit, I have to go grab something from my car. Do you guys want something to drink? I'm going to hit the cooler in the lobby."

"We have water and a few beers in the mini-fridge," Kate shares.

"I'm going to need something more caffeinated. I'll be right back."

A few people are checking in when I walk through the lobby and out to the parking lot. I find the cord behind the front seat; it must have slipped from my computer bag. Tucking it in my pocket, I head back inside.

The lobby is empty now and I turn my attention to the cooler. No Dr. Pepper, but they do have bottled iced coffee. I grab three.

Then my eyes drift to the shelves.

With my arms full, I walk up to the front desk and deposit my selections, when I hear a deep rumbling voice.

"Planning a long night?"

I spin around to find Lee standing there, a duffel bag slung over his shoulder.

"You've got to be kidding me," I exclaim. "Do I need to get a restraining order?"

"Is there a problem?" the hotel clerk asks behind me.

Lee's eyes shoot over my shoulder and he flashes a grin.

"No problem," he assures him. "My friend gets a little testy when she hasn't had her daily intake of sugar, that's all."

Before I can protest, he steps around me and up to the desk.

"Why don't I take care of that," he announces and drops a few bills beside my loot. "She may need a bag to carry everything, and I called earlier for a room. The name is Remington."

Lee

I've never encountered a woman harboring so much piss and vinegar.

Except maybe my nana, but she was almost six feet tall and weighed nearly three-hundred pounds. Pearl comes in a much smaller package, but she packs a punch.

I'm starting to get a kick out of needling her.

She stomps off to the elevator, the heels of her boots sharp on the tile floor of the lobby. Back ramrod straight, her head high, and a sexy sway of her little ass encased in what I'm sure are designer jeans.

Yeah, Pearl Han definitely has my attention.

It's by pure chance I ended up here. After talking with Amelia's parents at length, I stopped in at the police station. The detective who had been handed the missing person report was out on a call. The desk sergeant handed me a card with Detective Battaglia's direct line, but warned me he might not get back to me right away.

The city has apparently been swamped with a recent surge of violent crimes, including three murders in the past week they suspect are related to renewed gang activity. I can see how Amelia's missing person report might land at the bottom of the pile, especially if there is no evidence found of any crime, and it looks like she may have walked out of the house under her own steam. I left a message with the detective, found a place to grab a bite, and checked around for convenient accommodations.

It shouldn't surprise me I happened to end up at the same hotel as the GEM team. I'm sure we were looking for similar attributes; accessibility, proximity, and outside downtown.

I'm glad the Sherwoods called in GEM, they'll need all the help they can get to bring their daughter home. I should probably give Jacob Branch a call, as a courtesy, to let him know I'll be looking into this case as well. Wouldn't be a bad thing to compare notes.

My room is nothing fancy, pretty generic, but it suits my purpose. A bed, a bathroom, a small sitting area, and a desk. I'm glad to see the small fridge and microwave, making a mental note to pick up some groceries to keep on hand. I might be here a while.

It takes no time at all to stuff my shit into the empty drawers. I grab one of the complimentary bottles of water and take a drink before I sit down on the small sofa, put my feet up on the coffee table, and dial Jacob.

"How's the weather in West Virginia?" is the first thing out of his mouth.

I chuckle.

"Either you're tracking me or you just got off the phone with a pissed-off operative."

"That woman does not like you."

"Tell me something I don't know."

"It's interesting though," he elaborates. *"Something you have to understand about Pearl; she's generally indifferent. To men, to people in general. She cares about the team, but that's about it. The fact she feels any kind of emotion—even negative ones—is telling."*

I mull on that for a moment, because each one of my encounters with Pearl has been highly charged.

"That is interesting since she strikes me as fiery and hot-blooded."

I hear Jacob chuckle softly.

"Exactly. Now, on to business," he firmly redirects. *"I assume you're in Huntington for the same reason we are, did the family contact you?"*

"No, but I know them. I covered the child molestation case—"

"The uncle?" he interrupts.

"Yes," I confirm. "I interviewed the family back then and talked to Amelia's parents again this afternoon. That's why I'm calling, they told me they'd been in touch with GEM."

"I see. Is this simply a story you're after?"

I can't blame him for making that assumption, but it still feels like a slight.

"My first concern is finding the girl," I reply with a bit of an edge. "She was nine years old when I last saw her, but even then, there was something about her that stuck with me. She was on the soccer team."

It's silent on the other end and I give Jacob time to connect the dots on his own.

"That never came out at the trial."

"Because no charges were filed on Amelia's behalf. The family never admitted to anything, but I always had a suspicion."

"Yes, I guess that would've been hard to come to terms with," Jacob observes.

I remember the pained look in Derek's eyes when I asked if they thought his brother had ever been inappropriate with Amelia. It had been his wife who'd quickly denied it.

I wonder what their response would be if I asked them now.

Jacob has the same idea. *"Perhaps they're more likely to open up about that now? It would be helpful information to have, it gives us a better picture of the girl."*

"I'll stop by tomorrow morning and let you know."

"Good idea. What room number are you?"

"Three fourteen."

"Okay, I'll get my team to share any information we come up with as well."

I'd love to be a fly on the wall when Pearl gets those instructions. I'm willing to bet she won't be happy.

Funny how life can work out sometimes. For years I've been trying to find answers for the questions my mother's murder left me with.

She knew things, had seen things while working at

Transition House in Lanark. She'd tried reporting them to law enforcement, but her suspicions had fallen to deaf ears. It was only a couple of weeks after the place burned to the ground, supposedly with the youth home's program supervisor, Josh Kendrick, its director, Dr. Elsbeth Sladky, and the facility's owner, David Wheeler, inside. I'd always had my doubts. Even more so since finding out none of the remains recovered were ever autopsied. I knew then someone in law enforcement must've been involved.

Earlier this year, I had confirmation when the program director for a new youth center in Lanark turned out to be none other than Josh Kendrick, albeit under an alias and with his features dramatically altered.

That had been my first run-in with GEM. They were instrumental in taking down Kendrick, who didn't survive, but there is evidence it didn't end with him. My gut says the other two are still out there somewhere and I'm not alone in that belief. Jacob Branch and his GEM team seem equally convinced.

I know now Opal was one of the kids who lived at Transition House at one point, and I've wondered a few times if Pearl may have been a victim as well. Unfortunately, the home's records were burned in the fire and other than a list of faceless names I found in my mother's things, there isn't much else to go on.

It wouldn't surprise me if the others have some kind of connection to Transition House as well. Especially since the one time I tried to ask Branch about GEM's interest in the people who ran the former children's home, he shut me down quickly.

If I want Pearl's history, I'm going to have to get it from her.

Fat chance of that.

FOUR

Pearl

"Jesus, Janey, go to bed."

I have to blink a few times to make out Kate's shape in the shadows. I've been staring at my bright screens in the dark room for hours.

"I was there already."

I don't bother mentioning I barely managed two hours of sleep, but that's not unusual. Not when I have work waiting for me, and especially when I'm not making much progress.

"For a hot minute," she scoffs, padding on bare feet to the coffee maker in the small kitchenette. "How old is this?"

"I don't know, an hour? Hour and a half?"

"I'll chance it."

She pours herself a cup and takes a seat across the table from me.

"Any luck?"

I lean back in my chair, stretch my arms over my head, and work out the kinks in my neck. I'm getting stiff from sitting so long.

"Still working on it, but I need some fuel other than just coffee." I already cleaned out the snack food I got from the lobby last night, but I need something more substantive and preferably healthier. "I think I'm going to head out to pick up some food. Can I get you guys anything?"

"No, no need. I'm waking Mitch up shortly anyway. With Lee talking to the parents this morning, I think we'll head out to Charleston, see if we can talk to someone at the Evolution Quest offices. We'll grab something on the way."

At the mention of Remington, some of the anger I felt last night returns. When I left the Caymans, I half expected he'd be hot on my tail to Key West but he never showed up.

Jacob called back after he spoke to him to let us know we'd be sharing information. Apparently, Lee already knew the family and Jacob felt he might be more successful getting information from them. Knowing I'm likely going to bump into him again leaves me feeling unsettled.

"Sounds good. I'll let you know if I find something," I promise her, heading for my room.

I quickly brush my teeth and run a comb through my hair. Then I change into jeans, put on my booties, grab my purse, and move to the door.

According to my GPS, the closest grocery store is just a few blocks from the hotel. It's still only five forty when I pull into the Kroger parking lot and I end up having to wait for twenty minutes until it opens. While I'm waiting in the Chevy, I notice lights come on in a diner across the street. Maybe I'll stop in to pick up a jumbo-sized coffee and breakfast on my way back.

I beeline it to the produce section and grab a salad kit, a few apples, and a bunch of grapes, then toss a couple of bottles of veggie juice in my basket. I head for the checkout lane by way of the dairy section where I pick up a few yogurts. That should tide me over for a bit.

Feeling moderately better—a little more in control—I manage a smile for the barely awake cashier.

Rationally, I know the normally tight rein I have on my food intake stems from the years I spent at Transition House. What I chose to eat had been the only power I had left. It gave me the illusion of having at least some dominion over my body.

For the most part, I've relaxed a bit since then, allowing myself the occasional indulgence, like I did last night. But then that man showed up, throwing me off-kilter, causing enough of a distraction it threw me off my game. Not even the few hours of sleep I managed got me back on track.

Sadly, it's the bag of groceries I dump on the passenger seat that gives me back a sense of control.

I zip across the street to the diner. The only other vehicle parked in front is a public works truck, and through the window I see the pair of city workers sitting in a booth.

"Morning!" the waitress chirps when I walk in and take a seat at the counter, my back to the door.

The woman—Sheila, according to her name tag—flips over the cup in front of me and holds up a carafe.

"Coffee?"

"Actually, can I get an extra-large one in a to-go cup? I'd also like to order an egg white omelet to go. With spinach and feta, if you have it?"

"Sure thing." Her eyes slide over my shoulder at the sound of the bell attached to the top of the door. "Have a seat, I'll be right with you," she calls out to whoever just walked in.

I know even before the stool scrapes over the linoleum floor who is sitting beside me. My sixth sense proves correct when I hear his voice.

"I swear I did not follow you."

Sheila's eyes flit back and forth from me to him, an inquisitive expression on her face.

"Should I make that order to stay?" she ends up asking me.

"No."

"Yes," comes from the man beside me.

Sheila shakes her head and chuckles.

"Why don't I get you two started on some coffee while you figure it out."

The moment she turns her back, I whip my head around and narrow my eyes on him.

"I don't have time to sit around. Some of us have

actual work to do, since there's a young girl out there somewhere. In case you forgot," I add snidely.

I immediately regret it when I see him wince, but I'll be damned if I apologize. It's a show of weakness I cannot afford. Not to Lee Remington.

"Takes no longer to eat here than it does to eat back at the hotel, Pearl."

It's guilt that has me answer, rather ungraciously, "Fine."

Or so I tell myself.

"And? Do we have a decision?"

Sheila is back with a take-out cup for my coffee.

"We'll eat here," Lee answers for both of us as he glances up at the blackboard behind the counter. "I'll have the classic: three eggs over hard, hashbrowns, bacon, and sausage."

"White, whole wheat, or rye?"

"Rye, please. Do you mind if we grab that booth?"

Lee points to one farthest from the counter and the city workers.

"Have at it." Then she turns to me. "Still want this?" She holds up the large paper cup.

"Yes, please."

She fills the cup to the brim and hands it to me.

"Cream and sugar on the table," she indicates. "I'll get your egg white omelet and his classic ordered."

When I get off the stool, Lee gestures for me to lead the way. I walk over to the booth and sit down with my back against the wall so I have a full view of the diner. He sits down across from me, his elbows on the table.

"You really should make better food choices," I blurt out, uneasy under the intense scrutiny of his dark, amused eyes. "Bacon *and* sausage?"

"Don't forget the hashbrowns," he comments sardonically before shrugging. "Gotta grab fuel when I can, especially at the start of the day. You never know when or where you'll get your next chance."

I take a sip of my coffee, wincing at the strong dark brew, but I can't allow myself to indulge in cream and sugar. Next thing you know, I'll be stealing bacon from his plate.

"Are you suddenly on some kind of health kick?" he asks, tilting his head slightly as he doctors his own cup with copious amounts of both. "Or was last night's raid on snacks an anomaly?"

"That wasn't for me," I fib, trying to look down my nose at him. A hard thing to do when he towers over me by a good foot, even sitting down.

"Liar." He grins, looking much too smug. "So, are the egg white omelet and black coffee penance for last night's Reese's Peanut Butter Cups and chips? Because I don't think you need to worry about your weight."

I press my lips together. Little does he know weight is the last thing I'm concerned about.

"If I'd known your reason for having breakfast with me was to critique my dietary habits, I would've passed," I can't seem to stop myself from sniping.

To my surprise, he dissolves into laughter. To my annoyance it makes him even more attractive.

Suddenly, he leans across the table.

"Hey, Tiger, need I remind you who started it?"

Shit.

He's got a point.

"Let's talk about something else," I quickly suggest. "Why journalism?"

He follows my segue with ease, answering without hesitation.

"Justice."

"For your mother?" I probe.

I know his mother worked in housekeeping at Transition House and was supposed to have been killed for what she knew. During the years I was there, I recall a few black women on staff, but we weren't really given the chance to interact. It's possible one of them was Lee's mother.

"That's how it started, but now I simply want justice," he clarifies. "Money, power, and inequity often get in the way."

I hum in agreement. It's what I'm after as well, although I'm sure our idea of justice differs greatly.

"Wouldn't law enforcement have been the more logical choice?"

He snorts. "Not for me. Law enforcement not only could've prevented her death, but they were eager to write it off as an accident, ignoring evidence to the contrary."

He's referring to former Lanark police chief, Browning. He and his son—also law enforcement—are currently in jail on a laundry list of charges, including kidnapping and sexual exploitation of children. One of those assholes gave me a scar when one of their bullets grazed my head during the rescue of Mitch's daughter, Sawyer.

"Your egg white and spinach omelet? And one classic breakfast for you."

The waitress slides our plates in front of us and sets a thermos of coffee in the middle of the table.

"That way I don't have to bother you," she explains with a wink.

"That looks anemic," Lee comments, pointing at my plate.

Sadly, it does. The smell of bacon grease teasing my nostrils doesn't help, and my eyes drift over to his breakfast, which looks amazing.

"Oh, for fuck's sake," he mumbles as he grabs a couple of strips of bacon and deposits them on my plate. "Eat," he orders.

It's on my lips to tell him off, but instead I grab a piece. With a satisfying crunch, I sink my teeth into it, closing my eyes and groaning when the greasy saltiness hits my palate.

When I open them, I catch Lee watching, an unfamiliar gleam in his eyes.

Lee

After what started out as an inexplicable desire to

needle her, breakfast with Pearl ended up being surprisingly enjoyable.

She even appeared to relax a bit after a while.

I've never met a woman so on guard at all times. She seems to feel most comfortable asking the questions, which I take to mean she has a lot to hide. Especially since most women I know talk more than their share.

It makes the journalist in me curious, but I was able to curb it. I have a feeling she'd either turtle or her claws would come out if I tried to pry for more information. I figure if I can get her to relax around me, she's more likely to show me a little more of herself, and if that means I have to do most of the talking for now, so be it.

As we walk out of the diner, I notice the top of her head doesn't quite reach my shoulder. She's small everywhere, but even though my arm is probably thicker than her leg, she's not a stickpin. Her body is nicely toned, and my eyes zoom in on that ass at every opportunity. Makes me wonder what she looks like in spandex.

"Hey, do you work out?" I ask innocently when we get to her SUV.

I'm parked two spots farther from the door.

"Run, mostly, why?" she asks with narrowed eyes.

"There's a trail from the back of the hotel that runs through Ritter Park. I was thinking of taking a run down there tomorrow morning, if you feel up to it?"

I can almost see her shields slam firmly back in place.

"I run alone."

I lift my hands in a defensive gesture.

"Fair enough. If you change your mind, I'll probably

head out around six. Catch you later, and thanks again for breakfast."

Without waiting for a response, I turn and head for my vehicle.

I don't mind conceding a few wins—like letting her pay for breakfast which she announced would be expensed to GEM anyway—if it puts her at ease.

Pearl is already pulling out of the parking lot by the time I start backing out of my spot.

It's after seven, so instead of heading back to the hotel, I make my way into town. I'm pretty sure the Sherwoods will be up.

"Do you have news?"

Maggie opens the door wider and waves me in. The poor woman has aged at least ten years since I last saw her.

"Hey, Maggie. No, nothing yet," I inform her before asking, "How are you holding up?"

Her shoulders slump.

"I'm still standing. Derek said you came by yesterday, sorry I missed you."

"Not to worry."

"We're in the kitchen."

She starts walking toward the back of the house and I follow behind.

Her husband is sitting at the round table in the breakfast nook, staring out the window, when we enter the kitchen.

"Lee is here," Maggie announces, quickly following it up with, "No news." Then she turns to me. "Coffee?"

I've already had my share at the diner but nod yes anyway.

"Morning." Derek indicates a chair across from him. "Please, sit down."

"Hope it's not too early? I have a few things I want to go over with you both."

"No, we don't sleep much," he shares. "My mind is constantly trying to come up with things I may have missed, places she might be I haven't searched yet. That's the hardest part, you know? This feeling of impotence. It's been almost two weeks."

Maggie slides a mug in front of me and sits down next to her husband. Two terrified parents, each in their own version of hell. Side by side, but something tells me they might well be miles apart.

"We had some family and friends help us search last week, but people have to work. Life goes on, except for us. I almost wish—"

"Don't!" Maggie snaps sharply. "I know what you were going to say and I won't hear it. She's fine, she has to be. We just need to find her."

My heart hurts for these people, but it won't help anyone—least of all Amelia—if they turn on each other.

"Listen, I wanted to let you know I spoke with my contact at GEM yesterday," I divert the conversation. "We'll be working in tandem, sharing any information we come up with. Because you already know me—and if that's okay with you—we thought it might be easier for me to be your point of contact."

"Sure, yeah," Derek answers.

Maggie just nods.

"Good. A couple of things we need a little more information on. First of all, Evolution Quest, how did you find out about them?"

"I don't know." Derek turns to his wife. "Maggie?"

"Amelia," she answers. "She'd heard it mentioned somewhere and asked me to look into it. I checked with the school counselor, who had heard nothing but good things about it. She put me in touch with the parent of another student who'd gone on a trip with them in the fall and I got her feedback. It seemed a reputable organization. Why? Do they have anything—"

"No, no. There's no reason to think that," I rush to calm the woman, making a mental note to talk to the school counselor. "We're just trying to get a more complete picture."

Derek places an arm around his wife's shoulders and gives her a squeeze.

"That trip was months ago," he reminds her. "I doubt it had anything to do with Amelia's disappearance. Besides, she was so much better after she came back."

"She was struggling before?" I take the opportunity to ask.

"Yeah."

Derek's eyes don't quite meet mine and I tread carefully.

"I can only imagine the kind of trauma you suffered as a family since we first met, and I hate to open up old wounds, but it could be important. Was Amelia one of Donald's victims?"

Maggie visibly flinches before turning to bury her face into her husband's shoulder. Derek closes his eyes as he rubs his wife's back.

"We...it was...you have to understand," he stammers.

I hold up my hand.

"I'm not judging. If that was my daughter, I would've wanted to shield her as well. I'm sure it was a devastating situation already."

"She was in therapy until early last year," he admits. "She didn't want to go anymore, started having nightmares again, and became more difficult to handle. She was angry all the time."

Maggie lifts her head and turns to look at me, her eyes red from crying.

"When she came to us with that wilderness trip, her enthusiasm made us hopeful maybe it would be good for her. We were at the end of our tether and were desperate for something—anything—to help her. She seemed a lot better after she came back. Did we make a mistake?"

The plea is accompanied by a tortured look in her eyes and since I don't have an answer for her, I redirect with a question.

"Do you know if she made any friends? Someone she may have stayed in touch with?"

"She mentioned a girl she'd shared a tent with a few times." Maggie brings a hand to her forehead and pinches the bridge of her nose before huffing, "I can't think of her name now, my brain is mush."

"Josie," Derek fills in. "I think Amelia mentioned she was from Columbus, Ohio."

"Remember a last name?"

He shakes his head.

"Sorry."

Josie from Columbus, Ohio. A needle in a haystack.

It's not much to go on, but maybe those girls stayed in touch online. At least we have a name to look for, provided Pearl found a way to retrieve Amelia's online history.

Maybe I should check in with her.

FIVE

Pearl

"What do you want?"

I wince at the unfriendly greeting that leaves my mouth before I can check it.

Being bristly, especially when caught off guard, is a force of habit. My teammates easily recognize it for what it is—a defense mechanism—and tend to ignore it.

Lee, who is standing in front of my door, doesn't deserve it.

Not after we shared an impromptu, yet civil breakfast yesterday, which I surprisingly enjoyed. It had been a bit of a sobering realization, the guy I'd readily filed as just another asshole in the months since first meeting him turned out to actually be a decent guy. He didn't flinch at my relentless stream of questions—mostly to keep him from asking me any—and answered them easily.

It was...pleasant and definitely undeserving of the reception I just gave him.

He looks taken aback for a moment before returning sharply, "I came to share some information I uncovered yesterday, but I see it's not a convenient time."

Then he abruptly swivels on his heel and starts marching down the hallway.

"Wait!" I call after him, flipping the night lock on the door so it doesn't fall shut behind me and chasing his retreating back halfway to the elevator.

"Would you stop running?" I grumble, grabbing his arm.

He spins around.

"Only person running is you," he comments dryly, glancing down his nose at me.

"Only because you—" I catch myself snapping.

I didn't chase after him only to continue on the wrong foot, but apologizing doesn't come easy for me.

"You caught me off guard back there," I try, less than graciously, and quickly add, "I'm naturally suspicious."

Both his eyebrows shoot up and he barks out a sharp laugh.

"You don't say?"

I bite my lip in an effort to hold back the knee-jerk snide return I have ready to fire off and take a deep breath in.

"Sorry," I mutter almost inaudibly.

Jesus, that feels foreign, and to be honest, somewhat torturous. Especially when his expression turns into a sardonic smirk.

"That sounded painful," he mocks.

"It was," I assure him, tossing my bob back with a huff. "Why don't we try this again? Would you care to come in? I can make us some fresh coffee."

He responds with a nod, but when I turn back toward my room, I hear his mumbled, "Much better," behind me.

The moment we enter my room, I realize what a bad idea inviting him into my personal space is. The man's presence in the room I sleep in is instantly overwhelming, and I quickly usher him through the connecting door into the suite next door.

"So," I try again, after quickly putting on a fresh pot of coffee. "You said you have some information?"

"Yes, I met with Amelia's parents yesterday and was on my way back to the hotel when I got sidetracked."

"Sidetracked?"

When I turn around, I notice he's made himself comfortable at the table and is glancing at the screen of my laptop. Reaching over. I slap it shut.

"Was that Amelia's Instagram account?" he asks, not at all embarrassed to have been caught snooping.

I give him a stern look, which doesn't appear to have any impact. It shouldn't surprise me since snooping is basically his job.

"Yes," I inform him reluctantly.

"Does that mean you were able to retrieve the deleted info from her phone?"

I sigh and take a seat in front of my computer.

"So far only disconnected bits and pieces of it. Nothing to give me a clear lead, so I started poking around her social media. Hoping maybe I'll find something to tie things together."

"You mean you hacked into her account."

I roll my eyes. I'm sure Lee does a fair share of cutting corners himself.

"Semantics. Whatever it takes to find that girl fast."

He concedes my point with a curt nod.

"To that end, I may have something for you. A possible friend. A girl from Ohio she met on her wilderness trip. Josie."

I wait for more information, but there doesn't seem to be more forthcoming.

"That's it? Josie from Ohio?" I prompt, flipping open my laptop.

"Columbus, Ohio. It's all I've got," he tells me with a shrug.

I'm already pulling up her friends list on Instagram. Something about Columbus niggles at the back of my head, but I can't quite put my finger on it. I start scanning the names. No 'Josie' but the moment I see 'SciotoJo' I click on it.

The profile picture is of a young girl clinging onto a rock wall. Her head is turned and she's grinning at the camera, two dark-haired braids poking out from under her helmet.

Underneath the image is a quote I recognize from a Harry Potter book.

"Let us step into the night and pursue that
flighty temptress, adventure."

"How the fuck did you do that?"

I hadn't even noticed Lee had come out of his chair to stand behind me.

"I'll show you."

I'd managed to recover part of Amelia's browser history. One of the pages that had caught my eye was a map search from late April. That's what was niggling at the back of my mind. The search was for directions to Scioto Audubon, a large park just south of downtown Columbus.

I pull it up on my screen.

"No shit," he mumbles, leaning over my shoulder. "She looked up walking distance from the Greyhound bus station to the park."

I indicate the end point. "The rock-climbing wall, to be specific."

"Did she happen to visit the Greyhound website?" he asks.

"Not that I've seen from what little I've been able to recover." I twist slightly in my seat to look at him. "Are you suggesting she bought a ticket, hopped on a bus, and took off to Columbus by herself?"

His dark brown eyes land on me, and it hits me he's a little too close for comfort. Why I'm not scampering back to create some distance is a mystery, but I remain where I am.

"Hard to believe she wouldn't take at least her phone with her. Besides, you have to be fifteen to buy a bus ticket and travel by Greyhound alone," I point out.

"*If* she was traveling alone," he infers. "We need to talk to this Josie."

It takes me less than twenty minutes to find out 'ScotioJo' is in fact Josephine or Josie Kenner. She's a year older than Amelia and lives with her dad, Joe Kenner, in a small home in the Brewery District, just a couple of blocks from the park.

Lee shoves the piece of paper he jotted the address down on in his pocket and heads for the door.

"Where are you off to?"

He stops with his hand on the doorknob and swivels his head around.

"Where do you think? Columbus."

Then he opens the door and walks out.

"Hey!" I call after him, scrambling to shove my laptop in my bag. "Not without me!"

Lee

I listen with half an ear to Pearl's phone call with Mitch and Opal.

Apparently, they're in Charleston, looking into Evolution Quest, but it doesn't sound like they're having much luck so far.

"...on our way to Columbus to talk to the girl. I'm not sure when we'll be back."

I glance over but find myself looking at the back of her head. She's turned away, looking out the side window. I don't think she's looked at me once since hopping in the passenger seat.

She caught up with me by the elevator back at the hotel and seemed annoyed when I went straight for my vehicle in the parking lot. I get the sense she's not used to being a passenger and prefers to be in the driver's seat.

I do too, although I'm guessing it's about control for her, when it's about trust for me. It wouldn't surprise me if she ditched me somewhere on the side of the road, given half a chance.

Despite the shared breakfast yesterday morning—which I admittedly cornered her into—I don't for a second believe she's happy with my involvement in this case.

There's a competitive edge to this woman, a need to come out on top I find puzzling and intriguing at the same time.

"Yes, we," I hear her snap into the phone followed by a more subdued, "Remington is driving."

Someone must've said something on the other end to tick her off. I'd swear that was a growl just now.

"Whatever," she cuts them off. "I'll call if I have something to report."

I turn my eyes back to the road when she straightens

in her seat and wait for her to fill me in. After a lengthy silence I finally lose patience.

"I gather they're not having luck with Evolution Quest?"

It takes a minute for her to respond.

"No. They're back in Charleston today. The receptionist wasn't very forthcoming yesterday and suggested they speak to the program coordinator, who is supposed to be in sometime today."

Not exactly a surprise the receptionist is closed-lipped. Although it carries a good reputation, GEM doesn't have any official standing, so it makes sense information—especially when it involves children—is guarded carefully.

"It would help to have support of local law enforcement."

Pearl huffs.

"The cops in Huntington aren't even concerned with a missing girl, why would the Charleston police be?" she questions.

I shift in my seat and pull the business card given to me at the Huntington police station from my pocket and hand it to her. Something else I should've done already, but yesterday's events back home in Lexington put a halt on those good intentions as well.

"That's the number for the detective in charge of Amelia's case. His name is Battaglia. He hasn't called me back yet, but that's the lot of a reporter. Try him. He'll probably be more inclined to talk to you guys and would have connections in the Charleston PD."

She takes the card and pulls out her phone again, typing out a quick text.

"Passing it on to Mitch," she explains. "He still has that official air about him other cops seem to respond to."

It's clear she's not a fan of law enforcement. Another puzzle to Pearl Han I feel compelled to pick apart.

THE BREWERY DISTRICT IN COLUMBUS IS ONE OF those unique areas steeped in history, with a mix of industrial and residential buildings still remaining from the different breweries' heyday in the mid to late eighteen-hundreds.

The house Josie Kenner and her father live in is a modest cottage. Likely one of the original homes built here, but it looks to have been updated with new windows and a coat of paint covering the brick. Definitely well-maintained.

There is no driveway, but a work truck with a contractor logo on the side is parked out front. I pull up along the curb on the opposite side of the street.

"Let me go first," Pearl announces as she opens the door. "In case Amelia is hiding out here."

"Why? Amelia already knows me."

It's a bit of a stretch since the last time she saw me was years ago and we didn't actually speak much.

"Exactly," she unexpectedly agrees. "Which is why it makes more sense for someone who is not familiar to knock on the door. Less chance of her darting out the back door if she's here and doesn't want to be found."

She's got a point.

"Okay, I'll wait," I concede, which earns me a startled look.

"You're not going to argue?"

"Why would I? I have no trouble admitting when someone is right."

Unlike some, but I wisely keep that thought to myself.

Judging from the sharp glance she throws my way, she guessed it anyway. Then she gets out and darts across the road, walking confidently up the narrow path to the house.

A man, dressed in jeans and a checkered shirt, opens the door. He seems to listen intently as Pearl introduces herself, only to turn his head to look at something or someone behind him. The next moment Pearl turns around, motioning for me to join her.

"Lee Remington," I introduce myself to the man I assume is Josie's father.

"Joe Kenner," he confirms as he steps to the side. "You're lucky you caught us. We're just home for lunch. Come on in."

He directs us into the living room where a young, dark-haired girl is curled up on an oversized chair, a pillow clutched in front of her and a look of concern on her face.

Josie.

"What happened?" she asks the moment she spots us.

"We're hoping you can help us figure that out, but I'm curious why you're asking," Pearl returns.

The girl looks from her to me.

"Aren't you cops?"

"Investigators," her father answers for us. "They're looking for a missing girl. That new friend you've been talking to."

"Amelia?"

I've kept my eye on Josie, and although her voice and facial expression are meant to convey surprise, her body language does not.

She curls herself even tighter around the pillow she's had in a stranglehold.

"Josie?" Pearl prompts her. "Is there anything you can tell us that might help us find her?"

The girl darts a look at her father. Then focuses back on Pearl as she shakes her head.

"I don't know anything."

I catch Pearl's eyes reflecting the same thing I'm thinking.

Josie Kenner is lying.

SIX

Pearl

"More?"

I look over at Lee, who is holding out his container of fries, and it takes everything out of me not to snatch the whole thing from his hand.

I tell myself I was being polite when I took one the first time he offered, but I really just wanted a taste of that salty, greasy deliciousness. The truth is, my apple pecan salad doesn't quite offer the same satisfaction.

"Thank you," I mumble, grabbing a handful this time.

It had been Lee's idea to hit the Wendy's drive-thru a few blocks from the Kenner's place, for a late lunch.

After the girl's declaration she didn't know anything, we spent ten minutes trying to get any information from her. Aside from her confirmation she'd shared a tent with Amelia during the trip with Evolution Quest and only talked to her online sporadically, she didn't volunteer much more.

At some point, her father announced it was time for her to get back to school. Frustrated, I handed Josie my card and told her if she thought of anything else to call me, but on our way out the door I heard him remind her to grab her climbing gear.

The girl clearly had been holding back, and I suspect her father's presence was the reason. My initial thought had been to stake out her school and wait for an opportunity to talk to her alone, but hanging around outside any school is risky. It might draw the kind of attention we'd like to avoid.

Joe Kenner's reference to his daughter's climbing gear gave me a better idea. I checked for any after-school climbing programs online and found one at the Scotio Audubon Metro Park, which runs during the months of May and June. It fits right in with her Instagram account name and profile picture.

So, we've been sitting in the parking lot across from the rock-climbing walls in Scotio Audubon Metro Park, eating our lunch and waiting to see if Josie shows.

"You can have them all. I don't want any more," Lee states, handing me what remains of his fries.

Breathing in the mouthwatering smells of his bacon-burger meal in the SUV's confined space these past twenty minutes has taken its toll. I don't even feel guilty grabbing the container out of his hands, my half-eaten salad forgotten.

"I'm not surprised that salad you ordered didn't—" Lee wisely stops what he was about to say when I snap a hand up to silence him, while stuffing my face with the other.

"I don't eat junk food," I remind him primly after brushing off the last of the fries.

"Could'a fooled me," he returns right away. "I don't get it, you're tiny as it is."

Clearly the man has a short memory, since I already pointed out to him at the diner this morning that weight has nothing to do with making healthy choices. This is the reason I don't date. The few times I've gone for dinner with a guy, they always seem to feel they have to comment on my food intake.

Although I have to admit, after seeing me hoard chocolate bars and wolf down fries, I may have given Lee reason to be confused.

"And you obviously are a bottomless pit, but why don't we just focus on what we're here for, shall we?"

I focus my eyes across the road on the two large rock-climbing walls, even though it's only just after two. Classes don't end until two thirty, according to the school's website. It'll be a while before she gets here.

When Lee stays silent for a while, I decide to prompt him about something he said this morning. Something my curiosity won't let up on.

"So what was the distraction yesterday?" I look over and notice his confused expression. "You mentioned you were on your way back to the hotel and got sidetracked?"

Understanding settles over his much too handsome face.

"I got a call. An emergency."

I'd love to know what would constitute an emergency when we're trying to find a young girl who's been gone for two weeks already.

"An emergency," I scoff when I realize he isn't more forthcoming. "What could be more important than a missing child?"

"Only one thing," he replies in a low voice, adding, "My own daughter."

My head whips around. I did not know he had a kid and, believe me, I did a background check the first time I met him.

"You have a daughter?"

He drops his head and scratches the back of it.

"Her name is Yana and she's six."

Oh, *wow*.

I figured at least a teenage daughter, given his age, but I wasn't expecting a little girl. I'm tempted to ask about her mother when I suddenly remember what started this conversation.

"Wait, you said there was an emergency... Is she all right?"

He tilts his head to look at me.

"She will be."

"What happened?"

"Apparently, she fell during recess, hit her head and had a seizure. The school called an ambulance to take her to the hospital but couldn't get hold of Yana's mother, so they contacted me."

"Oh no," I mutter. "That doesn't sound good."

"It looked worse than it was," he explains. "My daughter has epilepsy. The seizure could be what caused her to fall in the first place, and she was kept overnight for observation. But as of this morning, she's the proud owner of four stitches, and back at home with her mother."

At home with her mother.

Curiosity wins.

"Then shouldn't you be home with her as well?"

One side of his mouth curls up.

"Are you fishing?"

Even though he's right on the money, I huff in response, annoyed I'm apparently that transparent.

"Lola and I had a brief thing going seven years ago. She'd already moved on to Mike—who is now her husband—when she discovered she was pregnant with Yana."

I'm not sure why I suddenly feel a distinct sense of relief. It's not like I have any designs on the man.

"I never knew you had a daughter."

"Not something I advertise, safer for her that way."

I nod. I get that.

In this line of work, family can be a vulnerability. Mitch found that out firsthand when his daughter, Sawyer, was abducted not that long ago. Lee's been chasing down scum of the earth, like the sick bastard who took Mitch's daughter, longer than we have. He just does it with a pen, but a hell of a lot more public, so that doesn't make him any less of a target.

"Anyway, Lola and Mike live in Fort Wright, close enough for me to see Yana when I can."

From the way he says her name, it's obvious he loves his daughter very much. Which, unfortunately, makes the man even more attractive. It's the last thing I need.

He must've misinterpreted the frown on my face because before I have a chance to say anything, he suddenly leans in close.

"I know it's not nearly enough, but my daughter is becoming more independent every day, and I'll damned well make sure it's as safe as I can make it before she starts spreading her wings."

"Whoa, easy. I wasn't—"

"Is that her?" he interrupts before I have a chance to set him straight.

Something must have caught his eye because he's peering over my head out the side window.

I turn, squint my eyes, and spot the girl walking toward the rock wall along the footpath.

"Yup, that's her."

Lee

"Can I borrow your ball cap?"

She points at the Chiefs cap tucked between the dashboard and the windshield.

"Sure."

She grabs it, tightens the strap, and puts it on, pushing all the hair away from her face and pulling the brim down over her eyes. Then she sits forward, tugs the dress shirt from her jeans, and starts unbuttoning it.

I'm not sure what the hell she's doing, but I'm not missing a second of it.

She shrugs out of the shirt, revealing a white tank top, before she ties the shirtsleeves around her waist.

"Wait here," she orders.

I don't get a chance to comment because the next moment she's out of my truck and heading across the road.

Her usual crisp march is replaced by a casual, lumbering gait, hands shoved deep into her pockets and her head ducked low. If I didn't know it was her, I'd have mistaken her for a teen.

Apparently, the ruse pays off, because Josie only glances up briefly when Pearl turns onto the path toward the small building housing changing rooms at the base of the rock walls. She's only a few steps ahead of the girl.

Smart move. By staying in front and making herself look like a peer, she's not perceived as a threat, and it minimizes the chance of Josie bolting.

Both disappear inside the building, and it takes everything for me to simply sit back and wait. Whether intentional or not, I've been effectively sidelined and forced to trust Pearl.

After sitting here twiddling my thumbs for a bit, it occurs to me this might be a good opportunity to check in on Yana.

"Hey, how's she doing?" I ask when Lola answers.

"Full of beans and bored. She wants to go to school and show off her stitches."

I grin. My little girl's condition has never slowed her down. Yana is a bit of a tomboy and full of energy, which gives her mother gray hairs. I knew Lola would have her hands full trying to keep her calm and contained for a day or two, as per the doctor's instructions.

"Every textbook says she should be sluggish for a while after a seizure. Why does our daughter have to be the exception to the rule?"

It's true. Yana is already unusual, in that her epilepsy doesn't seem to cause her fatigue, as it does with most others, but she also barely requires any recovery time after her seizures.

Luckily, these days, her seizures are few and far between, managed with medication. There was a time she had five or six a week.

"Because she *is* exceptional," I tell her mom, who scoffs.

"Easy for you to say from a safe distance."

Overall, Lola and I have an amicable relationship, but every so often—usually when life gets a little challenging —her barbs come out and she knows exactly where to strike for maximum effect.

"Below the belt. You know damned well that distance is necessary."

It's quiet for a moment on the other side before she comes back, her voice softer.

"Do you ever think of giving up the chase? Maybe focus more on your human-interest stories?"

It's not the first time she's brought that up.

Back when I thought she and I might have something we could build on, I made the mistake of confiding in her. The next week she broke things off and hooked up with Mike, a certified accountant, only a few weeks after that. I know the unpredictability of my job—not to mention the potential danger in my efforts to expose the lowest form of criminals—was something she wasn't comfortable with.

When she discovered she was pregnant with Yana was the first time she suggested redirecting my career into a safer direction. I explained to her then my objectives had just become bigger than finding justice for my mother's murder and the many faceless, nameless victims out there. It now included protecting our child the best way I know how.

She knows I'd do anything to keep Yana safe, even if it means I can't be a constant presence in her life, so I opt not to respond to her comment.

"Can I talk to her for a minute?" I ask instead.

Another pause, while she undoubtedly considers whether to push or let go. She finally chooses wisely for the latter.

"Yeah, okay, hang on."

A few moments later my daughter's chirpy voice sounds on the other end.

"Hey, Daddy."

"Hi, Baby-girl. How are you feeling?"

"I'm fine, but Mommy won't let me go to school."

"Good for Mommy," I return.

I'm rewarded with a dramatic whine.

"But, Daddy..."

"Yana..." I mimic her, and smile at her giggle before adding in a more serious tone, "You know why you need to take it easy for a few days. Don't give your mom a hard time, okay?"

"Okay. Are you coming to visit soon?"

Fuck. I'm still waiting for that question to get easier.

"Soon as I can, Baby-girl. Soon as I can. You be good for Mommy in the meantime, all right?"

"Okay. Love you, Daddy."

"Love you more, kiddo. I'll call you soon."

When I end the call, my heart feels heavy, like it always does after I've seen or talked to her.

I don't have a lot of time to sit and mull on it when just minutes after I tuck my phone away, I see Pearl exit the building, Josie in tow.

Pearl heads this way, but Josie veers off toward a group of five or so kids at the base of one of the walls.

As soon as she gets in the passenger seat, she whips off the cap, flings it back on the dashboard, and runs her other hand through her shiny black hair. Then she grabs her phone.

"She talked, but let me get hold of Opal and Mitch, I'll tell you all at once."

A few moments later she has them on speakerphone.

"I just talked to Josie Kenner," she starts. "She didn't

want her father to hear because it turns out the girls did secretly plan for Amelia to visit. She was afraid she'd get in trouble again. Especially since the plan was for a third person from their wilderness trip to pick Amelia up, but neither of them showed up."

"Who is the other friend?"

Opal beats me to the question just as Pearl locks her eyes on mine.

"She claims not to know who, but that she suspects Amelia may have had something going on with someone older," she answers.

"According to the program coordinator there are generally twelve kids in the groups, ages between twelve and sixteen," Mitch volunteers. "We just talked to him. He wouldn't give us specifics on Amelia's group."

"I got the sense she wasn't exactly referring to a sixteen-year-old," Pearl returns.

"What about staff?" I ask with an uncomfortable feeling in my gut.

Opal answers this time.

"One group leader—usually a social worker—and three group counselors, one per four kids. The counselors are often college students or former program participants," she explains.

A college student could be considered 'older' by a thirteen- or fourteen-year-old.

"We're going to need a closer look at Evolution Quest," I suggest. "We need some names."

"Doing our best," Mitch explains. "I spoke with

Detective Battaglia and he said he'd put a call in to the Charleston PD, but I haven't heard back from him."

"We can't afford to wait," Pearl pipes up. "I may have to get creative to get that information."

"Do what you need to do," Opal tells her.

Looks like Pearl is about to break some laws.

Again.

SEVEN

PEARL

"But enough about me…"

Shit. I knew that was coming.

It had been almost eight o'clock by the time we got back to Huntington. We hadn't stopped, mainly because I was impatient to get to my equipment and start doing a little digging, until somehow Lee talked me into grabbing a bite at a BBQ restaurant we passed on the Ohio side of the river.

I'd spent most of the car ride on the phone, checking in with Raj and briefing my boss. The moment we sat down in the restaurant, however, I asked him to tell me about his daughter, and when he'd fall silent, I'd question him about his work.

At first, I wanted to keep him talking to avoid him prying into my life—a curiosity I can feel every time he looks at me—then it turned into wanting to learn more about him. I can't say it was a hardship listening to his deep, resonant voice either.

Hell, I'd been so mesmerized I didn't even notice I'd almost cleaned up my order of pulled pork.

"What's your story, Pearl?"

Yeah, I knew it.

I shrug. "Not much to tell. I'm just a computer geek, my life isn't that interesting."

"I heard differently. Not only did you build a reputable cybersecurity company on your own, but from what I understand, you've got some serious martial arts skills as well. You fascinate me."

I'm not sure who of my coworkers gave him that understanding, but I suspect it may have been Jacob. Or maybe Mitch. Neither Kate nor Raj would ever talk about me to an outsider, and that's what Lee is.

GEM wouldn't be able to operate if our true identities were out there for everyone to know. It's ultimately my own decision to share personal details with someone I trust—like Kate did with Mitch—but it also makes me responsible for any potential fallout should that trust be abused.

"I dabble," I minimize. "I've had some luck. And the martial arts are just a hobby. A form of exercise where my smaller size turns out to be more of an asset than a hindrance."

"But you run too," he prompts.

"I do. Especially when I'm on an assignment and I can't get to my dojo."

So far, this conversation isn't nearly as bad as I'd imagined, but I no sooner have that thought when Lee decides to dive deeper.

"What about family? Siblings? Parents?"

"No one left," I answer, grateful to see the waitress approaching our table.

"Is there anything else I can get you?" she asks with a friendly smile.

"Just the bill, please," I beat Lee to the punch as I pull my credit card from my bag, handing it to the woman.

He leans across the table when she walks away with my card and our dishes.

"I distinctly remember it was my idea to grab a bite."

"Be that as it may, you've already bought me snacks, breakfast, and lunch. I'm paying for dinner," I return, matching the stubborn look on his face.

He slowly starts shaking his head, one side of his mouth pulling up.

"You're something else, you know that?"

Unsure how to respond to that, I opt not to say anything and focus on returning the condiments to their assigned places on the table, avoiding his penetrating eyes.

Luckily, the waitress is back quickly with the bill and my card, and a few minutes later we're on the road.

"So what's the plan?" he asks when he pulls into an open parking spot in front of the hotel.

"I'm not sure what *you're* doing, but I'm going to head up and start digging."

The instant he turns off the engine, I grab my bag and climb out. "Thanks for driving," I manage before closing the door on any response.

Of course, his long legs have caught up with me when I get to the elevator. The prospect of sharing yet another small space with him has my stomach suddenly churning.

I push the button and tilt my head back to watch the numbers slowly creep down.

"You're welcome, by the way."

From the corner of my eye, I see him casually leaning his shoulder against the narrow wall between the two elevator doors, his arms crossed in front of his chest.

He follows up with, "So tell me, when do you sleep?"

The unexpected question startles me into swinging my head around, and I feel an unfamiliar blush creep up my cheeks when I notice the heat in his eyes.

Holy shit.

"I..." I clear my throat and try again. "I don't need much."

Thankfully, the elevator I'm standing in front of arrives at that moment and I dart inside as soon as the doors slide open. Not that it does me any good; Lee steps in right behind me. I quickly press three for him, and the fourth floor for myself.

He doesn't say anything else on the short ride up, but when the elevator stops on the third floor, he doesn't get off.

I press the button to keep the doors open before turning toward him.

"I'll see you to your room first," he indicates when I look at him questioningly.

Instant panic makes me snippy.

"I'm more than capable of finding it myself."

"It's been a while, but I always see a lady home," he returns easily. "Mom ingrained that in me."

Cheap shot, bringing his mother into it. Now if I make a fuss, I'll sound like a bitch.

Instead, I turn my back and mutter, "It's not like this was a date," before letting the doors slide shut.

"Felt like one," I hear him whisper behind me.

What is that supposed to mean?

What the hell is happening here?

I'd thought, since it looks like we'll be working together, I should probably try to be a bit more civil and let down my guard a little. But now I wonder if that was a mistake.

I feel completely out of my depth and I don't like it.

Determined not to let on he's getting to me, I exit the elevator and walk as casually as I can muster down the hallway. The key is already in my hand when I get to the door, and I push it open the moment the lock flashes green.

"Night," I mumble as I step into the room.

Only to be tugged back by the strap of my bag.

When I swing around, Lee is already right up in my space. A few weeks ago, I'd have made him rethink crowding me, but like some wimp, I'm motionless. Then he leans in and my breath sticks in my throat.

His lips lightly brush my cheek.

"Get some sleep," he orders, shooting me a wink before he heads back to the elevator.

It's not until I close the door and lean my back against it that I take my next breath.

And what the hell was that?

Lee

"Hey."

I'm just walking toward the elevator, Pearl's subtle floral scent still muddling my brain, when the doors open and Mitch and Opal happen to step out.

"Hey. How'd you make out in Charleston?"

"Battaglia finally came through," Mitch answers. "We met with his contact in the local PD late this afternoon, but the Evolution Quest office was already closed so we ended up following the officer to the program coordinator's house. Unfortunately, he was no more forthcoming, but definitely more cooperative. He offered to check with the head office to see what, if anything, he can share."

"Raises a bit of a flag, considering a thirteen-year-old's well-being is in the balance," I observe wryly.

"Yeah, or he's just covering his ass legally," Mitch suggests. "At least the Charleston PD will now have them on their radar, even if Amelia's disappearance is not technically their jurisdiction."

"One thing we did discover," Opal pipes up. "Their next group trip is leaving the day after tomorrow. If for some reason we don't have anything better by then, we can always stake out the Evolution Quest parking lot."

The thought of two more days before we can check out this lead, with Amelia potentially in the hands of someone who means her harm, doesn't sit well, but we may not have a choice.

Unless...

I have an idea, but that requires the cooperation of my old editor at the *Charleston Gazette*.

A quick glance at my watch tells me it's already well after ten. If I want to catch him tonight, I need to get on it.

"I should get going, I've got a phone call to make."

I punch the elevator button again, because the car has long since left.

"Oh, you're not on this floor?" Opal asks innocently.

She doesn't miss a thing.

"No. One floor down, and yes, Pearl is in her room," I quickly add, already anticipating the next question.

That doesn't stop her though.

"Is she still up?"

Mitch grabs her firmly by the arm.

"All right, woman, let's go. You can find out for yourself."

With a wink for me, he steers Opal down the hallway.

"Mark, it's Lee. Sorry to catch you so early, did I wake you?"

"You're damn lucky you didn't fucking wake me, but it's six thirty in the morning and you're messing with other plans I had before hitting the shower."

I hear a disgruntled female voice call out, *"Mark!"* in the background.

Sounds like I interrupted something.

"I tried last night but couldn't get a hold of you. It's about Amelia Sherwood," I explain.

"Turned off my phone. Last day of school for the kids yesterday and they left for the trailer with my in-laws last night, so I was busy then too."

"Mark!"

"What? First time this year we had the goddamn house to ourselves. He's a guy, he gets it," he tells the woman I assume is his wife.

Yeah, I get the picture. Especially after waking up an hour and a half ago with Pearl's subtle scent still coating the inside of my nostrils, and my dick hard as a rock.

"Look, I have an idea I wanna bounce off you. Can you meet me for breakfast? Eight, at Shoney's. That gives you an hour and a half?"

Shoney's is a family restaurant right by the river and not far from the *Charleston Gazette's* offices. We've met there before.

"Killing me, man."

"It's about Amelia," I repeat, not above playing the guilt card.

"Fuck. Yeah, I'll be there."

Twenty minutes later, showered and packed, I get into my Highlander, tossing my bag in the back seat.

I took the stairs and left the hotel out the side door to avoid any run-ins with members of the GEM team. I fully intend to eventually share whatever information I can come up with if my plan pans out, but I've always worked best by myself. I don't need anyone questioning my every move while I'm doing it.

I turn into the restaurant's parking lot a little less than an hour later. It doesn't look too busy, only six or so cars parked out front.

I'm early but that doesn't stop me from heading inside. I'll wait to order breakfast until Mark gets here, but I'm ready for a decent cup of coffee, that dishwater coffee in the hotel room doesn't really count.

To my surprise, Mark is already sitting in a booth in the back corner, a waitress sliding a mug of the good stuff in front of him.

He responds to my raised eyebrows by grumbling, "Thanks for killing the mood."

My guess is his wife wasn't cool with him oversharing earlier and shut him down. Not my circus, I've got more important things to worry about.

Like a thirteen-year-old girl still missing after two weeks.

"I'll have one of those as well," I tell the waitress, sliding into the booth across from him.

Then I get right to the point.

"Have you heard of Evolution Quest?"

"Isn't that some kind of kids' camp? I believe they occasionally run an ad in the paper. Why? And what does it have to do with the missing Sherwood girl?"

An experienced newsman, it's clear his wheels are already turning. I wait for the waitress to serve my coffee and drop off a couple of menus before responding to him.

"What I'm about to share has to be off the record."

"Christ, Lee..."

"I mean it. There's too much at stake, both for Amelia and other people involved in trying to find her."

GEM's involvement in trying to locate a missing child is entirely above board. However, Pearl hacking into accounts to get the lead we're following, is not. The last thing I want is to hang her out to dry.

"Fine," he bites off.

When I'm done giving him some background—enough to clue him in—he sits back in his seat, a mix of anger and disbelief on his face.

"Are you saying that organization is involved in her disappearance somehow?"

The waitress circles by again to take our orders.

A few more folks walk in and thankfully choose a booth near the door, out of earshot.

"Not necessarily, although I can't rule it out. Something smells. At the very least, we have reason to suspect someone who works there might have been involved. So far, we're hitting a wall trying to get information from management."

"You know, I'll never, ever understand what drives people to prey on young kids. Sick fucks."

No argument there.

I've seen and heard enough over the years to haunt me for the rest of my days.

"So what do you want from me?" he prompts.

"I want you to have me do a feature piece on Evolution Quest. Or at least pretend to. The fact they advertise in the *Gazette* only makes that more feasible. They have another so-called *quest* going into the Appalachian Mountains of Virginia tomorrow. I want to go on that trip."

He nods. I don't have to explain I'm more likely to get unsanctioned information from staff than I am from management. Especially, if I have a good reason to ask.

"And you don't think they'd be a little nervous about your motivations? Especially since that last article you did about the Youth Center in Lanark."

The article he's referring to was picked up not only by his newspaper and the *Lexington Herald*, but syndicated to several news agencies nationwide. It had been just the tip of the iceberg when it comes to the full scope of the underlying story, but enough to stir general interest.

"Not if we sell this as a contrast piece. Showing the good versus the bad when it comes to organizations working with troubled, traumatized, or disenfranchised kids."

He's quiet for a moment, a faint smile tugging at his mouth. Then he nods, grabs his phone off the table, and wags a finger in my face.

"Just so you know, I'm using that line."

By the time the waitress returns with our orders, he's secured me a meeting at ten o'clock at Evolution Quest with the program coordinator, Rod Purvis.

EIGHT

Lee

"Have a seat."

Rod Purvis is a bulky guy in his mid-forties, if I'd venture a guess. Bulky in a healthy sense. He looks like he'd feel right at home in the great outdoors, chopping wood or wrestling bears. His balding head and metal-framed glasses don't appear to detract in any way from his lumberjack looks. His casual jeans and plaid shirt seem fitting for an organization specializing in outdoor adventures.

Oddly enough, the only thing out of place about him seems to be the degree hung on the wall behind his desk featuring a PhD in Clinical Psychology. It doesn't really mesh with the framed image of the man smiling at the camera as he rappels down a sheer rock face hanging right beside it.

"How can I help you?" he asks, sitting down himself.

"Your editor gave me an outline, but I'd like to know what you envision for the article he's wanting you to write, since it seems a bit of a departure from your earlier work."

Straight to the point and no time wasted on niceties, which I appreciate. I also make note of the fact he's clearly done his research. I'm going to have to sell this hard.

"I've spent the better part of the past twenty years reporting on all the ways the system has failed disenfranchised kids. When Mark came to me with the idea to do a story on a reputable organization that's really helping those kids, it was actually a relief. A lot of the stories I investigate involve the most heinous kinds of crimes against children and it starts to eat at you from the inside out. An article on something positive, more hopeful, is a welcome change to be honest."

He seems to be buying into it, his head bobbing in understanding.

I find it's always better to stick as close as possible to the truth, and I'm not lying when I say the trauma I encounter in the course of my work has a profound effect on me. I'm willing to bet that's something he recognizes.

Funny enough, even though I've just met the guy, he feels like a straight shooter. I get the sense he wasn't trying to hide anything when he resisted sharing information with the GEM team, but was simply being cautious and protective of the kids and his staff.

Yeah, I'm not getting any red-flag vibes.

"And you want to go on a quest?" he prompts.

I shrug. "Absolutely. I need to know what I'm writing about."

He narrows his eyes on me and I hold his gaze without flinching. Finally, he nods slowly.

"All right. On a few conditions," he stipulates. "Every trip we have four kids to each counselor; twelve kids in total, three counselors, and one supervisor. My staff has their hands full with the kids and can't afford to waste time looking after you out there. You'll have to look after yourself."

"Not a problem," I tell him.

"This isn't a walk in the park. The terrain is rough, the hikes are challenging, at times through water or up cliffs. You'll need to carry your own tent, make your own camp, cook your own meals, just like we ask of the kids. Except you won't have anyone holding your hand."

"Like I said, no problem," I repeat.

"All names are confidential," he adds. "And no interviewing the children. You're free to talk to staff, they're all adults, but you won't hound them for information if they don't want to share."

I nod my consent

"Also, no pictures."

None of these stipulations are particularly surprising.

"No one is going to read an article without a visual," I argue. "This isn't my first rodeo; I won't shoot images that can identify the kids, and you'll have final say over any pictures I want to use in my article."

It's his turn to nod. "Very well, then. I have a trip leaving in two weeks you can—"

Fuck. I can't wait two weeks; Amelia may not *have* two weeks.

"I understand you have one leaving tomorrow," I raise.

He lifts an eyebrow.

"I thought you might like some time to prepare? Why the rush?"

I scramble to come up with a valid reason when a perfect one occurs to me.

"Congressman Doug Melnyk's trial starts June 18th. He's one of the accused in the Lanark Youth Center scandal. I'm supposed to be doing a follow-up story."

Not a word of a lie, although I'd hand that assignment off to someone else in a heartbeat in favor of looking for Amelia.

"As for preparing," I add. "I'll be ready in time."

I'll need to run back to Lexington to get my gear together, but getting back here for tomorrow morning shouldn't be a problem.

Purvis puts his meaty hands on the desk and pushes to his feet.

"Very well. I'll get the group leader up to speed. Her name is Vera Jackson." He rounds the desk and reaches out his hand, grabbing mine in a firm shake. "The bus leaves at eight forty-five. It won't wait."

I grin. "So noted."

Walking out of his office, I nod at the girl manning the reception desk before I head out to the parking lot. It's already after eleven by the time I hit the road.

I'm not looking forward to the almost three-hour drive

home to get my gear, only to drive back again. A better plan is maybe to crash at home, if I leave at five or so tomorrow morning, I'll be back here in plenty of time.

Traffic is light and I use the opportunity to cancel my room at the hotel in Huntington, give Mark a quick call to let him know how things went down, and check in with Amelia's parents. I've just hung up with them and am about to make one more call, when someone beats me to it.

Jacob's name pops up on the screen in my dashboard.

"Branch."

"Where are you?"

"On the road. Why?"

"You weren't answering your phone so Mitch went to knock on your room."

So that was who tried to get through when I was talking to Mark. I'd almost forgotten about it.

"Housekeeping was in there cleaning, and said you'd checked out."

"I did. In fact, I was about to call you. Has Pearl been in touch about the new possible lead we got?"

"Yeah, that's why Mitch went looking for you. She got hold of Evolution Quest's personnel files."

Pearl

My head is still foggy when I step into the shower.

Thank God for decent water pressure.

I'm content simply standing under the steady stream, letting it hit the tight muscles in my neck and shoulders I woke up with.

I'd still been bent over my computer this morning when Kate came out of the bedroom, my eyes dry and gritty from lack of sleep and too many hours of staring at the screen. Taking one look at me, she insisted I get some rest. Since my back was killing me and it was becoming hard to ignore the dull throbbing in my head, I didn't argue.

I prefer working at night, when it's dark and quiet, there are no interruptions, and I can concentrate with singular focus. I'm a bit of an insomniac anyway, having a hard time getting my mind to shut off, and often don't fall asleep until the early morning hours.

There's something about the dark that makes me feel more vulnerable. Working helps me keep those shadows lurking at the edge of my memory at bay.

I know it's not healthy—most nights catching only three or four hours of sleep if I'm lucky—but there are some benefits. Like being able to hand Kate a list of employee names I'd been able to uncover before I dragged my ass to my own room.

I'd set my alarm for nine thirty—allowing myself to sleep for three hours—so it takes a few moments for my head to clear. Then I grab the ridiculously small hotel bottle of shampoo and quickly run through my shower routine.

When I walk through the connecting door to the suite, I find Kate on the phone. She holds up a finger indicating she'll be a minute, so I head to the small kitchen instead. Someone made a fresh pot of coffee, which is exactly what I need to get my mind sharp.

"Who was that?" I ask Kate when she walks up to refill her cup.

"Sawyer. She was looking for her dad."

"How is she doing?"

Sawyer—Mitch's daughter from his first marriage—is a well-adjusted teenager, but still struggling with the fallout of our recent investigation into the Lanark Youth Center. Not only was she abducted by an old nemesis we were after, but her own stepfather turned out to be involved in the plot to exploit minors.

"She's doing okay, Raj is working with her, but apparently her mother is a mess. Sawyer needs a breather and wants to stay with us for a bit. With school out for the summer, she's going nuts stuck in the house with Becky."

I can imagine. I've only met Mitch's ex briefly, but she struck me as a bit high-strung. I guess finding out your husband is a sick predator may have played a part in that.

"Where *is* Mitch?"

"We heard you get in the shower so he went out to fetch us some breakfast. Oh, and he was going to check on Remington. He's not answering his phone."

Memories of his dark, smoldering eyes, and those strong lips featherlight against my skin come flooding back. I feel a flush rise on my cheeks.

"Why does he need Lee? What did I miss?"

I grab my cup and sit down at the table, hiding my body's response to the mention of his name behind the screen of my computer. Kate sits down across from me but doesn't seem to notice my burning face.

"I was able to track down Cody Guilford, one of the names from your list. Talked to him earlier. He's been a group counselor for Evolution Quest for the last two years, but landed his dream job earlier this month as a park ranger with the National Park Service."

"Interesting timing," I observe, instantly suspicious.

"That was my initial reaction, but something tells me he doesn't have anything to do with Amelia's disappearance," Kate shares. "For one, he mentioned he's still scheduled to go on this next trip because of staffing issues at Evolution Quest. But more convincing were the pictures Mitch found of his wedding to a lovely-looking man."

The cynic in me wants to hang on to suspicion a little longer, but I have to admit, it's a pretty compelling suggestion Guilford is not likely Amelia's *older* boyfriend.

"Staffing issues?" I lock in on something Kate mentioned in passing.

"That's what Cody said," she shares. "Apparently, it's not unusual for there to be a higher than usual turnover at the start of the summer season. With schools out there's an uptick in kids and therefore more trips scheduled, but with less staff to cover them. The program coordinator called him because two counselors unexpectedly quit recently."

"Sounds like this guy didn't have a problem talking to

you," I point out. "Does he know why you contacted him?"

"Well, he thinks I got his name from the head office for Evolution Quest, but yes, I told him we were looking for a missing teen who was on one of their trips. He didn't seem too surprised and suggested that in dealing with troubled kids, this isn't the first he's heard of that happening. Unfortunately, before I had a chance to mention Amelia's name and ask him if he remembers her, he had to go. His shift was starting."

"Too bad," I commiserate. "I also wonder if he knew either of the two who quit, and would love to find out if one or both of them may have known Amelia."

"But I'm not sure what it has to do with Lee?" I prompt her, trying not to sound too interested as I get up for a refill.

"That was Jacob's idea. Raj is tied up this morning but as soon as she's available, he wants a meeting and suggested Lee should sit in on it."

Great. I was hoping to avoid the man after spending all day in his proximity yesterday, but it looks like that's not going to happen. He makes me feel unsettled anyway, but that chaste kiss when he dropped me off yesterday had my stomach jittery and my heart hammering well into the night.

With the way my body seems to respond just at the mention of his name, I'm not sure I can hang on to my usual impassive mask.

"And he's not answering his phone?"

When I turn to face her, Kate is studying me with a slow shake of her head.

"No. Did anything happen last night?"

"I would've told you if it had," I return, unable to keep the sharp edge from my voice.

Of course, she picks up on it and raises an eyebrow. I feel put under a microscope and try not to squirm.

"Maybe he mentioned plans for today," she suggests.

No sooner have the words left her mouth when the door to the suite opens and Mitch walks in with a few paper bags. I brace myself to see Lee following him inside, but Mitch shuts the door behind him.

"Bacon and egg sandwiches, hash browns, and a couple of yogurt parfaits with fruit," he announces as he pulls the food from the bags and sets it on the table.

"That's too much food," Kate observes before adding, "Unless Lee is coming?"

Mitch grunts. "Doubtful, since he apparently checked out early this morning."

"Checked out?" I echo.

Mitch's mouth is already stretched around one of the sandwiches so he opts to nod.

"That's weird. Did he say anything to you last night?" Kate asks me.

"Nothing."

Despite being more than a little flustered last night, I'm pretty sure I would've remembered. I feel oddly disappointed he didn't mention anything.

To give my hands something to do, I grab one of the egg sandwiches and take a bite.

"You'd think he'd have let one of us know," Kate mutters. "Have you tried to call him again?"

Mitch shrugs. "I let Jacob know and he said he'd follow up. Who knows? He may have had an emergency."

My mind immediately goes to his little girl.

Yana.

Did the hospital send her home too soon?

Did she have another seizure?

The bite of egg in my mouth turns to sawdust at the thought.

———

"Send Onyx a list of things you need and she can swing by your place to pick them up before heading out there."

As usual, when Jacob has his mind set on something he's like a bulldozer.

"Covert operations are Opal's thing," I try one more time. "You know I'm not good at pretending. Besides, you need me on the computer."

"Then this'll be the perfect opportunity to challenge yourself. Can't hide behind that computer forever, grasshopper."

I grind my teeth. Trust him to have an answer for everything. The tone of his voice invites no further argument. I look around the table and realize I won't get any support from my teammates either. Kate is biting her lip in an effort not to laugh, and Mitch isn't even trying to hide his grin.

Fuck. I guess I'll be joining the quest tomorrow.

I don't know how Jacob manages to get these things done. No one knows who the man is or what he looks like, but his persuasive powers are legendary. Hell, he talked me into working for him, and I don't deal with anyone I can't run a background check on.

Somehow during the course of the day, he was able to connect with Cody Guilford and roped him into helping us. I'm sure some money was exchanged, but as a result Cody had a very convenient family emergency come up and contacted Evolution Quest to let the program coordinator know he wouldn't be able to make the next quest. His good college friend, Pearl Han, however—experienced working with children and an avid outdoors person —was able and willing to take his place.

Given the staffing issues, Rod Purvis had no choice but to agree.

Looks like I have no choice in the matter either.

"Fine," I concede ungraciously.

"Excellent, that's settled then. Opal, you'll stick as close as you can for any backup Pearl needs."

It's getting to be annoying; the way Jacob insists on using our operator names, even when it's just us he's talking to. You'd think he'd occasionally slip up and call us by our real names, but the man is a robot, he doesn't make mistakes.

"Mitch, I want you to stay in Huntington and use your connections in law enforcement to maybe rattle some cages," he continues. *"And Onyx will be there tonight. She*

can work the computers and also act as liaison for the family."

"Wasn't Remington supposed to do that?" I find myself asking.

I've been wondering all day where the hell he went off to and finally caved and sent him a message, asking where the hell he disappeared to, but I've had no response.

"Remington is doing something else. He's not going to be around."

Well, isn't that convenient. Just now things are starting to heat up here.

Asshole.

NINE

PEARL

"I can't walk around with those things in my ear."

I try to hand the small sat-com earbuds back to Raj. She showed up last night with my hiking pack, boots, and the rest of my gear. Apparently, she packed communications equipment as well.

"Look," she states calmly. "You need a way to communicate with Kate. There likely won't be cell reception, and a satellite phone is going to be bulky and stand out." She holds up the earbuds in the palm of her hand. "These fit in your pocket, or can tuck away in your backpack, and could pass for regular earbuds from a distance."

"Fine."

She smiles at me sympathetically, making me feel even more like a petulant child.

This is not me.

I'm levelheaded, control my emotions, and present

myself as unaffected. Some would probably label me as cold and emotionless, which doesn't bother me in the least. It serves my purpose.

However, right now I feel all but levelheaded or unaffected.

I hate to admit it, but the whole Lee Remington thing already has me unbalanced. Add to that this undercover assignment, and I might've well just landed in quicksand.

What causes me the most anxiety is the fact I won't have my laptop. Jacob wasn't far off when he suggested I hide behind it. It's my window to the world, and I can be whoever I want to be without putting myself out there.

I tuck the earbuds in my pocket and sit down on the edge of the bed to lace up my boots, while Raj goes over the details again.

"The group leader's name is Vera Jackson, a thirty-nine-year-old social worker, divorced, no kids. She's the veteran in the group, with four years under her belt. Jason Weir is one of the counselors, twenty-three and a nursing student at UC-Beckley. This'll be his second year. The other counselor is on loan from the Knoxville, Tennessee office; Remi Hogan, twenty-two."

"Got it."

I get up, grab the ball cap I asked Raj to pack, brush my hair back, and fit it on my head. Then I turn toward her for inspection.

She scans me top to toe, taking in my T-shirt, the hoodie wrapped around my waist, and the cargo pants I tucked in my boots. Then she nods.

"Good. You look the part. Now, do you remember it?"

I was given a fictional background Jacob assured me would measure up under scrutiny.

"Twenty-five, studied phys ed and coaching before switching to a major in wildlife resources at Potomac State three years ago. I'm currently home at my adoptive parents' place in Madison for the summer. No siblings, no current boyfriends, avoid social media, and spend most of my time outdoors," I rattle off.

"Perfect. It's getting late though. Kate's already gone, she had to pick up her rental and will probably get there before you. You need to get on the road."

I hoist my pack over my shoulder and walk out of the room, Raj right behind me. In the elevator she hands me a set of keys with a ridiculous stuffed bunny keychain.

"What are those for?"

"Your ride."

Oh, hell no. My gorgeous black-cherry Chevy Traverse is parked right outside.

"I have a ride," I declare stubbornly, trying to hand the keys back.

"Unless they're from a wealthy family—which, by the way, your pretend family is not—no college student drives around in a brand-new, high-end SUV."

She's right, dammit. Even more reason to hate this assignment.

"What is it?" I ask as I lead the way through the lobby.

"2010 Subaru Outback. It's a pretty nice ride," she adds.

"For a hippy mobile," I grumble.

Her soft laughter follows me as I make my way to the ugly, baby-poop-colored station wagon.

"The rest of your gear is in the back!" she calls after me.

I flip her the middle finger over my shoulder.

MY STOMACH IS IN KNOTS BY THE TIME I PULL INTO the parking lot behind Evolution Quest.

A few people are standing beside a big coach bus. They appear to be loading gear into an open cargo bay. A Paul Bunyan look-alike breaks away from the small group when I get out of the car and starts walking toward me.

"Are you Pearl?"

"That's me."

"Thank God." His offered, shovel-sized hand easily swallows mine. "I'm Rod Purvis, I'm the program director, and you're a lifesaver. I hope you're a quick study too. I'm afraid we don't have time for a full introduction to our program, but I printed off some information for you to read on the bus. The rest you'll have to pick up on the fly."

He points at the back of the Subaru. "Is your gear in there?"

"Yes."

"We should get that loaded up. The kids should start arriving shortly, and you and I still need to go over a bit of paperwork first."

I feel his scrutiny when I open the gate and reach in

for my pack. I quickly clip the coil of climbing rope and my harness to the side of my pack, and strap the hammock tent and sleeping bag to the bottom of the aluminum frame. Then I hoist it over my shoulder and lock the car.

"You look well-equipped, but you don't need your climbing gear, we provide it. It'll save you some weight."

Not on your life. If I'm going to hang off the side of a mountain, I'll do it on my own ropes. I'll gladly carry the extra ten or so pounds it adds.

"I prefer to use my own, if you don't mind."

"Not in the least. Let's get that gear on the bus."

He quickly introduces me to Vera, the group leader, Jason—who is one of the counselors—and Roman, our driver. Then he whisks me inside.

"Cody tells me you worked at Eagle Landing?" he asks me as he takes a seat behind the desk.

"Yes, I was the wilderness guide for the summer program there for a few years."

"Good. Any experience with troubled kids?"

It's on my lips to point out it's a little late for an interview, but that might not set the right tone.

"Not specifically," I dodge, since I'm not really familiar with the types of camps Eagle Landing offers. "But there are some in every group."

He nods. "I guess that's true."

Then he grabs a folder from the corner of his desk and pulls out a document he slides in front of me.

"This is a pretty basic contract. There are a few extra forms attached you need to sign. One is a waiver indemnifying Evolution Quest in the event of injury or accident. The other is a confidentiality agreement."

I don't take much time skimming over the contract and scribble the required signatures before handing it back.

"I included a copy with your package," Purvis shares as he hands me a manila envelope. "The drive is a little over three hours, so you have some time to read the rules and regulations and leaf through the rest. If you have any questions, you can ask either Vera or Jason. The third counselor on the trip is Remi, who left earlier with a crew to set up base camp at Lake Moomaw."

By the time I walk out of the building, a crowd is forming in the parking lot. A few parents stand off to the side, watching their kids load their belongings before they get checked off a list by Vera, and waved onto the bus.

The temptation to jump in the car and take off is over-whelming, but that won't help Amelia.

It's the fear of what might be happening to her these two weeks since she's been gone that propels me toward the bus.

Lee

I groan when I'm finally able to stretch my legs.

Over three hours stuck in the back of the bus, folded up like a goddamn pretzel, cursing fucking Jacob Branch.

There's no doubt in my mind Pearl showing up just as I was finding a seat is no coincidence. A brief moment of panic had me dart to the back of the bus. Not that she noticed me, she had her ball cap pulled low and her head down.

If it wasn't for that counselor, Jason, taking the seat beside her, I would've gone down there and asked her what the hell she was doing here. I assume she's posing as either a student or a counselor. I'm betting on the last.

Either way, I guess we both have our parts to play and can't risk letting on we know each other.

Too late to warn her now since she's already getting off. I just hope she has a good poker face when she catches sight of me.

I'm the last one off the bus and my eyes immediately search for Pearl, who is standing with a group of four kids next to a trailer carrying eight canoes. She has her back to me and there's something about her body language that has every alarm bell going off in my head.

However, before I have a chance to figure out what has me on edge, my name is called.

"Lee?"

I turn around to find Vera approaching me. She introduced herself earlier when I arrived at Evolution Quest. There'd been no sign of Purvis, but he'd obviously given his group leader the heads-up, since she seemed to know my first name and why I was there.

"You brought your own tent, correct?" she asks.

"I did."

"Good. I hope it's easy to take down and set up again, because we'll only be here for one night to give the kids some basic skills before we pack up and load the canoes."

She points to what looks like a trail heading into the woods.

"Remi—he's one of our counselors—just took the first group to base camp. Follow that path, you'll catch up with him. He can tell you where to pitch your tent."

"Great, thanks."

I fetch my gear from the cargo bay under the bus and start walking.

"Oh, and, Lee?" Vera calls after me. "You should probably stop and introduce yourself to our new counselor. She's with that group by the canoes. Her name is Pearl."

Great.

The group with her consists of three girls and one boy I noticed as he was getting off the bus. Not a very big kid, in fact, he's probably the smallest one in the bunch. He's standing off to the side, his shoulders stooped, and his head hanging low.

As I approach, I notice Pearl focusing on the boy, saying something to him before helping him adjust the pack on his back.

"You must be Pearl," I announce from a distance.

Her head snaps up and for a brief moment shock registers on her face, before angry eyes narrow on me.

"Vera told me to stop by and introduce myself," I tell her when I reach the group. "My name's Lee. I'm doing a story on Evolution Quest for the *Charleston Gazette*."

"You're a reporter? Cool!" the only Black girl in the group pipes up. "Are you going to interview us?"

She appears excited at the prospect, unlike the other kids who display varying degrees of panic.

Pearl beats me to a response.

"No. I'm sure Lee is only here to observe," she states firmly.

"Your counselor is right, I'm afraid. I'm only tagging along, trying to keep up with you guys."

I glance over at Pearl, who is eyeing me with an expression on her face I can't decipher.

"Which reminds me, I'd better get going and find out where I should pitch my tent. I'll see you all later."

With a nod in Pearl's direction, I take off into the woods.

When I catch up with the other group, they're already walking into a small clearing right on the lake, where I notice a group of small, green, two-person pop-up tents already set up. My guess is two kids per tent and staff each get their own.

I wonder where Pearl is going to sleep.

Hanging back while the children are assigned their shelters, I don't pay too much attention to the young guy directing them until he turns around.

Then I have to fight to keep the shock off my face.

Very unexpected, but it explains the tension I could see radiating from Pearl earlier.

This cannot be a coincidence.

"Are you Remi?"

His pale blue eyes are assessing as he approaches me. Either he's a brilliant actor or he really doesn't know who I am.

"Yes, and who are you?"

"Lee. Vera told me you'd be able to show me where to pitch my tent?"

"Sure."

He doesn't ask me why I'm here and I'm not volunteering.

I'm too busy trying to wrap my head around the fact the guy who slipped through our fingers in the Caymans shows up in the Appalachian Mountains.

Not to mention in the middle of an investigation of yet another missing girl.

Definitely not a coincidence.

TEN

PEARL

"Say what?"

I wince. Even through the crackle of a poor connection, Kate's high-pitched squeal pierces my ear.

"Jesper Olson? Are you sure?"

Oh, I'm positive. Took my heart a long time to slow down after I caught sight of him.

Not because of any threat he poses me—he wouldn't know me from Adam—but because of what his presence here implies.

We've always suspected the child exploitation ring operating from the Lanark Youth Center not that long ago was part of a larger organization. One that appeared to have roots in the former Transition House, which is going back over two decades.

Ironically, the one-time group home for teens is the connective tissue for the GEM team members as well. It's the carrot Jacob Branch dangled to lure Kate, Raj, and myself into working for him. I know what motivates the three of us, but what drives Jacob is still a mystery.

Jesper Olson was just a grunt in the depraved plot to groom disenfranchised youths and sell them to sick fucks with deep pockets to feed their perverted sexual fantasies. In a way, I guess Jesper probably started out a victim too, but he was also the only remaining connection to the other big players we suspect are still out there. Which is why I spent the past few months trying to track him down, hoping he could lead us to them.

Only for him to drop right into my hands.

"It's him," I confirm, keeping my voice low.

I had to wait for everyone to go down for the night before I had a chance to sneak away from camp and give Kate a heads-up.

"What do you want me to do?"

"Nothing," I tell her. "As sick as it makes me to have him this close to other kids, we'll give up any advantage if we take him in. I stand a better chance getting information if I let him believe I'm his peer."

"True enough," she agrees. *"What are the odds, huh?"*

Pretty good, apparently.

Of course, moments after I watched Jesper disappear down the trail, I got another shock when Lee showed up.

"FYI, Remington is here under the guise of doing a story."

I expect surprise, but that's not what I get.

"I know. Found out from Jacob this morning."

That bastard. He's playing games again.

"Figures. You tell Jacob Branch to brace; I have a thing or two to say to him. Hell, I'd kick his ass if I knew where to find him."

"You know Jacob, he likes to meddle."

"Tell him his time is better spent trying to find the connection between Evolution Quest and Glan Industries," I tell her. "Olson showing up is not an accident. I'd bet my computer their hands are all over Amelia's disappearance."

"On it," Kate's voice crackles.

At the sound of a branch snapping, I whip my head around, peering into the dense, dark forest.

"I have to go," I whisper, ducking low behind a tree trunk.

"Okay. You be careful."

I remove my earpiece and shove it in my pocket.

Something is moving through the trees. I hear the rustle of clothing and watch the small beam of a penlight scanning the underbrush. I can't make out who it is, but they're approaching from the left, the direction of the camp.

For a moment, I consider trying to move to my right and make my way back to my hammock the long way, but the likelihood I can do that without drawing attention is slim. Besides, whoever is out there is closing in.

I have no choice but to stand up, step out from behind the tree, and pretend to zip up my jeans.

The narrow beam of the penlight hits me square in the face. Blinded, I immediately reach for the can of bear spray clipped to my belt and hold it out in front of me.

"Whoa, it's just me."

The light disappears from my eyes as Lee aims the beam at himself.

"See?"

"What the hell are you doing here?" I hiss at him.

"I saw you get out of your hammock. You were gone a while, so I came to look for you. You know you don't have to walk half a mile to relieve yourself, right?"

"I meant, what are you doing here, Lee? In the mountains, in Virginia? Did you know Olson was going to be here?"

I squint, trying to read the expression on his face, but it's too dark.

"Fuck no. I was following a hunch. Like you." I can see the white of his teeth when he grins. "Looks like we both had the right idea."

"Wasn't my idea," I grumble. "I was conned into this scheme, but I suspect you already knew that."

When he stays silent for a few beats, I'm sure I hit the nail on the head.

"What will it take for you to trust me?" he finally sighs, his voice laced with disappointment as he takes a step closer.

Close enough for me to see the angry frown between his eyebrows.

"Are you telling me you didn't talk to Jacob?" I ask, suddenly not so sure.

"Yes, I talked to Branch all right. I filled him in on my plans and assumed he'd share them with the rest of the team. You're not the only one who was manipulated."

"Oh."

To be honest, it wouldn't surprise me if Jacob played that game on both of us.

"Yeah, oh," he echoes.

Then his eyes drop down to my mouth and my damn heart picks up the pace.

"Don't..." I whisper, lifting my hand to his chest.

"Don't what, pretty Pearl?" he mumbles, taking a step closer so my hand is caught between us and I feel his breath stroke my skin.

It would take little effort to shove him away, drop him to the ground where he'd roll into a fetal position while clutching his tenders, but somehow my fingers curl into his shirt instead.

I'm mortified when a pathetic whimper escapes my lips.

"Kiss you?" he taunts. "I've thought of little else since the first time you used that fine mouth of yours to spew venom at me. And trust me, not for lack of trying."

I hold my breath when he bends down, brushing my nose with his.

"But here we are..."

I feel a brief moment of panic, trapped between the trunk of a tree at my back and Lee's large body caging me against it. But it's gone when his lips brush mine with an almost hesitant tenderness.

It's by far the gentlest touch I've ever felt.

"Okay?" he whispers as he lifts his head.

"Mmmm," I mumble, using his shirt to pull him back down.

This time I initiate the kiss, slightly tilting my head as I press my mouth against his. His deep, rumbling groan resonates against me and I open my lips to the first stroke of his tongue.

It's like coming alive, hyperaware of every sensation as synapses throughout my body start firing off impulses. Somewhere in the back of my mind I know I'll probably regret this later, but for now I can do little more than exist in the moment.

Losing control never felt this amazing.

Then the screaming starts.

Lee

The entire camp is awake by the time we burst into the clearing.

Pearl is leading the way and the only reasons I am even remotely able to keep up with her are my long legs and my damn pride.

Blood is rushing in my ears and I'm gasping for air when we join the small group standing outside one of the tents.

"What's going on?" Pearl demands to know.

She addresses Jason, who is standing off to the side with one of the older boys who'd been assigned to share a tent with Ricky, the scrawny kid from Pearl's group.

The big kid—I think his name is Alex—is clearly shaken.

Vera's soft voice can be heard from inside the tent, intermittent with subdued crying.

"Sounds like Ricky had a nightmare," Jason informs us.

"He was moaning. I just wanted to wake him up," Alex jumps in. "But when I touched him, he started screaming."

The poor kid looks like he might be on the verge of tears himself.

"Show's over, guys. Back to bed," Vera orders firmly when she crawls out of the small space dragging a sleeping bag.

Jesper, aka Remi, starts hustling the other kids back into their tents.

"Let's go, Ricky, you can bunk with me," Vera announces as the small boy crawls out after her.

He keeps his head down and follows her for a few steps but then suddenly stops.

"Can I stay with Pearl?" he asks in a timid voice.

Shooting a sideways glance at Pearl, I catch a brief look of panic on her face which is quickly replaced with a tiny smile.

"If she's okay with it," Vera tells him.

"Sure, except—"

"Take my tent," I interrupt her. "We'll swap, I'll take the hammock."

Vera hands Pearl the boy's sleeping bag. "Great. That's settled then."

"Sorry," Alex mumbles when Ricky passes him.

"S'okay," is the muted response.

My tent is pitched on the far side, closer to the tree line, and only a few feet from where Pearl strung up her hammock. The other tents are set up facing the lake in a semi-circle around the firepit.

When I walk by, I see the embers are still glowing from the fire the kids built earlier. One group had been sent into the woods to collect fallen trees and branches, while a second foursome hauled rocks up from the shore, building the pit. The third group was responsible for actually building the fire, using only a flint and steel to create a spark.

The kids were left to figure things out by themselves, and whoever their assigned counselor was only intervened if they really got stuck or any disagreements—and there were a few—threatened to get out of hand.

Vera had simply observed, probably making note of the different personalities and group dynamics the assignments brought forth.

"Let me just grab my sleeping bag," Pearl mentions when we get to my tent.

She hands Ricky his own bedroll and heads for her hammock.

The kid tries to look anywhere but at me.

"I hate nightmares," I comment casually, tilting my head back to look up at the sky. "Don't get them that often anymore though, but I still hate that feeling when I startle awake and it takes a few moments before I remember where I am."

His voice is so soft, I almost miss his whispered, "Yeah, me too."

This far away from light pollution, the stars are plentiful on a clear night.

I point up. "That's the Big Dipper."

"Actually, that's Cassiopeia," he corrects me.

From the corner of my eye, I see him step up beside me, pointing a more northerly direction. "That's the Big Dipper,"

"I see."

"What are you looking at?" Pearl asks as she comes up behind us.

"Stars," I tell her, turning around. "Ricky knows his stuff."

A faint smile tugs at those lips I have trouble keeping my eyes off of.

"I bet he does, and I'd love to hear more about it...*after* I get some sleep." She reaches over and ruffles the boy's unruly mop of hair. "Come on, Copernicus, let's hit the sack."

"What's a Copernicus?" he asks, allowing Pearl to nudge him into the tent.

"A very famous astronomer, who lived five hundred and fifty years ago."

I grin to myself, trust Pearl to know shit like that.

"Cool," Ricky reacts, his nightmare all but forgotten.

I look over my shoulder at the hammock, stretched between two sturdy trees, wondering how the fuck I'm going to get in. Better yet, how I'm going to *stay* in.

I turn my head at Pearl's voice beside me.

"Don't forget your sleeping bag."

"Almost did." I take my bedding from her hands and tip my head toward my perch for the night. "Any tips on how to get into that contraption?"

"Very carefully."

Even in the darkness, I can see the mischievous glimmer in her eyes.

"You making jokes now?"

I bump her shoulder as she snickers at my expense.

"Come on, I'll show you how it works." She ducks down and sticks her head in the tent. "I'll just be a minute, okay, Ricky?"

Judging by the boy's muffled response, he's already half asleep.

"Okay, show me," I tell her when we get to the trees.

I watch as she spreads out my sleeping bag and swiftly heaves herself into the hammock. She makes it look easy.

There's something about seeing her lying back, those dark eyes looking up at me, that stirs my blood.

"Does it fit two?"

From the narrowing of her eyes and abrupt way she gets to her feet, I'm guessing I should've kept that thought to myself.

"You try," she prompts, moving on from that awkward moment.

I manage, not quite as gracefully as she was able to, but at least I'm in and I don't plan on getting out again. It's a bit of a juggle to get my boots off but when I drop them to the ground, Pearl shakes her head.

"You don't want to do that. The nights are cool and snakes like to find warm places," she warns.

She bends down to pick them up and zips them into a pouch hanging from the hammock by my feet.

"Thanks."

I lie back, fold my arms behind my head, and look up at her.

I'm liking this view too, but rather than put my foot in it again, I change gears.

"Find out anything useful?" I ask in a whisper; in case someone is within earshot.

I'd noticed her sitting down next to Jason at the bonfire.

She matches my low volume. "Other than his girl-friend is not a fan of his job? The only informative thing I got from him was the fact he went on the last trip as well."

"The one Amelia was on?" I ask, sitting up so abruptly I almost launch myself out of the hammock.

"Yup. But then he launched into his girlfriend trou-bles and I couldn't get him back on subject without it being weird. I'll try again tomorrow. You?"

"Didn't get much. Talked with Vera a bit, but stuck to general questions about the program."

"And Jesper?"

I shake my head.

I'd planned to try and engage him in conversation but am having a hard time checking my anger around him. This guy is neck deep into some sick shit and is as much a predator as the people he works for are.

I have been watching him though. Especially when

he's interacting with the kids. If I notice anything that doesn't sit right with me, all bets are off.

"I'm keeping my eye on him."

"Yeah, me too."

I catch her stifling a yawn.

"You should get some rest," I tell her, lying back.

"Yeah. You too, tomorrow will come soon enough," she mumbles.

But instead of heading back to the tent, she leans over and covers me with my sleeping bag. Then she pulls down the flap hanging over the hammock and starts zipping it up, but stops halfway and stares down at me.

"What?"

Her bottom lip disappears between her teeth. I reach up and pull it free with my finger.

"What?" I repeat.

"I, uh...I trust you."

She's gone before the weight of those words hit me.

ELEVEN

PEARL

"How is he doing?"

We just pulled the canoes to shore in one of the inlets on the other side of last night's camp. The rest of the group went ahead to find a new camp for tonight, while Vera and I stayed behind to pull the canoes on land and secure them.

It took us close to three hours to traverse the lake, a trip that should've taken no more than a good hour of solid paddling. Of course the kids' inexperience slowed us down, which made it an exercise in patience, something I don't have a lot of.

Two kids and one adult to a canoe with the exception of the two oldest kids, who claimed to have some experience. I had Shamyra in my canoe along with Ricky, who hasn't let me out of his sight since last night. Even when I was helping the others break down camp while he gave

Lee a hand taking down his tent and my hammock, his eyes were on me every time I checked.

Of course Shamyra talked incessantly, like she's done since we got here. She's easily one of the most vocal kids in the group. Ricky was quiet for most of the canoe trip, but oddly enough the two seem to get along fine.

"I haven't really had a chance to talk to him much," I tell Vera, handing her the paddles from the last canoe. "He slept well enough the rest of the night, as far as I could tell, but generally doesn't seem the talkative kind."

I leave out that it suited me just fine, since I'm not a big talker either.

"He seemed to do well paddling," she observes.

"Yeah, he picked it up quickly," I agree. "He uses whatever strength he carries in that small body very effectively."

Something I'm not a stranger to; intelligent strength beats out muscle size every time.

"He's a smart kid," she comments. "Sadly, wise beyond his years."

"Sadly?" I prompt.

"Yeah, I suspect his home life isn't the greatest. He lives with his father, who signed him up. I'm not sure where his mother is, but Dad claims Ricky is hard to manage at home and a troublemaker."

That boy is about as timid as they come so I find that hard believe.

"Ricky?"

She glances at me and raises an eyebrow. Clearly she's not buying it either.

We work together to hoist the last of the canoes up on shore and flip it over. When we hoist our packs on our backs and start up the narrow trail bisecting the heavy undergrowth, I voice what's been on my mind since the incident last night.

"Was he abused?"

She stops and looks back at me.

"Wouldn't surprise me if there was abuse in the house. Could well be he witnessed it or incurred it himself. Either way he'd be a victim." She shakes her head. "Look, the only reason I'm telling you this much is because Ricky seems to have taken a shine to you. I don't normally share this kind of information because it's important to the success of the program for all of the kids to start on equal footing. Knowing their backgrounds can impact the way counselors interact with them versus the others, which would be counterproductive. They're here to build confidence, learn about themselves—their strengths and weaknesses—and have a better idea of who they are or could be by the end of the week."

She resumes moving up the trail and I follow in her tracks.

"Hardly seems long enough," I note.

"In most cases it isn't, but maybe it's a start, and even if only one out of a group like this walks away empowered, I consider it a success."

Vera seems genuinely passionate about the program and the children. I'm having a hard time envisioning her as part of some kind of elaborate abduction scheme.

"And the others?" I probe. "What happens after they leave?"

"All of the kids are referred to an after-care program."

That piques my interest.

"Also run by Evolution Quest?"

"No." She looks over her shoulder at me. "It's an unaffiliated, free program providing online counseling, geared toward teenagers and run by licensed therapists offering their time pro bono. It's voluntary and the kids can access it independently from any computer or phone."

Jesus, a program like that would be like shooting fish in a barrel for child predators. Every hair on my body stands on end.

I wish I had my computer so I could look into it, but sadly I had to leave that behind in my hotel room back in Huntington. I wonder if Amelia accessed those online services. Any evidence of that would be on her electronics and I left those behind as well.

I'm tempted to dig for more details but am afraid I'll raise suspicions if I ask too much. Maybe it's less obvious if Lee probes a little deeper, it's his job after all. I can try my luck with Jason again if I get a chance.

The spot where the group chose to set up camp is a fairly level clearing on an elevation, with a view of the lake below, and a steep, rocky hillside rising up behind us.

I look around to find Ricky helping Lee set up the tent. I note my hammock is already hanging a few feet away, one end tied to a tree and the other fastened around a large boulder at the base of the cliff. I'm not sure it'll be far enough off the ground with Lee weighing it down, but I guess he'll find out tonight.

Some of the kids appear to be struggling trying to set up the tents they just took down this morning. Not a surprise, since the ground here is mostly rock, making it almost impossible to set stakes down.

"Would you mind slapping some sandwiches together?" Vera asks me. "We're running a little later than I'd hoped."

"Sure."

I'm used to carrying what I eat in my pack when I hike. Mostly protein bars, MREs, and gel-packs for quick energy. I don't need much though. These kids, however, need their calories, so we brought across a large tub containing mostly nonperishable foods, which Jason and one of the older kids hauled up here.

While Vera jumps in to help set up camp, I pull out a couple of loaves of regular sandwich bread—the white stuff I normally don't touch—as well as a tub of peanut butter and a jar of jam.

I was told yesterday there are no kids with allergies or dietary restrictions, otherwise I'm guessing peanut butter would've been left out of the supplies. As it is, it makes for a decent serving of protein, and what kid doesn't like PB and J.

Using the lid of the bin as my table, I get started on assembling about twenty double sandwiches.

"Need help?"

I glance up to find Alex—the kid who shared a tent

with Ricky—standing a few feet away, looking a little tentative.

"Is your tent up?" I ask, peering over his shoulder.

"Yeah."

"Then sure. I'll do peanut butter, you do jam?"

"'Kay," he mumbles, sinking down on his knees on the other side of my makeshift table.

I got the sense his offer of help had an ulterior motive, and he doesn't make me wait long.

"Is Ricky okay?"

"I think so. You know that had nothing to do with you, right? Nightmares happen to everyone," I assure him.

"But this was a bad one."

"I could hear that."

He's quiet again as we work our way through the second loaf.

"He's got scars."

That gets my attention and I ask, perhaps a little too sharply, "What do you mean?"

"When I touched him... I guess when he was rolling around his shirt had pulled up. When I touched his back, I could feel them."

I have to resist the urge to reach behind me to touch my own marred skin.

"I think I hurt him, 'cause that's when he started screaming," Alex adds.

"You startled him, that's all."

Any pain Ricky would've felt was probably etched into his skin long before this trip.

Lee

"...your own dinner."

Loud groans go up among the group of kids, but Vera ignores them and plows ahead.

"Remi's group, you guys are going to catch us some fish. You'll have to make your own rods with the fishing line and hooks I have here. It also means you're responsible for cleaning the fish you catch."

There's a variety of responses to that, mostly dependent on gender. His group has only one girl and she looks a little green around the gills at the prospect.

"Everyone in Pearl's group is going foraging."

Shamyra pipes up, "What is that?"

"You'll be looking for things we can eat that grow in nature. Wild mushrooms, plants, and berries."

"And what about us?"

Vera turns to the third group.

"You guys have the most important task because we can't cook dinner without..."

Several voices shout out, "Fire!"

"Bingo."

"That's easy," the kid who spoke up earlier says. "We did that yesterday."

"Not so fast," Vera returns, holding up the flint and steel before tucking it in her pocket. "This time your only tools will be your hands. Jason will show you what to do."

She lifts both hands to silence a few protests going up.

"Don't worry, we'll be doing the same thing tomorrow and the day after as well, but we'll rotate so each group has a different job every day. Now, this is not a competition, it's a collaboration. For the best result you need to be able to work together, help each other out." She claps her hands. "Time's ticking, let's get going."

Each of the groups takes off in a different direction and even though part of me wants to follow Pearl, I stay put and watch as she leads her group into the woods. Right before she disappears into the trees, she turns her head and glances back at me. I give her the slightest of nods.

We didn't really have an opportunity to talk but while everyone was eating lunch, Pearl managed to pull me aside for a moment and quickly filled me in on a conversation she had with Vera that raises a lot of questions.

Questions she wants me to ask the group leader.

When I turn around, I notice Vera sitting down on a boulder near the drop-off, where she has a clear view of the lake below. She glances up at me when I walk up.

"Do you mind?"

I motion to the rock.

"Not at all."

I sink down beside her, stretching my legs out in front of me.

"I thought this might be a good time to ask you some questions? If that's okay with you?"

"Sure. As long as you don't mind me keeping an eye

on those guys." She points at the group arriving at the water's edge. "Remi is new and he's young."

"Oh, I didn't realize he was new."

"Technically, he's on loan from a branch of Evolution Quest in Kentucky, but he's new to me," she states firmly.

Interesting. Clearly there's something about Jesper/Remi, that has her Spidey senses going off.

"What about Pearl? She's new," I point out, playing devil's advocate.

"Never had an issue with a female counselor before."

"Suggesting you've had issues with the male variety?" I probe.

She briefly takes her eyes off the group below to give me a side-look.

"It's not as big an age gap as you'd think, between our kids and our staff. Which, I have to admit, has its benefits; the kids tend to be more responsive and open to those they can still recognize as contemporaries. But it also has its drawbacks."

She pauses and I decide to take a stab at what she is trying to tell me.

"Teenage boys are not nearly as appealing to young women, as teenage girls are to young men."

"And vice versa," she adds. "Some of these kids come here with a ton of baggage. Girls especially crave any kind of positive attention."

"I gather you've had to step in before?"

She shrugs but keeps her eyes fixed on the tableau in the water.

"Only on a few occasions and, for the most part, I was

able to nip it in the bud with a caution."

"For the most part?"

"Well, it didn't work on Remi's predecessor; Paul," she retorts with distaste. "The idiot crossed the line with one of the girls, and I ended up tossing his ass to the curb at the end of our last quest."

Fucking bingo.

I have a hard time not pumping my fist, and attempt to keep my tone casual.

"What happened to the girl?"

Still, something in my voice has her twist her entire upper body in my direction. Her eyes are narrowed to slits and her tone is sharp.

"Wait a minute, you're not going to print any of this, are you? This is a great program and the last thing I want to do is put it in a negative light."

I shake my head and smile to hide my discomfort at lying to her. She seems a decent woman.

"That's not what I'm after, Vera. Besides, you being vigilant about possible fraternization speaks *for* the program, not against."

"Oh, you're smooth." She wags her finger at me. "You're dangerous, and if I weren't swinging for the opposing team..."

She lets the sentence drift off and resumes her vigil, but her expression is grim. I don't make an effort to break the silence—I figure I pushed my luck enough—but I quietly wonder if Vera was told Amelia is missing.

Because I'm convinced that's the girl she was referring to.

TWELVE

Pearl

If I didn't know his real identity, he'd probably have me fooled too.

I'm forcing myself to think of him as Remi so I don't accidentally call him by his given name, but it makes it difficult to remember what I know he's capable of.

I can see why kids are drawn to him. It's hard to believe behind those good looks, ready smile, and natural ease, hides a master manipulator. A predator.

Even Ricky, who's been mostly quiet and subdued, has fallen victim to the guy's charm. He seems to be coming out of his shell tonight. Of course, it helps he had a very successful day.

This morning, Vera had each group build a raft, something I'd certainly never done before, but Ricky seemed to know what he was doing. To my surprise, he took the lead on the project and the other three kids—all girls—didn't seem to have a problem following his instructions. His design had been the only raft to stay afloat under the weight of their group.

Then, this afternoon, Vera had us switch things up. I took Jason's group foraging while my kids went fishing, and Ricky ended up with the biggest catch of the day.

That's what has all the kids in stitches now. Remi is mimicking how Ricky landed his monster fish, turning it into a slapstick the kids think is hilarious.

Including Ricky.

"Scary, isn't it?"

Lee lowers himself on the log beside me.

I growl low in my throat.

"I wanna throttle him."

He chuckles softly. "Don't think that's gonna be productive."

"Maybe not, but it'll be satisfying," I counter.

"Maybe you'll get a chance after we find Amelia."

Right. *Amelia.*

Last night, I had a chance to slip away and contact Kate. She told me she'd get in touch with Cody Guilford to see if he knew this Paul-guy Lee learned of. I also passed on what little information I have on that online pro-bono counseling service the kids are referred to after a trip. Jacob will need to do some digging into that.

"I just feel so restricted in what I'm able to do from here and I'm getting frustrated. Especially knowing Amelia is out there somewhere and the longer it takes to find her, the harder it's likely going to get."

I feel Lee's hand on my knee as he gives it a squeeze.

"Incoming," he whispers.

I turn my head just as Ricky walks up.

"Pearl? Is it okay if I go back to my own tent tonight?"

"You mean, with Alex?" I peer past him at the older boy who is glancing this way.

It looks like everybody else is getting ready to turn in for the night, but Alex appears to be waiting.

"Yeah." He brushes the dirt with the toe of his sneaker. "He's pretty cool."

"Sure. That's fine by me."

More than fine, actually. I haven't slept well the past few nights. I much prefer my hammock.

"And for the record, you're pretty cool yourself," I call after him.

The boy tosses a grin over his shoulder as he rushes back to his waiting friend.

"I'll go grab my stuff out of your tent," I announce, wasting no time.

On this afternoon's excursion the kids and I discovered a small stream with clear mountain water feeding into the lake. Since the closest I've come to a shower these past days is a quick rinse with a bucket of lake water, behind the tarp we stretched between a couple of trees for privacy, I'm craving a good soak.

I'm already hauling my things from the tent to my hammock when Lee catches up.

"You can stay in the tent if you want. Now that I've mastered getting in and out of the hammock without causing myself physical harm, it's actually quite comfortable."

"Thanks, but I think I'll sleep better in here."

Not to mention it'll be easier to slip out of unseen, since I'll have the cover of the trees rather than be out in the open where Lee's tent is pitched.

I roll up his sleeping bag and hand it to him.

"Sure?"

"Positive," I assure him.

For a moment we stand there, eyes locked as we both still hold on to his sleeping bag, and I'm sure he's going to kiss me again.

I want him to.

A peal of laughter coming from one of the other tents breaks through the suspended anticipation.

"See you in the morning."

The rich, warm timbre of his voice seems to hold a tinge of regret.

"Goodnight," I answer, turning back to hide the disappointment I'm afraid will show on my face.

What the hell is wrong with me? I don't fawn over a man, *any* man.

I shouldn't even like Lee; he's arrogant, intrusive, unpredictable, and stubborn, but somehow, he's starting to grow on me. Of course, he's also quite beautiful, which should be a strike against him, but instead I find myself fascinated. So much so I can't seem to keep my eyes off him.

There's an ease about the man, the way he interacts with people effortlessly. He has the kind of natural confidence I'm missing and have been trying to emulate most of my adult life. It doesn't help he seems to be really good with the kids.

Annoyed with myself, I quickly brush my teeth, rinsing with what's left in my water bottle, and climb into the hammock. I don't bother taking off my boots and only zip up the cover halfway.

Lee's scent lingers and I can't stop my mind from fantasizing about him while I wait for the camp to fall asleep.

I must have dozed off myself, because when I peek out of my shelter a faint trickle of smoke is all that remains of the fire, and the camp is completely silent.

Easing out of my hammock, I try not to make any sound. I grab my microfiber towel, roll in clean underwear and a fresh shirt, and slide the tin with my biodegradable shampoo bar into my pocket.

With my bear spray strapped to my belt and the beam on my flashlight set low, I find my way through the trees to the small creek we bumped into this afternoon.

It seems to be overcast, making visibility limited, and I hear the flow of water before I see it. I undress quickly, shivering lightly at the cool air hitting my skin. Leaving my clothes and my towel on a large rock on the edge of the water, I dip my toe in the freezing water.

Fuck, that's cold.

Maybe this wasn't such a great idea but I've come this far, I may as well push through.

The water isn't that deep, only halfway up my thighs. I bolster my courage and sink down, ducking my head under. The rush of cool water takes my breath away and I sharply suck in air when I surface.

By the time I've shampooed my hair and washed my body, I've already adjusted to the temperature. When I lie back in the water to rinse my hair, I allow myself to float for a few moments.

Above me the clouds break open, revealing a deep indigo sky dotted with a million stars. The three-quarter moon reflects on the water, making it look silver and luminescent.

This is why I enjoy being out in nature; this peaceful stillness. It's the only thing that can calm the churning of my mind.

It seems a little too still though.

Sitting up, I squeeze the excess water from my hair as I scan my surroundings, listening for the normal sounds of the woods, the buzzing of cicadas and insects, the screech of an owl or the flapping of its wings when it dives after prey. So many noises, mostly drowned out in daytime, seem to come alive at night.

The forest is quiet, though. Too quiet.

I rise from the water, trying to listen beyond the sound of water sluicing off my body.

That's when I hear it; a soft rustling of fabric.

Lee

I'm not sure what wakes me up in the first place, but as I roll over on my other side, I hear the distinct sound of a zipper.

My eyes pop open and I see a flash of light hitting the roof of my tent before it's gone.

A thunderstorm?

I listen for rain hitting the tent fabric, but there's none, just a faint rustling in the woods. Not unusual, there's plenty of wildlife active at night, but they don't generally carry a flashlight.

Because that's what I decided that beam of light was.

Pushing my sleeping bag down, I grab my flashlight and boots, shoving my feet inside. I try to be as quiet as possible to get the zipper up halfway before ducking outside.

It appears to be quiet again.

I glance around to look for movement anywhere but see nothing in the camp. Then my eyes drift farther out, catching a brief glimmer of light disappearing in the trees. My first thought is maybe someone tending to a call of nature, but the makeshift latrine—a tarp shielding a hole in the ground—is on the opposite side of camp from where I saw the light.

My eye catches on Pearl's hammock and I notice the zipper is open and the cover is hanging loose. I could've sworn the zipper I heard was farther away, but maybe I heard it wrong.

I walk over and peek into the hammock, which is empty. Sliding my hand into the sleeping bag, I find it cool to the touch. If she'd just slipped out, I would've expected it to still hold some of her body heat.

She's been gone a while, which means someone else is out there with her.

I let my eyes drift over the rest of the camp, looking for anything out of place. I find it when I notice the bottom of a tent flap moving in the breeze.

Unease prickles the back of my neck as I turn back in the direction I saw the light. It's gone now but it gave me a good indication of direction.

The moon starts breaking through the thinning cloud deck, giving me enough light to see my way without needing to use my flashlight. I'm careful not to make too much noise while still moving at a decent clip. A few times I stop to listen for any movement, but I can't hear any snapping branches, or rustling in the underbrush.

I'm about to head back to camp when I hear the sound of moving water.

Immediately I change course, careful where I put my feet. If anyone is there, I don't want to announce myself until I know who it is.

I make my way around a large boulder just in time to hear a splash and see a figure sitting up in the water, like some kind of forest nymph.

The moment she raises her hands to brush the ink-black hair back, it hits me I'm looking at Pearl's back.

Her very naked back.

Manners my mother instilled in me have me avert my eyes and take a step back to give her privacy, when a

splash draws my eyes back. Her wet skin is almost irides-
cent in the moonlight as she rises to her feet.

Then I notice a darker crisscross pattern bisecting the
lower part of her back and the top of her buttocks, and I
couldn't drag my eyes away now if I tried.

I fucking knew it.

All of a sudden, she whips around, looking right
at me.

When she opens her mouth, I immediately press my
fingers to my lips. She instantly clues in and swivels
around, peering into the dark shadows. Then cool as a
cucumber, she makes her way to the edge of the water
where I can see her clothes piled on a rock.

She's covered in a thin towel by the time I get to her.
Not that it matters, in the brief moments I've seen her
naked I have mentally mapped out every inch of her.

"Talk to me," she hisses.

"Someone else is out here."

"Who?"

I raise an eyebrow, which apparently tells her enough.

"Jesper?"

I nod but she's already grabbing for a slinky pair of
underwear from her pile of clothes. Then she bends over
to step into them. My eyes are glued as she starts shim-
mying the dainty scrap of fabric up her legs.

"Excuse me, some privacy please?"

My gaze travels up her body to her eyes, which are
shooting fire at me right now.

"I just saw you naked," I point out.

"Oh, I'm aware, thank you for the reminder, but you'd

better enjoy that mental image, because you won't be getting another chance."

Like hell I won't, but I'm keeping that thought to myself. Instead, I compliantly turn my back and give her what she asks for.

"Do you know where he went?" she asks when she's finished dressing.

Regrettably.

"Just a general direction, which I was following when I stumbled on you."

"Well, he didn't come by here or I would've heard him."

"Fair enough," I concede, but she's already moving.

I quickly fall in step with her.

"You know you're heading back to camp, right?"

I get hit with a sideways glance.

"I do."

"You don't wanna go after him?"

I'm surprised.

She stops and turns to me. "And then what? He could be anywhere at this point. Besides, I don't want to waste time blindly searching these woods when it's possible he made his way back to his tent by now."

Good point.

We don't talk on our way back, even though I'm full of questions. It's in my nature to dig until I find answers, but something tells me Pearl wouldn't respond well to badgering. Especially not on what is sure to be a sensitive topic for her.

I can't unsee what I saw though. It appears to confirm what I suspected all along, but I'd like to hear it from her.

When we get back to camp, I point out the flap on his tent is still partially unzipped.

"He's not back yet," I observe.

"I see that," she confirms as she lifts the flap of her hammock and dumps her stuff inside. Then she starts moving toward Olson's tent. "I'm gonna have a quick look."

Before I have a chance to voice my concern, a loud rumble sounds, immediately followed by the snap of a lightning strike, which brightens the night. Up ahead, Pearl abruptly stops as the skies open up and rain starts coming down in sheets.

I leap forward and grab her by the arm, pulling her toward the shelter of my tent. She doesn't object and dives inside the moment I have the zipper up.

I'm just about to duck in after her when I catch a flash of movement at the edge of the trees. At the next lightning strike, I see a tall figure ducking his head as he runs for the camp.

Olson.

It's hard to hear anything over the noise of the pounding rain, but for some reason he turns his head in my direction right before he dives into his tent.

"You're gonna drown," I hear Pearl's dry voice from inside.

I whip my soaking-wet shirt over my head and drop it before I crawl inside.

"He was out there," I inform her as I kick off my boots and set them by the opening.

"Jesper?"

"Yeah. Came tearing out of the woods and made a beeline for his tent."

I turn around and see her sitting in the far corner, her knees pulled up to her chest and her arms wrapped around them. It's an unusually defensive pose.

"Are you okay?"

"Fine," she snaps, but when a flash of lightning strikes, I can see her jerk.

Definitely not fine.

She looks scared out of her mind, which is completely out of character. The woman is a badass.

"Here, let me take your boots off."

I reach for a foot.

"That's okay, I should probably get to my hammock anyway. This could last all night," she says, but she doesn't move from her spot.

"Doesn't sound like a good idea, seeing as you left the cover open and your sleeping bag is probably drenched." As I'm talking, I slip her boots off her feet. "You can crash here."

When she doesn't respond, I grab my sleeping bag, unzip it, and spread it out. Then turn around and I dig through my pack for a clean T-shirt.

"Here..." I toss it over my shoulder at her. "It's dry."

I take my time putting on a flannel shirt myself, hoping to save my last clean shirt for another day. Then I lie back on the sleeping bag and pat the makeshift bed beside me.

"Come on, let's get some rest." I twist my head and meet her eyes. "I'm beat, Pearl, I need some sleep."

I'm guessing it's because I wasn't focusing on her that she finally moves out of the corner and stretches out on the sleeping bag, stiff as a plank. I slide my arm around her, pull her into my body, and press a kiss to her forehead.

"Relax, Pearl. I've got you."

It takes a few minutes, but she finally relaxes against me and I let my eyes close.

"Lee?"

"I'm right here."

"It's Janey..." she whispers. "My name."

I lift my head and look down at her for a beat before I lower my mouth to hers for a soft kiss.

"Get some sleep, Janey."

THIRTEEN

PEARL

I'm almost afraid to breathe.

Waking up with a large hand covering my ass and my head resting on a wide shoulder is not my normal MO. In fact, it's been many years since I've been in bed with a man, let alone woken up with one. In a tent, of all places.

It feels good though. *He* feels good, which is why I don't want to risk waking him up, because then I have to pretend I'm not enjoying this.

It's still dark outside, but daylight can't be far off because I can hear a few birds starting their wake-up call. The storm must've passed over at some point because I can't hear the rain or thunder anymore.

Thank God. I fucking hate storms. It's the one fear I haven't been able to conquer, the only thing I have absolutely zero control over. Already somewhat outside of my comfort zone, I was completely unprepared for last night's sudden weather change.

I totally freaked, in the middle of an assignment.

There are a lot of things I could blame it on but the truth is, I flipped out and am grateful Lee was there.

Not that I'm about to tell him that.

"Are we gonna talk about it?"

The sleepy sound of his voice startles me. I never felt his breathing change, it's still as steady and even as when he was sleeping.

I immediately try to sit up, but his hand on my ass moves to grab on to my hip to keep me in place.

"There's a lot to go over from last night before people start waking up," he rumbles in my hair. "We may as well be comfortable doing it."

I'm about to tell him I'm not that comfortable, but he's a step ahead.

"And don't waste your breath lying, you've been awake for at least fifteen minutes and haven't bothered to move yet."

I take a moment to consider whether to fight him or not, but decide I'm not really in that much of a hurry to get up.

"So talk."

Instead of starting with the easy stuff—like asking what I was doing in the middle of the night, or even why a thunderstorm had me curled into a ball—he goes straight after the heavy subject. The one thing I haven't allowed myself to think about.

I know it's coming when his hand slides to the small

of my back and his finger starts tracing the webbing of ugly ridges on my skin.

"Who did that to you, Janey? Who put those marks on you?"

"That was a long time ago, and you should be careful calling me that."

"I realize that, and don't worry, you'll be Pearl in public. But you gave me Janey, and I'm gonna call you that when it's just us."

Damn. It's ridiculous how much I like that.

Unfortunately, despite that rather sweet sentiment, Lee will not be deterred.

He squeezes my hip. "Who was it?"

"No one who matters now."

He lets go of my hip and rolls me on my back, leaning over me.

"Matters to me," he whispers, his eyes locked on mine.

"My mother," I find myself admitting.

He looks surprised. "Your mother did that? Why?"

I shrug, letting my eyes drift over his shoulder. To be honest, I've never quite understood it myself.

I wasn't a bad egg, did well in school, I had nice friends, and I didn't get into trouble. Looking back, I was a pretty good kid, and oddly enough that's what seemed to trigger her.

"I remember the first time," I muse out loud. "I'd just turned eleven and my father had died of cancer the year before. I'd won a school speech competition. I was excited because I'd be representing our school at the regionals. I guess she got angry because I was happy."

"That's fucked up," Lee points out.

I'm surprised after decades of pushing those memories away, how easily the words come to describe them.

"I know. At least I do now. At the time I thought I'd done something wrong and did everything I could to do better, be better. It seemed the harder I tried, the more angry she became. When I realized that even just being in the same room with her could be a trigger, I did my best to become invisible."

I only now notice Lee's thumb gently stroking along my jaw. His eyes are locked on my face, soft and attentive.

"I was in class one day when a kid noticed blood on the back of my shirt. Child Protective Services was called in and they took me."

"And that's how you ended up at Transition House," he guesses.

It doesn't surprise me; I could tell he had his suspicions. Other than in GEM circles, I've never discussed my connection to the home, but for some reason—maybe because of Lee's own history with the place—I'm comfortable sharing with him.

"Yes," I simply confirm, realizing if anyone outside of my team members understands what that infers, it would be this man.

He drops his forehead to mine, the tips of our noses touching.

"From the fat into the fire," he mumbles.

Yeah, he gets it.

His lips brush mine briefly and I find myself wanting more.

"What happened to your mother?"

"I didn't know for years, not until I left Transition House. It turned out she killed herself just days after I was removed from her care."

"Jesus."

"It was probably for the best," I continue, having long ago come to terms with it. "I think she died years before when my father took his last breath. Became a cold empty shell."

Lifting his hand, he traces my features with his fingertips.

"You're a bit of a miracle, aren't you, Janey Han?" he whispers using my cover name.

"Actually, it's Fisher. Janey Fisher."

The smile he throws me is beautiful, but the searing kiss that follows steals my breath.

As his tongue slides between my lips, I briefly wonder if I'm falling for the man, but then coherent thought is no longer possible when all my senses overflow with only him.

His warm palm slides along my neck, over my shoulder, and down my arm, before moving under my shirt and up my rib cage. Every nerve ending comes alive in its path, and by the time his hand curves around my breast, barely brushing the nipple with his thumb, I feel like my body is set alight.

He changes the angle of the kiss as he shifts his body to cover mine. I spread my legs to accommodate him, and my moan vibrates against his lips when I feel the prominent evidence of my impact on him hard against my core.

I'm no stranger to being the subject of desire. I was taught that lesson way too young and learned to use it to my benefit. But those men left me cold, dead inside, and nothing like the fire Lee seems to stoke in me.

Sex has always been a task for me. A chore, something I realized was part of life, like a dental appointment, or doing taxes. I won't claim I didn't occasionally feel pleasure during the act, but I've never wanted to actively participate like I do now.

With my hands on his back, I trail my fingers over his soft skin and map the ridges and valleys underneath, when I feel him still in my arms. His head comes up abruptly.

"What?"

He puts his finger to his lips in response.

Then I hear it.

Lee

"Shamyra...where the hell are you?"

A girl's voice. Sounds like she's moving toward my tent.

I roll off Janey and reach for my boots, but she's already darting out the tent on bare feet.

"Julie? What's going on?" I hear her ask in a low voice.

I quickly lace up my boots and button up my shirt.

When I step outside, the first hints of daylight are starting to filter down. I have no trouble spotting the girl heading in the direction of Vera's tent, while Janey looks to be moving for the trees...in bare feet.

Cursing under my breath, I duck back into the tent and grab Janey's hiking boots before darting after her.

"Wait up," I hiss.

She spins around and I immediately recognize the stubborn set of her mouth. Without giving her a chance to say anything, I shove her boots at her.

"You can put them on while you fill me in."

"Shamyra is gone. Julie says she ducked out after everyone went to bed, claiming to go to the latrine. She blew off Julie's offer to come along for company and said she'd be okay. Julie must've fallen asleep because she just woke up, and it doesn't look like Shamyra came back."

"Olson was out there last night," I bring up.

The eyes she turns to me are troubled. "I know."

"So what's your plan?" I prompt her.

"I'm going to look for her."

Before I have a chance to point out we may do better organizing ourselves first, Vera comes running up and takes charge right away.

"Julie's waking up Jason and Remi. The four of us will search," she directs, addressing me. Then she turns to Janey. "Pearl, I want you to stay here with the kids. No one goes anywhere without a buddy."

"I'm searching," Janey responds in a firm tone. "Shamyra is one of my kids."

I throw her a look of caution—I'm pretty sure she's about to blow her cover—but she completely ignores me as she stares down the woman who's supposed to be calling the shots.

I get it, and I agree the missing girl is more important than safeguarding her real purpose for being here, but I'm afraid of what it may mean for Amelia, who is still out there somewhere.

"Someone has to stay with the kids," Vera points out, breaking the standoff.

"Then Lee can stay, but I'm going. We're wasting valuable time."

I'm not sure whether to be pissed I just got tossed under the bus, or impressed at the way Janey stands her ground.

Vera throws her a lengthy, pensive look before nodding once. "Very well."

They're joined by Jason and the Olson kid. Hard to remember he is still a kid. His alter ego, Remi Hogan, may be listed as twenty-two, but Jesper Olson is only nineteen. A kid in my books, but one who is up to his pretty blue eyes into some shady shit.

Vera came equipped with four two-way radios and hands them out to Janey and the others.

"Sorry," she directs at me. "I'd leave one with you but I don't have another one."

I wave her off. It makes more sense for the search party to have means to communicate. I didn't even know she had those. While she gives instructions on what channel for everyone to tune in to, I can feel eyes on me. I turn my head to catch Olson staring.

It takes everything out of me not to pound the snot out of him—there's no doubt in my mind he has something to do with Shamyra disappearing—but for the sake of the investigation, I hold myself back.

Instead, I shoot him a *I know you know I saw you last night* look before I turn around and head back to camp.

I'm not happy I've been sidelined, but admittedly, Janey is skilled and probably better equipped for the search than I am. Vera and Jason know the terrain, and I definitely wouldn't want Olson in charge of the camp.

———

Twenty minutes later I'm wrangling kids—the commotion in camp woke up most of them—and am trying to get some kind of breakfast going.

"Why can't we go out to look?" Alex asks.

He's not the first one.

"Because the last thing we need is more kids getting lost."

At least I hope she's simply lost, I'm not willing to consider anything else happening right under our noses.

"Can you grab bowls and spoons?" I give the boy something to do.

"What is that anyway?" he asks, peering into the large pot I'm stirring.

"Oatmeal."

He makes a face. "Looks gross."

"It's not only delicious," I correct him. "It's brain food, it's highly nutritious, it's a great source of energy, and—unless you have a better suggestion—it's what's for breakfast."

He doesn't look convinced, but scuttles off to do what I asked, I hope. Moments later I hear him call my name. I glance behind me and spot him standing near the ridge, looking out over the lake and pointing at something.

"Could you keep stirring?" I ask Julie, handing her the wooden spoon. "I'll be right back."

The girl's been my shadow since the search group went out earlier. She hasn't said much, but I'm sure is scared for her friend.

So am I.

I walk up to Alex.

"What is it?"

"There. Off the point."

He's referring to a rocky outcropping the kids were fishing from yesterday. When I let my eyes drift over the water, they catch on someone in a canoe, halfway across the lake. The canoe looks like it could be one of ours.

I immediately step closer to the edge and peer down to where eight canoes should be pulled onto the rocky shore.

I see seven.

My eyes go back to the water.

"Alex, check the tub for the binoculars, will you?"

I don't want to take my eyes off the canoe, which is

moving at a decent clip to the other side of the lake. A moment later, the boy hands me the field glasses.

"Who is it?" he asks when I peer through them.

The good news is, there's only one person in the canoe. The bad news, the blond hair is easily identifiable as Jesper Olson's. I'm guessing the moment the search group split up to cover more ground, he backtracked, steering clear of the camp, and headed straight for the canoes.

That fucking lowlife. I knew he had something to do with Shamyra missing. This confirms it.

My stomach rolls thinking of what that might mean for the spirited girl.

I'd love to go after him, but I can't leave these kids to fend for themselves, and there's no way for me to contact the others. I wonder if he still has his radio on him or ditched it. Leaning over the edge, I scan the area around the canoes but I can't really see anything from up here. If only there was a way for me to contact someone.

I remember Janey talking to someone when I caught her in the woods the first night. I didn't see a satellite phone or anything else in her hands, but I suspect she was talking to her team. She may have had another way of communicating. An earbud, maybe?

"Who is it?" Alex asks beside me.

"Not sure," I lie. I want a chance to talk with Janey first. "Can you help Julie start dishing out the oatmeal? Remember it has to feed everyone. I've gotta check on something."

He grumbles, but turns back to the fire he helped me build earlier.

I head for Janey's hammock. Odds are she's got whatever it is on her, but I want to make sure. If there's any way to get hold of someone at GEM, they might be able to pick up Olson.

"What are you doing?"

I'm rifling through Janey's pack when Ricky's voice startles me.

"Looking for something."

No use in lying since he already caught me red-handed.

"Aren't those Pearl's things?" he probes, his expression suspicious.

From the way the normally timid boy is standing up for Janey, I'd guess she's made an impression.

"They are, but—"

I'm not really sure how to explain without blowing her cover and my own. A sound from the woods behind us saves me the trouble.

I spot Janey weaving her way through the trees with Jason right behind her.

He is carrying the missing girl.

FOURTEEN

PEARL

"What the hell is going on?"

I ignore Vera and continue talking to Kate, who luckily answered right away.

"I'll get on the horn now to dispatch a boat. As for Olson, I'm not sure if I can get there in time, but I'm doing my best," she promises.

"Okay. An FYI; my cover is blown."

"Then let's just hope no one else is involved who can make life difficult. Gotta go."

I turn to catch Lee crouching next to Vera, who is attending to the girl.

I found her less than five-hundred feet from where I was having a bath in the creek last night. It already feels like ages ago.

She'd wedged herself in between two larger boulders, I'm guessing to take shelter from the storm. Her ankle looked misshapen and her skin was cold to the touch. I had a hard time getting her to communicate, she was sluggish, and I could barely understand a word she was saying.

I'd put out a call on the radio and, within minutes, Jason showed up and easily lifted Shamyra in his arms.

Then when we got back to camp, Lee pulled me aside right away and whispered he saw Jesper Olson in a canoe, crossing the lake.

"Are you going to explain?" Vera looks up at me with an angry expression on her face.

"Yes," I respond, looking at her pointedly.

No way to put the genie back in the bottle, so I might as well fill her in, but I'd rather not do it in front of the children. They'd flocked around us when we entered camp and seem to be following everything closely.

Lee surprises me by taking charge.

"Okay, guys, give Shamyra some space and let us figure out how to deal with this. Breakfast is getting cold."

They move hesitantly at first but eventually every kid has moved to the fire, where Alex starts dishing out oatmeal. The only ones left are Vera, Jason, Lee, and myself, and of course Shamyra, but she still seems out of it.

Vera had splinted the girl's ankle and given her some pain medication, before covering her in a sleeping bag. She'd been too cold.

"Have you heard of GEM?" I dive right in. At Vera's affirming nod, I continue, "We search for missing kids and were called in to help find Amelia Sherwood. She was on your last trip and has since gone missing."

Straight to the point is the best way to make it clear what I am doing with the group, posing as a counselor.

"But you knew that already, didn't you?" I throw at the woman, keeping the upper hand by putting Vera on the defensive. "Amelia was the girl one of your staff couldn't keep their hands off of?"

This earns Lee a dirty look from Vera, who knows that information came from him.

"That was months ago."

"Perhaps so, but we have reason to believe Amelia kept in touch with that employee, and was supposed to meet up with him when she suddenly disappeared."

"That was Paul Gibson," Jason volunteers. "I told him he was an idiot when he started flirting with the girl. She's only thirteen."

"How long had Paul been with Evolution Quest?" Lee follows up.

Vera takes the question.

"That was his second trip. I'd already warned him on the first trip for being too hands-on with the kids. Literally. He always seemed to be touching or hugging the kids. He blamed it on growing up in a demonstrative family, but promised to keep it in check. He appeared to heed his promise that second trip, until I caught him trying to hide he was paying Amelia special attention. I ended up giving him his final warning."

"Who hired him?"

Vera turns to me.

"He was a transfer from another office."

"Which one?"

She opens her mouth to answer but quickly closes it. Then she suddenly looks around. "Where is Remi?"

"He took off with one of the canoes. I saw him cross the lake earlier," Lee volunteers.

The look on Vera's face is one of shock, and then it's like watching the puzzle pieces clicking together in her mind.

"Let me guess," I help her out. "Paul Gibson was a transfer from the Knoxville office as well, wasn't he?"

Her sharp nod confirms it.

"One more thing you should know," I continue. "Lee saw Remi leave his tent last night."

I purposely leave out Remi wasn't his real name or the fact we were already on his trail.

"Maybe he needed to use the bathroom?" Vera offers, but I can tell she doesn't really believe it herself.

"It could be," Lee responds. "Except he went the wrong way. In addition, I also saw him return quite a while later and again from the opposite direction of the latrine. From the same general area where Pearl found Shamyra."

"Are you with GEM as well?" she fires at Lee.

"No, I'm a journalist, but I occasionally work side by side with GEM. We're focused on the same types of cases."

A bit of a stretch of the truth, but I'm not about to call him on it.

"Is Rod aware you are who you are? Rod Purvis?"

I shake my head. "No. He's not."

When Shamyra softly moans, I change course.

"I think we should discuss how to get these kids back to civilization."

"But there are still two days left," Vera brings up.

"You want to continue on with eleven kids to you and Jason? Because I've got transport coming for Shamyra, Remi is already gone, and Lee and I need to go after him."

Vera drops her head, looking defeated.

"This is not going to look good for Evolution Quest."

"Probably not, but that's the least of our concerns. Amelia is, and now Shamyra as well, who, by the way, we should get closer to the fire until the boat gets here."

"I've got her," Lee claims when both he and Jason simultaneously reach for the girl.

Vera lingers when the two guys walk over to where the kids are gathered. She turns to face me, her expression pained.

"Don't think I don't care—because I do, a lot—but this is an amazing program that has helped so many kids, it hurts me to see its reputation damaged by a scandal like this."

"I'm afraid that's out of my hands, or yours for that matter. It looks like Evolution Quest is already involved, whether voluntarily or involuntarily," I share gently.

I don't believe this woman is in any way involved and judging from Jason's reaction, he was not aware of what was going on either. I feel bad for anything blowing back on them, as it likely will.

Still, it won't stop me from taking down anyone in my way of finding Amelia.

———

Lee

"Does this mean I have to go home already?"

Ricky keeps his back turned to me and keeps paddling as if he just asked a casual question.

Except, it's obvious to me there's nothing casual about it. The scars on his back say otherwise.

I take a moment to think about my answer, which turns out to be a question instead.

"You don't want to go home?"

His shoulders slump but he stays quiet.

"Ricky?" I prompt him carefully. "If you don't feel safe going home, there are people who can help you make it so you don't have to."

Slowly he twists his body to look at me, the expression on his face cuts right through me.

"How?"

Shit.

I wish I was already on shore with Janey or Vera to consult. I'm familiar enough with Child Protective Services in Kentucky, but not in Virginia, which is where we are. Every CPS agency is bound by the same laws and federal requirements, but the way they operate and apply their services can differ from state to state.

"You'd probably have to start by telling someone why you don't want to go home. Or if someone had reason to believe you were being abused at home, they would need to report it to the authorities."

I'm cautious in my phrasing as I paddle a little harder to get to land, where I can see some of the others already pulling their canoes on shore.

Vera decided to pack up and paddle out right after the small motorboat with EMTs left, taking Shamyra with them. Most of the kids had been a little shell-shocked after what happened to her, and didn't put up too big of a fuss when the premature end to their trip was announced.

Janey, being the lightest of the adults, had volunteered to take two kids with her. To my surprise, Ricky ended up claiming a spot in my canoe.

I'm disappointed as I watch Ricky straighten in his seat, facing forward. Wondering if I ended up saying the wrong thing, spooking the kid.

Then he suddenly reaches behind him and pulls the shirt from his shorts, exposing a network of crisscross scars, some still scabbed over, covering his back.

Nothing can stop the surge of anger, or the resulting curse that flies from my mouth.

"Son of a fucking bitch!"

In front of me, the boy instantly drops his shirt.

"I'm sorry that happened to you, buddy. So fucking sorry."

I probably shouldn't be swearing in front of the kid, but I figure it's already a little too late for that.

"Your mom?" I ask, remembering Janey's story.

He shakes his head.

"Mom died when I was ten," he shares without turning around.

I put him at twelve so that was just two years ago. Fuck, that poor kid.

The shore is a bit closer, but both of us have stopped paddling now, so we're just drifting.

"That's tough, Ricky. Was she sick?"

Another headshake. "Car crash," he clarifies.

It hits me right in the chest.

I'm far from a qualified professional, but I know a thing or two about losing your mom that abruptly, even if I was twice as old at the time.

"What happened?" I ask softly.

He shrugs. "A truck. She wasn't looking..."

I wait for more but it takes him a while.

In the meantime, my eye is caught by some movement at the water's edge. It's Janey, pacing back and forth with what looks to be a phone to her ear. Strange, because I'm pretty sure there's no reception here, unless she somehow got her hands on a satellite phone.

Then suddenly it hits me; how does the kid know his mom wasn't looking? Unless...he was in the vehicle with her.

I'm about to ask him about it when he starts talking again.

"She was yelling at me. I'd gone home with Tyler

after school to play this new game he got, even after she said I couldn't. She was mad she had to come pick me up."

What the hell do you say to that? It's not a stretch to see how guilt would be eating at him, and I have a nagging suspicion he's not allowed to forget.

I'd love to get my hands on his father.

"They say she died instantly."

"And you survived."

"Yeah. It would've been better—"

"Hey," I stop him, knowing where he's going with this. "I didn't know your mother, but I can guarantee you, she wouldn't have wanted any other outcome."

He finally twists in his seat to look at me.

"Dad would."

And there it is, the full, tragic picture. I don't understand it, but I can see it clearly.

"Remington!"

I look at shore to find Janey waving us in. Then I notice Opal standing right behind her.

"We should go," Ricky mutters, sounding resigned as he faces forward again, slipping his paddle in the water.

Whatever Janey's urgency is, I'm not going to leave this kid hanging.

"We've gotta go," she announces the moment I pull the canoe on shore.

"Hey, Opal," I address the other woman before turning back to Janey. "I need five minutes."

"We don't have five minutes," Janey fires back stubbornly.

Ricky, who is standing a few feet away is looking down at his toes. No way I can leave things like this.

Taking Janey's arm, I pull her out of Rickey's earshot.

"What are you doing?" she protests. "Opal missed Olson by a hair, but she talked to a few hikers who saw someone by his description get into the passenger side of a navy pickup truck at a trailhead, just north of here, a little over two hours ago. I'll give you details in the car, but we've gotta hustle."

"Five minutes, Janey. Ricky opened up as we were paddling over here."

Her eyes widen with curiosity.

"It's bad," I inform her. "I've gotta make sure Vera can give him the help he needs, but he can't go back home."

It doesn't surprise me she clues in right away as her mouth forms an angry line. Then she nods.

"Five minutes. We'll wait, but after that we're heading out, with or without you."

"Okay." Not really thinking, I tag her behind the neck and pull her close for a hard kiss on her lips. "I'll be there."

As I let her go and start heading back to where Ricky is waiting, I realize that kiss drew some attention. The boy's chin is hitting the ground, and a few steps from him Opal is wearing a shit-eating grin as she gives me the thumbs-up.

I ignore Opal and ruffle Ricky's hair.

"Let's go, kid. We're gonna have a chat with Vera."

"I thought you had to leave."

"In five minutes," I tell him. "Long enough to get Vera up to speed. Are you ready?"

He looks a little pale around the gills, but nods yes. I put my hand on his neck and give him an encouraging squeeze.

"I wouldn't leave if it wasn't really important, Ricky." I decide I need to give him a little more than that. "There's a girl missing, she's about your age, and we need to find her."

"Missing? Like, she ran away?" the boy wants to know.

"It's possible," I tell him, even though I know better. No need to load more on the kid's narrow shoulders. "Either way, it's important we find her as soon as possible, which is why we have to hustle out of here."

He nods his understanding and I give his neck another squeeze. He's a good kid.

"I don't want you to worry though. I'm gonna make sure you're looked after. You don't have to deal with this on your own anymore, and I'll touch base with you as soon as I can."

Vera must've seen us coming, because she breaks away from the group and starts walking toward us.

"Everything all right?"

"I'll let Ricky tell you."

The boy throws an insecure look my way and I nod my encouragement.

"I don't wanna go home."

Vera darts me a glance before focusing on Ricky.

"Why don't you want to go home?"

He takes in a deep breath before blurting out, "My dad beats me."

While he answers a few questions Vera has for him, I keep half an eye on Janey, who appears to be loading my pack in the back of an SUV. Opal's, I presume.

"Will I need to go back home?" I hear Ricky ask.

"No," Vera allays his fears. "We'll have to call Child Protective Services though. They'll help us figure out a place for you to stay."

I'm torn. As much as I'd like to see this through for Ricky, I really have to get going. Amelia is still out there somewhere.

"I'm sorry, kiddo, but I have to run." Then I hand my phone to Vera. "Mind putting your number in? I'd like to be able to follow up."

She enters her number and I send her a quick text so she has mine.

"I'll be in touch, Ricky."

It's clear from the look on his face he's not really buying it, which only makes me more determined.

"*Thank you,*" I mouth at Vera.

I start moving toward the waiting vehicle when an idea occurs to me and I quickly turn back.

"Here," I tell Ricky as I remove the strap from my wrist. "Keep this safe for me."

I hand him my watch.

"This is very special to me so I'll be back to collect it, okay?"

"Okay."

This time when I walk away my wrist feels naked, but my heart feels light.

Opal is behind the wheel and Janey took the back seat, so I get in the passenger side. The moment my ass hits the seat, Opal starts up the SUV. As she backs up the vehicle, Janey leans forward and taps me on the shoulder.

"What was that you gave him?"

I swallow hard, hoping I did the right thing.

"My mother's twentieth birthday present to me."

FIFTEEN

LEE

"They noticed the Tennessee license plate," Opal explains.

Janey takes over from the back seat.

"And get this; they said the plate stood out because it was one of those novelty ones. This one had a fish jumping out of the water, and you'll never guess the license number."

"I give up," I tell her preemptively.

"It said B A 1 T Z," she spells.

It takes me a second to clue in, and when I do it brings a sour taste to my mouth.

Sick bastards.

"Jacob checked DMV," Opal picks up. "It's listed to a navy blue GMC Sierra, owned by a Paul Gibson from Knoxville, Tennessee."

The fact Gibson and Jesper know each other isn't

exactly a surprise, not since finding out they're both from the Knoxville office of Evolution Quest. What *is* a shock is the guy was apparently still close enough to come pick Olson up.

It makes me wonder if it means Amelia could be closer than we think.

"Olson must've had a way to contact him for a pick-up," I suggest. "Since there's not much of a cell signal here, I assume it was a satellite phone."

When we checked his tent earlier, we discovered he'd somehow managed to collect his pack without anyone noticing before he took off. If he had a phone in there, it makes sense that he'd taken a chance to come back to camp.

"Not something every nineteen-year-old carries in their pocket. Those things can be expensive," Opal points out.

"So is a 2022 GMC Sierra, which is what Gibson is driving. Serves to prove someone with deep pockets is pulling the strings," Janey concludes. "A satellite phone would also mean they prepared for contingencies, which suggests a well-planned scheme."

"Amelia's disappearance was not an isolated incident," I observe.

"No," Opal confirms. "Jacob found two other names of missing girls who, at some point, before they disappeared attended one of the Evolution Quest camps. He's working on digging up more parallels with Amelia, but it's taking time."

"Has he had any luck on that after-care program?" Janey asks her.

"Not so far, but he's working on that too."

For the first time, I notice a route mapped out on the SUV's GPS.

"Where are we going anyway?"

"Bath Community Hospital in Hot Springs," Janey clarifies. "It's where the ambulance took Shamyra, and Onyx is going to meet us there with my SUV and our stuff. She should be there by now. She's going to stay with the girl, see if there's anything she knows that might—"

"Wait," I interrupt her. "*Our* stuff? *My* stuff is in my Jeep, which is locked, and parked in the—"

"Evolution Quest parking lot," she finishes for me. "We know. That shouldn't be a problem for Onyx."

I'm trying to visualize the reserved and well-put-together Onyx, with her classic looks and cultured voice, breaking into vehicles. It's not something I would've associated with the woman, but then I don't think it was necessarily her idea. I wouldn't put anything past Jacob Branch though. It's not so difficult to see his hand in this.

Which leaves me to wonder why.

"I'm sure there's a bigger picture to all this, but I may need some help seeing it," I admit.

"I'm heading back to Huntington," Opal clarifies. "Mitch and I will continue to hammer away at Rod Purvis and his staff, and stick close to the Sherwoods in case something happens there. Jacob wants you and Pearl to be mobile and ready to move."

"Move?"

"OnStar," Janey clarifies, leaning forward between the front seats.

I'm trying not to get distracted by her proximity and her subtle scent suddenly surrounding me.

"Standard on the newer GMC trucks," she continues. "I assisted in upgrading their cybersecurity years ago and still have a contact in their tech department. He should be able to backdoor me into their system once I have my computer."

Which will allow her to track down the location of the navy blue Sierra.

"I see."

Yeah, I see the picture now, but I think I need to have a talk with Branch. I'm a freelance journalist for a reason; I'm not a fan of getting bossed around. Last time I checked I wasn't on his payroll, and if he's going to give me orders he better make it worth my while.

The next ten or so minutes no one talks, until we pass the first sign for Hot Springs.

"So, Lee..." Opal drawls. "What's with that kiss back there?"

"Exactly what it looked like," I return, not surprised she brought it up. I was expecting it.

Janey makes a strangled sound from the back seat.

"It looked hot."

I glance over at Opal and catch the amused expression on her face.

"That's probably because it was," I share.

No use in denying a fact.

The muffled, "Oh God," behind me puts a smile on my face and has Opal bark out a laugh.

"You know she'll never let it go now, right?" Janey complains.

I twist in my seat and look at her.

"Relax, Janey. I have no intention of letting it go either."

Talk about laying your cards on the table, but she may as well know she's not just a diversion for me.

"It's been too long a road from when you busted my nose for me to give up now," I add.

She keeps a straight face, but her eyes look surprised.

"Well, I, for one, am thrilled my bestie finally found a slice of happiness," Opal shares.

"Who says I'm happy?" Janey grumbles behind me.

"Oh, honey, if you aren't already, I have a feeling Lee will get you there soon enough," her friend implies, aiming a wink at me.

Glad as I am for the vote of confidence, I'm grateful when my phone pings with an incoming text. I quickly glance at the message.

"It's Vera. She's letting me know she's contacted Charleston CPS about Ricky. They'll have someone waiting for him when the bus gets back to Evolution Quest, so he doesn't have to face his father."

"Who is Ricky?" Opal wants to know.

"One of the kids," Janey explains.

"Mom died suddenly two years ago, and Dad decided to take his grief and anger out on the kid," I fill in.

Opal glances at Janey in the rearview mirror and comments, "Sounds familiar."

"You have no idea," is her response.

She doesn't elaborate, but I know she's thinking about the matching marks on the boy's back.

A few minutes later, Opal pulls into the parking lot of the Bath Community Hospital. Onyx must've been on the lookout, because she's already waiting by the entrance.

"Lee," she acknowledges me when we walk up.

I return her smile, even as Janey grabs the computer bag from her teammate's shoulder.

"And hello to you too," Onyx snarks, letting go of the strap. "There's a cafeteria next to the front entrance where you can plug in."

Janey is already heading inside when Opal speaks up.

"Any news on the girl?"

"She should be out of surgery any time. Her ankle was broken in three places and dislocated, so they need to put in some plates and screws to stabilize it. I only saw her briefly before they took her up, so I didn't get into how she came to be out there, but she seemed very demure and a little sad."

"That doesn't sound like Shamyra," I inform her. "The girl I saw was outspoken, lively, and animated."

"Could just be the aftermath of the incident," Onyx suggests. "Or the effects of the pain medication they gave her."

It's possible, but I can't help wonder if the realization

Jesper Olson had left her out there all night, exposed to the elements, may have been to blame.

"You don't look convinced," Opal observes.

"I'm not a teenage girl, but if I'd been left in the woods during a thunderstorm by a cute older guy, I may have had a crush on, I imagine my feelings would be hurt. I might be embarrassed as well," I suggest.

Onyx nods.

"You have a point."

Pearl

"How is it going?"

I look up to find Lee looming over me.

"Is that it?"

He points at the flashing dot on my screen I just zoomed in on.

"It is."

I enlarge the map again so he can see the general area.

"New River Gorge National Park?"

"Yes, in the middle of nowhere, it appears," I point out. "On the bank of the New River. Nothing much around there.

"How far is that from where we are?"

"A little over two hours and a third of the way to Knoxville."

I expand the map a little farther to show him.

"So what are we waiting for?" he wants to know.

"Two things. First, the truck is parked at that spot and it hasn't moved in the past half hour, which to me suggests that's where they're likely staying for the night since it's already late afternoon." I share. "The second reason is this."

I minimize the tracking screen and pull up the live satellite feed of the area. Then I zoom in on the grainy image of what I suspect is part of the roof of a camping trailer, and poking out from under the tree cover you can still make out the bed of a dark truck.

"That is a current view, this is not."

Then I flip to a set of still shots side by side. Each is dated. One for earlier in the week, the other two weeks ago.

In each image the trailer is visible and the truck looks to be parked in the same spot.

"Gibson's been holed up there for a while," Lee observes.

Then I pull up a third and fourth screenshot, showing the same location, but this time only one of them shows the truck and trailer.

"These ones were taken a day apart." I point at the date on the image of the empty campsite. "The day after, the trailer was there, and hasn't moved since."

"That's the day Amelia was discovered missing," Lee clues in. "It's where he's keeping her."

"It's definitely a possibility," I agree.

"So why the hell not get out of here?" he insists.

"Because I don't want to rush this," I push back.

I've been sitting here doing my research on the park, trying not to think about Amelia alone with those two dirtbags in that trailer. I've been digging for trail maps, access points, logging roads, or anything to do with the park that could help me plan a covert approach. One that won't alert those two guys and push them into some rash decision that might turn out even worse for the girl.

If she's actually there, and that's not the only big question mark. I'm hoping my buddy at OnStar will be able to answer that.

I called and asked him to try and trace back any place the truck may have stopped for any length of time, from when it was spotted at the trailhead earlier this afternoon to where it is parked now.

I also put a call in to Jacob but barely had a chance to finish updating him when he mentioned he'd get back to me and hung up. Not unusual behavior for him, but frustrating when it means I have to sit around and wait for him to return my call.

So I get why Lee is agitated, pacing back and forth. Still, at his next pass I shoot out my hand and grab him by the wrist.

"Look, why don't you grab something to eat while I wait for a couple of callbacks? We may need to rush out of here, and who knows when you'll next have a chance."

His dark eyes burn into mine. "And what about you? I can't recall you eating anything today."

"I'm not really hungry," I mumble, lowering my eyes to the computer screen and out of range of his scrutiny.

Lee—being Lee—is not deterred by my evasiveness. He hooks a finger under my chin and lowers his mouth to mine. By the time he lets me up for air, I've forgotten what we were talking about.

Lee apparently hasn't.

"I'll grab us some sandwiches for the road. Preferences?"

My scowl doesn't seem to impress him so I end up giving him what he wants.

"Egg salad or ham and cheese, if they have it."

"Done," he confirms, briefly pressing his lips to my forehead before walking to the counter to place an order.

My eyes are glued to his ass until an incoming message snaps me out of it.

It's another still image, time-stamped for two thirty-seven this afternoon. The caption states:

Beckley WV—bus station. 15 min stop

I PULL UP THE MAP AGAIN. BECKLEY IS JUST southwest of the park. The bus station in Beckley is only a half-hour from the truck's current location.

After forwarding the message to Jacob, I call the bus station and speak with a friendly gentleman, who is able to confirm there are two security cameras on the premises.

It took me a while last time to access the video feed. I don't really have that luxury now. Then it occurs to me, there may be another way to get the information I want.

"By chance do you have a bus leaving for Knoxville, Tennessee today?"

"No direct routes, but we have three buses heading for Wytheville, Virginia. There's one bus leaving for Knoxville from there early every afternoon."

That means, even if Jesper managed to get to Wytheville, he'd have to wait until tomorrow to catch the next bus heading for Tennessee.

"I appreciate your help. I have one last question; is it possible to buy a ticket to Knoxville from you?"

"Well, sure it is. It's funny though, I don't get a whole lot of folks headin' for Tennessee, and suddenly I got two in a single day. I just sold a ticket this afternoon."

I pump my fist, trying not to celebrate vocally.

"Appreciate your help, sir."

I end the call and immediately call Jacob.

"Jesper Olson bought a bus ticket to Knoxville," I blurt out the moment he answers my call. "But the bus doesn't leave until early tomorrow afternoon from Wytheville. We may be able to intercept him."

"Leave it to me," Jacob says.

"It's a two-and-a-half-hour drive from here, and three hours for Mitch to get there from Huntington."

"Pearl. I said leave it to me."

"Okay, good, because if Amelia is in that trailer, it'll be a lot easier to get to her with only Gibson to worry about."

"About that..."

SIXTEEN

LEE

"I don't understand why I can't drive."

I dart a sideways glance and catch the familiar stubborn set of her chin. It's not the first time in the past twenty-five minutes she's brought it up but clearly isn't able to let it go. She still has a hard time not being in control.

"You could if your legs were a couple of inches longer, or if this thing had adjustable seats," I remind her.

"Why couldn't he have gotten us a newer model?" she complains.

He being Branch, who had arranged for us to pick up this old Winnebago motor home in Shady Spring, West Virginia. Just south of Beckley, it wasn't too far off the route to New River Gorge National Park, and we were able to leave Janey's SUV parked at the RV rental place.

Janey, who'd been driving all the way there, had been

mortified when she got behind the wheel of the old motor home and could barely reach the pedals with the tips of her toes, even with the seat as far forward as possible.

"Probably because the newer ones all display the rental company's logo," I offer.

It's getting dark out, and I have to focus on the narrow, winding road ahead. Last thing we need is to end up in a ditch or hit some wildlife crossing the road.

Jacob's plan is for us to park about a quarter mile downriver from Gibson's location where, according to him, we should find another dispersed camping spot. Far enough away not to be visible, but close enough to do some exploring on foot.

The RV is obviously for cover, and if we encounter anyone, we're just another couple camping. Even if by chance we encounter Gibson himself, the cover would hold since he wouldn't know who we are. It would've been a different story had Olson still been with him.

"In six-hundred meters, your destination is on your left."

I glance at the GPS monitor mounted on the dashboard and notice the location Branch gave us the coordinates to is supposed to be just past the next bend in the road.

"Keep your eyes peeled," I tell Janey. "There's probably a dirt road or something we have to follow to the edge of the river."

I slow down the lumbering vehicle when I come out of the curve. The only light we have is from the headlights, so I slow down to a crawl.

"Is that it?"

Janey points at a narrow break in the dense vegetation between the road and the river. You can just see two tracks leading into the dark shadows.

"You have arrived," the GPS chirps.

"I guess that's a yes," I conclude.

I turn the Winnebago and crawl across the road and onto the parallel ruts, looking like they haven't been used in years. Hope to God this damn thing doesn't get stuck, it's not exactly built for off-roading.

"Put on your high beams."

"I don't want to risk him catching sight of the lights," I tell her. "I'll go slow."

The trail is longer than I expected, but finally I notice a glimmer of water through the leaves up ahead. Soon the path opens up into a small clearing, bordered by tall trees and the river on the far side.

Janey leans forward to peer out the windshield. "Nice," she mumbles.

It is nice, the light of the moon reflecting off the water makes visibility a lot better here than back on the trail.

I park the motor home on a spot that looks pretty level and turn off the lights and the engine.

"Shit."

I turn to look at Janey who is fiddling with her phone.

"What is it?"

"Barely any reception, dammit."

"Didn't you bring your satcom earbud?"

"Yes, but I can't hotspot my laptop to it. I want to be able to pull up the OnStar feed so I can keep an eye on the truck," she explains. "And this single bar isn't enough."

"Didn't the guy back at the RV place say something about this rig being upgraded with solar power and a signal booster?"

I get up from my seat and climb into the rear where I tossed the binder with information the guy handed us. We were in a hurry to get out of there so we didn't bother looking at it.

I take a seat on the ancient jackknife sofa and start flipping through the pages. Janey joins me in the back and starts unpacking her gear on the dinette table.

"Here it is." I slide the binder on the table, open to the page with instructions on how to add appliances to the signal booster.

"Good call," she mutters a few minutes later, with her laptop already open. "I should have OnStar up and running shortly."

She doesn't look up until I unzip my bag and take out my navy hoodie and my camera.

"What are you doing?" she asks as I pull the sweatshirt over my head.

"Recon," I answer as I struggle to get my arms into the sleeves in the motor home's confined space.

Janey lifts an eyebrow at my response.

"Not on your own, you're not. Just give me two minutes."

Jacob wants us to get confirmation Amelia is in the trailer before we make any moves. The idea is to pinpoint where in the trailer she's being kept, so that when an opportunity presents itself, we'll have a plan to extract her.

I'm not exactly on board waiting for Gibson to head out for supplies or make a phone call or something before we can act. Sure, I'm all for avoiding a confrontation, especially in such close quarters, where Amelia might get caught in the crossfire, but there may be something we can do to get him away from the trailer and minimize that risk.

"There he is," Janey mumbles.

I glance over at the screen where the little light is still flashing in the same spot. The truck hasn't moved.

She gets up, brushing against me as she moves to the bedroom in the back. My body takes notice and I stifle a groan. It'll be a challenge to keep my hands off her and my focus where it needs to be with the two of us moving around this narrow tin can.

In the sparse light the computer screen casts, I watch her ruffle through the bag she tossed on the bed earlier and come up with a dark sweatshirt of her own, along with a ball cap. It's early June so the nights are still bound to be cool.

"We should close the blinds," Janey suggests. "If anyone shows up while we're gone, it'll look like we're sleeping."

I take care of the large side windows while she tackles the one in the bedroom. Next, I reach over the driver's seat to take the keys from the ignition and shove them in my pocket, before shutting the heavy curtain separating the cab from the rest of the RV. Then I loop my camera around my neck and open the side door. I go outside first, pulling out the stairs for Janey to get down.

"Ready?" I ask when she stands beside me.

"One sec." She fishes her earbuds from her pocket and slips them in her ears. "I am now," she confirms, already on the move.

Despite the instinctive need to shield her, I don't bother trying to take the lead. I'm starting to figure out it has less to do with trusting me than it does with Janey not trusting herself unless she's in control of a situation.

Still, I'm only a few steps behind her when she disappears into the trees.

Pearl

I wince when a branch snaps under Lee's size thirteens behind me.

Luckily, the sound of rushing water should drown out any noise we make.

I'm sticking close to the shore, using the river for navigation. Even though there's only about two hundred and fifty yards between campsites, it wouldn't take much to get lost in the dark, dense forest. But aside from a few pesky mosquitos buzzing around my head, it's been pretty easy going.

"Can't be too far now," Lee mumbles behind me.

He's right, which is why I've had my eyes peeled for any light or glow coming from the trailer I know shouldn't be too far away.

It's still another minute or two before I see a brief flash of light reflecting off something shiny between the trees, maybe fifty feet or so up ahead.

"See that?" I whisper over my shoulder.

"Yeah. Probably the truck," he returns in a low voice. "Doesn't look like there are any other lights on."

I inch my way forward until I can see the outline of the trailer on the other side of the parked truck. There don't seem to be any lights on inside, and the only thing I hear is the rush of the river and my own rapid heartbeat.

From here it looks like the windows are covered but maybe there's one on the other side, tucked up against the trees, I can see into.

I turn to signal Lee to stay put while I check things out, but he clearly had a similar thought. He's already moving away from me, sticking close to the tree cover as he starts circling the clearing.

For a moment, I'm unsure whether to stay put and keep an eye on any movement from inside, or follow him. The first option would probably be the smart thing to do, but still, I find myself following his broad back through the woods.

As we round the trailer, I notice the blinds covering the window on this side don't quite seem to reach all the way to the bottom. Once again, Lee beats me to it. He's already approaching the trailer, his camera in his hand.

He ducks his head, peering inside with the naked eye first, before he lifts up his camera.

The sound of the shutter closing—although faint—seems loud to my ears, but I remind myself it's unlikely to be heard from inside the trailer. Still, I'm on pins and needles, waiting for him to finally back away, dropping the camera back around his neck.

"She's in there," he mouths when he reaches me, a grim look on his face.

Then he takes my arm, pivots me around, and with a nudge in the small of my back, prompts me to move. I don't stop until we're back on the other side of the clearing and at a safer distance.

"What did you see?" I whisper, but instead of answering, he hands me the camera.

"Not much until the infrared sensor kicked in," he shares, indicating the small digital screen on the back of the unit.

It takes me a moment to orient myself and identify the lumpy covers on the bed as a human shape. The camera is angled to the rear of the trailer, which would put the head of the bed against the back wall.

When I flip to the next picture, I realize the figure in bed must be Amelia, because this one shows the edge of the trailer door and the top half of a man lying on a couch. One of his arms is tucked behind his head and the other crossed over his chest. Just visible on the pillow beside him is the grip of a gun, within easy reach of his hand.

Shit.

I'm armed, but the last thing I want is bullets flying, or

some kind of hostage situation, either one of which is likely if we were to force our way inside. We're going to have to wait until Gibson moves away from the trailer and the girl.

"Check the next one," Lee prompts me. "I zoomed in on the bed."

The image is focused on what looks like a metal plate with a ring, fastened above the head of the bed. Looped through is a length of chain disappearing into the pile of covers. I can't help but notice the thick strand of long hair, tangled in the links.

Memories flood my mind and I'm suddenly back in the basement of Transition House, my wrists shackled together and my arms stretched over my head. I can still smell the dank air and feel the lumpy mattress against my back.

Conditioning, she called it, the woman whose soothing voice became front and center in the nightmares that followed for many years after. Unspeakable things would happen to my body as her soft words in my ear repeated how special I was. How beautiful and *precious*.

"Janey?"

The moment his hand touches my shoulder I drop the camera and twist away, doubling over. I brace myself with my hands on my knees as I wait for the wave of nausea to subside.

Thankfully, Lee doesn't push, and when I finally straighten up and start heading back to the motor home, he follows silently.

"We have to wait," I announce once we're inside.

"I know," is his response. "I figured as much when I saw the gun."

"Yeah, can't risk it. Hopefully, he has reason to get out of that trailer at some point tomorrow."

"As long as it's not pouring rain, I'm convinced he will be," Lee declares with confidence. "I noticed a generator tucked under the trailer hitch and a jerry can in the bed of his truck, which suggests he uses enough power for it to run out of gas. He'll have to come outside to start it up."

More evidence of his observation skills, which is probably a bonus in his line of work. Good point too.

"In that case, we should probably get some rest while we can," I propose. "I can set up my computer to sound an alert if for whatever reason the truck moves during the night."

Not that I expect to be sleeping a whole lot anyway.

Twenty minutes later, I'm lying in bed, staring at the ceiling, and listening to Lee take a shower in the teensy bathroom. I find myself smiling at the occasional thud or bump against the paper-thin walls, inevitably followed by a couple of healthy curses.

I have to admit, I was a little disappointed when Lee offered me the bed and insisted he'd be fine on the couch, but I appreciate the fact he's giving me my space.

Whether I want it or not.

SEVENTEEN

LEE

I grind my teeth.

For the past hour or so, I've been listening to her restlessly moving about in bed. Finally, ten minutes ago it got quiet, but not long after that the moaning started.

I'm starting to regret my decision to give her space after her profound reaction to seeing the close-up picture I took of the chains. It honestly hadn't occurred to me it might trigger that kind of response. She looked shaken, physically ill, and the way she recoiled from my touch clued me in she might be reliving an experience of her own.

So I've been battling my instincts to wrap her in my arms and hold her close, thinking she probably wouldn't welcome my touch right now. But it's been torture.

The moaning turns into mumbling, and then the thrashing starts.

I whip my sleeping bag open and sit up, dropping my head in my hands.

The keening builds slowly, the sound cutting me to the bone. I can't fucking sit here and listen to this.

I get to my feet and, in two steps, bridge the distance to the bed.

"Janey," I try on a whisper first, but she wouldn't be able to hear me over the sound of her own voice.

So, I try again, this time louder.

"Janey!"

I narrowly avoid getting kicked in the junk by grabbing her ankle when one of her feet shoots out. Her movements still instantly.

"Hey, Janey, it's me. You're dreaming."

Abruptly, her head lifts up from the pillow, her wet eyes wild as she looks straight at me.

"Lee?" Her voice is raspy.

"Yeah, just me."

She blows out a sharp breath as she sits up and rubs her face with her hands. Then she's suddenly on the move.

"Excuse me," she mumbles as she tries to get out of bed.

I take a step back, only to have her dart past me into the bathroom, slamming the door behind her. Standing here for a few moments, I realize it's a little creepy, hovering outside the thin door and listening to her go to the bathroom. I return to the couch, lie back down, and wait.

The door opens a few minutes later and I hear the

squeak of the bed when she climbs back in. Shortly after the rustling of her sleeping bag starts up again.

It only lasts for a few minutes when it suddenly goes quiet, and I'm starting to wonder if she's fallen asleep again. I roll on my side, pull my sleeping bag up under my chin, and close my eyes.

"Lee?"

Her voice is no more than a faint whisper, but it may as well have been a foghorn, I shoot upright so fast.

"Right here."

"Are you tired?" she asks.

Exhausted, but I'm not about to tell her that. It doesn't sound like she's ready to try sleep again.

"Not really."

"Why? Is the couch not comfortable?"

I sit up and look in her direction. I can see the outline of her head and shoulders framed against the soft moon filtering through the curtains behind her.

"Janey?"

"Yeah?"

"Ask the question, Tiger."

She takes her time responding and it takes every ounce of patience I possess not to fill in the blanks for her, but I need to hear her ask it.

"Would you lie down with me?"

I'm already on the move.

Janey scoots to the side of the modestly sized bed to make room for me. As soon as my back hits the mattress, I reach out my arm for her. She doesn't hesitate to curl up against me, her head on my shoulder.

"Better?"

"Much."

There's nothing I can do about my body's response to her. The soft skin, her small but shapely body pressed against me, and that subtle, enticing scent she seems to carry around have an immediate impact on my heart rate and my cock.

Still, I'm happy simply holding her like this all night, if that's what she needs right now. She's in the driver's seat.

First the fingers of the hand she has resting in the middle of my chest begin drawing small circles over my shirt.

Then she starts to talk.

"Seeing her chained to the bed triggered memories I thought I had securely buried. But apparently not as well as I thought." Her hand stops moving as she scoffs, "Not the only thing I've failed to keep in check lately."

"What do you mean?" I ask, stroking my fingers up and down her upper arm.

It takes her a while to answer.

"I was engaged once," she starts unexpectedly. "He was a nice man and I thought maybe I could have a normal life. I met him through a few friends I'd made in my building. He didn't even seem to care I was dancing at a strip club at the time."

She pushes up abruptly and fixes her eyes on my face.

"Does that bother you? That I was a stripper?"

I grin at the challenge in her voice.

"I washed dishes at a gentleman's club to get myself

through college," I volunteer. "So no, it doesn't bother me."

"Good." She settles back against me. "Because I liked it. Made great money doing it. Steve seemed okay with it too, until that story came out."

I'm guessing Steve was the intended, but I'm more interested in the story she's referring to.

"What story?"

"We'd had an assault in the parking lot. A few days later I was cornered by this reporter, who claimed to be doing a story on it. Except, it turned out to be an exposé on the sex trade. He somehow managed to get a shot of me dancing and used it—with just my eyes and the juicy bits blurred out of course—to illustrate his article."

Well, that explains her initial animosity toward me.

It's on my tongue to ask whether she sued the reporter or the newspaper, but I hold back. I don't want to derail her from the direction she's taking me in with her story.

"Guess Steve wasn't as okay with it as he thought, and I became *persona non grata,* both at work and with my so-called friends."

What a douchebag. I bet he felt quite the man to have a beautiful woman other men drooled over in his bed, but wasn't man enough to stand by her when her profession became public knowledge.

"All this to explain why I've actively closed myself off from forming any kind of personal connection or bond."

Janey takes in an audible breath before she continues.

"But you've made that difficult."

Not exactly a declaration of love by any stretch, but fuck, coming from Janey's mouth it almost might be.

"Yeah?"

I try not to sound too pleased with myself but clearly fail.

"No need to be smug," she scolds me. "So far all of this is very unsettling, and I clearly don't do well with it."

I gently roll her on her back and prop myself up on an elbow. She looks up at me in a way that betrays her vulnerability. I gently stroke the back of my fingers over her cheek.

"My guess is you'll do great once you stop thinking," I suggest.

"And how am I supposed to do that?"

I grin, recognizing my cue.

"I bet I can help you with that."

One side of her mouth pulls up in a lopsided grin.

"How is it I feel I'm coming apart at the seams, yet coming alive at the same time?"

Pearl

"I can show you," he whispers.

I watch as he pushes himself up on his knees. A feat in itself given the limited space. He narrowly avoids banging his head on an overhead cupboard as he pulls off his shirt.

His eyes gleam with heat as they track down the length of my body. Despite the shirt and boy shorts I wore to bed; I can feel his gaze like a warm touch on bare skin.

His hand curls around my ankle, stroking up to my knee.

"May I?"

This is what I asked for, and yet he wants to be sure. Leaving me in charge while asking for control. I trust I'm safe in his hands and still I tremble with anticipation as I nod.

His eyes lock on mine, while his hands travel up my body, unhurried.

"Arms up," he instructs softly.

I comply, feeling the light abrasion of fabric as he undresses me. An involuntary shiver runs down my body when I'm completely bared to him. It's the look in his eyes when he sits back on his haunches, taking in every inch of me.

I recognize the hunger, but I'm not familiar with the sheen of tenderness. It suggests a level of caring I'm not sure I've ever had aimed at me.

"*Fuck*, you take my breath, Janey Fisher."

Next, to my surprise, he climbs out of bed. I can't help notice the size of his erect cock, which is barely restrained by the stretch of his boxer briefs.

"Hold on to that thought," he mumbles as he turns his back and ducks into the bathroom.

I hear him ruffle through his shaving kit. He returns a

moment later with a foil-wrapped condom he tosses on the mattress. Then he reaches for my ankles and pulls me closer to the edge.

"I need room for this."

For what, I discover seconds later when he sinks to his knees, lifts my legs over his shoulders, and, with one hand on my lower abdomen and the other wedged under my ass, covers my core with his mouth.

For a brief moment, I consider how strange it is I was never a fan, but Lee's skillful mouth quickly obliterates any ability to think.

My body is driving on instinct, restless, trembling, as my muscles coil and my fingers dig into the mattress searching for purchase. One hand finds the short bristles of his close-cropped hair and holds on for dear life, as I clamp my thighs around his head and tilt my hips into the merciless onslaught of his tongue.

My heart thunders in my ears, and my chest hurts from lack of air, as I desperately seek release for the deep throbbing between my legs. There's a brief moment of pain as every muscle in my body contracts before I finally fly apart in tiny fragments.

It feels like melting. A moment in time when it seems every molecule in my body bursts from its original place, floating aimlessly, before slowly rearranging itself in a better place. *Transformative.*

What follows is a deep sense of completion.

As I catch my breath and feel my heart rate slowing, I look down to find Lee's sparkling eyes on me as he kisses his way up my body.

"Wow," is the only word that comes to mind.

"Yeah." He lifts his head and grins, his lips and chin still shiny with the evidence of my release.

The next second, he's bending back down, closing his lips around my nipple. Small charges ripple through my body like little aftershocks, as he pulls me into the heat of his mouth.

I mourn the loss of his mouth moments later, but then he wraps me in his arms and rolls us, ending up on his back with me draped over him.

At some point he must've ditched his underwear, because I can feel his cock pressed against my stomach.

"Kiss me."

He doesn't need to ask twice.

I move up his body and taste myself on his lips as I slide my tongue into his mouth. His large hands stroke down my back to cover my butt, squeezing briefly. Then he lowers them to the backs of my knees, encouraging me to straddle him.

I moan in his mouth when I feel the hard ridge of his erection between my legs and I instinctively rub myself against him. It feels good, so I rock my hips harder.

"Janey," he mumbles against my lips. "Please...put me out of my misery."

His hand comes up with the condom, holding it up. I grab it, scoot back to sit on his thighs, and swiftly rip the foil with my teeth. Then I wrap my free hand around his cock, shiny with the juices I just rubbed on him. I'm tempted to put my mouth on him first, but I don't get a chance before he snatches the condom from my hold and rolls it on swiftly.

"Next time," he promises as he reaches for me.

I position myself over him as he guides us, one hand on my hip and the other positioning his cock at my entrance. Then he lifts one hand, folds it behind his head, and places the other loosely on my leg.

"Take me, Tiger."

Still wet and pliable, I easily open around the first inch or so of him. Letting my head roll back on my shoulders, I take a moment to enjoy the feeling of him inside my body.

"As slow as you need to. You set the pace," he mumbles, misinterpreting my pause.

I open my eyes, look at him, and place my palms on his chest. Then I slowly, but determinedly, sink myself down his full length. Tears sting my eyes at the stretch, but when I try to move, he squeezes my leg.

"Give it a minute."

I shake my head. "You don't understand. I welcome the burn. I *feel* it. I feel everything."

His hand shoots out, curling around my neck as he pulls me down to his mouth, kissing me deeply. Then he moves both hands to my ass, lifts my hips, and starts driving his cock up into me.

Plastered chest to chest, our mouths still fused, I fly apart for the second time as he grunts with his own release underneath me.

A little later, after a quick cleanup, I crawl back into bed and snuggle against him.

"Sore?" he asks, moving his hand to my ass.

"Yes. In the best possible way," I add when I feel him tense up.

His grumbled, "I'm glad," is accompanied by a butt squeeze. Then he continues with, "Because there's no fucking way I can go back to keeping my hands off you."

I lift my head and press a kiss to his lips before resuming my position on his shoulder.

"You won't get any complaints from me," I mumble.

His chest moves with his deep chuckle.

"That's what I was aiming for."

Closing my eyes with a smile on my face, I'm fast asleep in seconds.

EIGHTEEN

LEE

"Shhh."

Janey whips around, her finger to her lips. Then she points into the woods to her right.

Despite the sparse early-morning light, I have no trouble making out the bulky, dark shape of a black bear—fairly rare for these parts—scratching the bark off a trunk maybe fifty yards from where we're standing.

I know Janey carries bear spray—I saw her clip the can to her belt when we were getting ready—but it's still a little intimidating to encounter one out here.

We watch him drop to all fours and for a moment he appears to catch our scent, lifting his nose in our direction to sniff the air. He seems to decide we're no threat and casually lumbers off.

I turn back to Janey, who mouths, *"Okay?"* and I nod in response.

Despite having slept only a couple of hours, I feel surprisingly refreshed, although I would kill for a coffee.

We were still tangled up in each other's arms when Janey's phone woke us up at five. It was Jacob Branch.

Last night when we returned to the motor home, Janey had sent him a message with the pictures I took to confirm we'd found Amelia. He'd sent a text back to tell her he'd be in touch.

While we were getting dressed, Janey put him on speakerphone so I could listen in. He explained he had Mitch contact his former CARD team for assistance and wanted Janey to wait for them to mobilize backup, but she wasn't having it. Neither was I. I felt guilty enough this morning, knowing while we were sleeping—and in other ways occupied—Amelia had been shackled to a bed within walking distance.

One of the requirements in investigative journalism is the capacity to compartmentalize. This line of work exposes you to all kinds of trauma and human suffering and, without the ability to turn it off long enough to eat and sleep, the job would eat you up.

I'm sure it's no different for Janey, but she has her own trauma haunting her as well, making it harder to shut down.

She expressed to Branch, in no uncertain terms, we'd be making our move this morning before more harm could come to Amelia. The only concession she was willing to make was that she'd stick to getting the girl safe, but wouldn't take any big risks trying to take down Gibson before backup got here.

The plan is for me to focus on getting Amelia out of the trailer. Amelia should still remember who I am, which may help. Janey plans to take care of Gibson. I can't say I'm happy with that part of the plan—the guy has a fucking gun—but so does Janey, and even without, I'd put my money on her ability to take him down.

As we approach the campsite, I hope to hell I'm right.

Like last night, we make our way around to the other side of the trailer. This way we'll have the cover of the trees to shield our approach and get much closer.

The trailer is still quiet. No lights on and no one is moving about. Janey stops and motions me over when we're still thirty or so feet away.

"I need you to get as close to the back as you can," she whispers. "As soon as he comes out and moves away from the steps, you go for Amelia."

Then she unholsters her gun and tries to hand it to me, but I hold up my hands.

"Not taking your gun. You'll need it," I hiss.

She shakes her head. "I have bear spray and my skills. I don't intend to give him an opportunity to get near his weapon, and I don't want to end up killing him. Dead men can't talk. But on the off chance he finds his way back into the trailer, you need a way to protect Amelia. Her safety is priority."

I hate the idea of her facing off with an armed man using just her hands and a fucking can of bear spray, but I can't argue with the need to protect the girl at all costs.

Conceding, I take the gun from her and tuck it in the

back of my jeans. Then I tag her behind the neck and press a hard kiss on her mouth.

"Careful," I mumble, before ducking low as I make my way closer to the trailer.

Janey waits for me to get in position—crouched low with my back against the side of the trailer near the rear bumper—before she moves in. I watch her assume a similar position near the hitch at the front, the can of bear spray in her hand at the ready.

I'm not sure how much time passes, but it's long enough to have my legs cramping up from crouching, and the sky to brighten up overhead.

As I'm about to stretch out a leg for relief, I suddenly feel the trailer behind me move. My eyes snap to Janey, who is looking back. She felt it too. There's a brief pause, followed by a faint creak as the trailer shifts again.

There's movement from inside. I use my fingers to indicate to Janey someone is walking around. She nods her understanding.

The bathroom must be just on the other side, because a few seconds later I can hear who I assume is Gibson taking a piss, and then flush. A bit more shifting follows, and time seems to slow down to a crawl as I wait for the sound of the door.

When it finally comes, I duck down, hoping to get an eye on the guy. At the front of the trailer, Janey appears to do the same.

I hear the creak of the steps a second before a pair of hiking boots appears. They stop at the bottom of the stairs, and I hold my breath while I wait to see which way he turns.

The moment he starts moving left, I turn to look at Janey, who is already on her feet mouthing, *"Go."*

I almost stumble when I start moving while my body is still turning toward the rear of the trailer, but quickly recover. There is nothing but the rush of blood in my ears until I round the back.

"What the fuck?" I hear Gibson's voice come from the front of the camper, followed by what sounds like a scuffle.

I dart up the steps, hoping to fucking God Janey is kicking the guy's ass and not the other way around. Once inside, I immediately turn to my left where I saw the girl chained to the bed.

I can barely see Amelia under the pile of covers. It doesn't look like she's moved much, which is a bit worrisome.

"Hey, Amelia?"

I approach the bed with caution, not wanting to freak her out, but even when I reach out and pull down the top of the covers, she doesn't stir.

Her hair is matted and covering most of her face, but to my relief I see she's breathing. It wouldn't surprise me if that fucking scumbag kept her drugged.

Then I catch sight of her wrists, the pair of handcuffs she's restrained with, and the scabbed and inflamed skin around them. A hot rage surges through me. As if that poor kid didn't have enough trauma in her young life already, now she has more scars to remind her for the rest of it.

I'm about to see if I can find something to open them with when I hear feet pounding up the steps.

By the time I turn around I have a gun aimed at my face.

Pearl

I'm ready for him.

The moment he turns the corner I depress the trigger to blast him in the face with a hit of bear spray.

Except...nothing comes out.

"What the fuck?"

Shit.

I try to push the trigger again with the same result, wasting precious time and giving Gibson a chance to reach for his gun.

So much for a clean takedown.

I pelt the faulty canister at him, and immediately launch myself after it, hoping to keep the element of surprise. My aim is the gun, throwing my shoulder into his chest while grabbing on to the arm holding it with both hands.

Paul Gibson is no scrawny kid. The impact of my shoulder barely moves him and probably hurts me more than it does him. Still, as long as I can stay pressed against him and keep his arm extended, he won't be able to get off a shot.

I slightly shift my stance, hoping to use my hold on his arm as a pivot point to flip him over my hip. The kid is no dummy though; he clearly anticipated the move as he uses my sudden shift in balance to target the back of my knee while trying to wrench out of my hold.

I go down, but don't let go of his wrist. Twisting to my back, I yank on his arm and simultaneously kick out my foot, catching him square in the groin. Using my weight and his own forward motion, I manage to heave him over my head.

Almost.

The toe of his boot hits me in the face, and all I see is stars.

As I feel him scramble away from me, I realize I lost my grip on his arm at some point. Still blinded, I roll in the opposite direction, ending in a crouch, making my body as small a target as possible.

But instead of the sharp crack of a gun, I hear heavy footfalls on the metal steps.

Oh hell, no.

Getting to my feet, I blink furiously, trying to clear my blurred vision as I stumble toward the trailer door. I'm not even halfway there when the shot goes off.

For a second I freeze, the mental image of Lee lying bleeding on the floor as clear as if I were looking at it, making it hard to breathe.

The next instant I'm running up the steps, ready to

rip that lowlife to shreds with my bare hands, a primordial howl bursting from my throat.

But I come to a grinding halt when I find Lee kneeling next to a curled-up Gibson, who is sniveling and clutching his shoulder.

"Jesus, Pearl. You're bleeding."

I haul out and kick that dirtbag in the kidney. He cries louder. *Good.* He'll be begging for mercy by the time I'm done with him.

"Easy, Tiger."

Lee gets to his feet.

"Where's my gun?" I demand to know, still seething.

"I already shot him," Lee assures me.

"Then I'll shoot him again."

The guy on the ground whimpers.

Lee takes a step closer and lifts his hands, palms out.

"Calm down."

Guess he never got the memo those two words only add fuel to a woman's fire. The top of my head feels like it's going to blow off, so I kick Gibson again.

The next thing I know, I have my arms pinned to my side and my feet are dangling inches off the floor.

"Pearl, get a grip," Lee grunts when I try to wrestle free. "Amelia needs us."

Mentioning her name is like throwing a bucket of cold water on my rage.

"Where is she? Is she okay?"

"She's in one piece." He carefully lowers my feet to the floor and lets go of me. I notice he doesn't say she's fine. "But this guy needs something to stem the bleeding.

He's got a hole in his shoulder. And you have a nice gash over your eye that needs looking after."

"I can wait." I look around me and see a pile of dirty clothes on the floor next to the couch, grabbing a shirt from the top and shoving it at Lee. "Here, use this. I'm going to check on her."

I step over Gibson, resisting the temptation to stomp on him, and peek around the half wall between the small kitchen and the foot end of the bed.

The girl is curled up on her side, her body covered up to her shoulders and her hands clasped together by her head, still bound. Her face is obscured by long, dark hair. I carefully brush it back and see her eyes are narrow slits and her mouth is slack.

"That punk drugged her," I call out.

"I know," Lee answers over the sound of ripping fabric. "There are bottles of Ambien, Xanax, midazolam, and a couple of boxes of Dramamine. I'm guessing she's had a cocktail."

"Fucking hell, he could've killed her," I mutter.

I put my fingers to the carotid pulse in her neck, which seems much too slow.

"Search his pockets, I need keys for these damn handcuffs," I tell Lee.

"Give me a second," he returns. "Almost done."

A sharp cry from the other side of the wall is music to my ears as my anger flares up again.

While I'm waiting to release her, I gently fold down the cover to make sure she's not hurt anywhere else. My heart squeezes when I realize the girl is naked except for an adult diaper.

Jesus.

I quickly cover her up with the sheets when Lee pokes around the corner. Then I take the key from him and carefully unlock the handcuffs, sliding them from her wrists. She doesn't even flinch.

Taking the cuffs with me, I walk into the main part of the trailer where Lee seems to have made an impromptu dressing with the shirt I handed him. He's even tied Gibson's hands behind him. That explains the cry I heard, that can't be comfortable.

Kneeling behind his back, I undo the strips of fabric from his wrist, and none too gently slap the damn handcuffs on him.

"They're too tight," he whines.

I grab a handful of his hair and yank his head back so he can see my face.

"Ask me if I fucking care," I grind out, before dropping his head abruptly.

Then I pull my phone from my pocket and dial Jacob.

NINETEEN

LEE

"Who is Dr. Stern to you?"

The guy shakes his head, averting his gaze.

"I don't know," he mumbles.

Janey grabs his ear and twists viciously.

"Not helping yourself, you disgusting lowlife," she snarls. "You have five minutes before the feds get here. You'll get hauled off and locked in a cage with a whole other level of predators. The kind who'll fight over a new piece of ass, and like to give child molesters a taste of their own medicine. That's what's waiting for you, Gibson. And unless you start talking, no one will lift a fucking hand to help you."

Wow. Janey doesn't hold back any punches. If I were Paul Gibson, I'd be shitting my pants.

She looks pretty intimidating too, with that gash

above her eyebrow and her face still streaked with the blood she hasn't bothered wiping off yet.

What little color Gibson had left quickly drains from his face.

"She's ...she's my doctor. Those are mine."

He's referring to the collection of medications lined up on the kitchen counter. All the labels list him as the patient, but the medications were collected from different pharmacies. Branch did some calling and came up with the name of a Dr. Elenor Stern as the prescribing physician.

It's clear why he had to get different pharmacies to dispense this range of medication, because otherwise all kinds of red flags for contraindications would go off.

The puzzling piece is why one doctor would prescribe all of them.

"What kind of doctor?"

"A shrink, okay? She's my shrink."

A rustle sounds behind me and I turn to catch Amelia moving her legs under the covers. The worst of the drugs may be starting to wear off.

Janey had told me to take off the T-shirt I'd put on under my hoodie so she could cover up the girl with it. She refused to dress her in any of the clothes belonging to Amelia's captor.

She didn't remove the girl's diaper though. She left that for Onyx to deal with, who is apparently on her way with the CARD team. Janey mentioned she is better equipped to deal with any physical trauma Amelia may have suffered.

It would appear Onyx Baqri is GEM's resident field medic. Another name I'm sure is an alias. I already know Opal was a Transition House victim, and Janey confirmed she had been as well, so I think it's safe to assume Onyx falls under that same category.

"Why is she prescribing you enough drugs to bring down an elephant?" Janey persists.

I'm used to being the one asking questions, but it doesn't look like she needs any help. I'm happy to sit back on this one.

"I don't know."

"Bullshit. Are you telling me it was your idea to bait a little girl, groom her into trusting you for months, before finally abducting her? Keeping her chained to a bed and drugged out of her brain? You're saying you were able to con your shrink into writing you those scripts? Trying to convince me you're the one who came up with that plan?" Janey rants. "Fat chance. It's way too well thought out of a scheme for a dumbass punk like you."

She pauses to take a breath as Gibson appears to shrink under the barrage of her words.

"Where can we find her?"

He glances at me, maybe hoping for rescue, which won't be forthcoming from me.

"I don't know," he repeats.

Oddly enough this time he sounds almost sincere.

At the sound of vehicles approaching, Janey gets into his face.

"Hear that? This is your last chance before I hand you over to be thrown in a cell with a three-hundred-pound sadist named Bubba, who'll be thrilled to have a fresh bitch to play with. Choose wisely."

"I'm telling you the truth; don't know, okay?" he whines in a panicked voice. "I've never met her in person."

Outside I can hear car doors slamming. Gibson's attention focuses on the door.

"She'd email me the prescriptions. I swear, we only ever talk online," he rushes to share.

I catch Janey's eyes over his head. I'm pretty sure we're both thinking the same thing.

The next moment we hear footsteps coming up the stairs, and Matt Driver—Mitch's former boss and head of the CARD team—walks in the door.

The first thing out of his mouth is, "Fuck, Pearl, your face is a mess," followed by, "Is he our perp?"

"That's him," Janey confirms. "He doesn't enjoy the idea of bunking with Bubba and just started to volunteer some information."

"Excellent, we'll see what more he has to share," Matt says, hauling Gibson to his feet by his good arm. "Let me just put the trash away so there's room for Onyx to deal with the victim. She's right behind me."

"Hey, I need medical attention," Gibson complains when he's marched outside.

"All in good time," Matt tells him.

Onyx walks in a moment later, a red first aid bag slung over her shoulder. She takes one look at Janey and simply shakes her head before reaching into the bag, pulling out a stack of sterile gauze and a bottle of hydrogen peroxide she hands to me.

"Clean her up while I have a look at Amelia, will you?" she instructs, giving me a little shove away from the bedroom opening.

To my surprise, Janey doesn't protest as I scrub the drying blood off her face and barely winces when I focus my attention on her already swollen eye. She's going to have an impressive shiner.

I try my best not to listen to the soft whimpers coming from behind the flimsy partition.

The bleeding seems to have slowed down, but I suspect the cut will need a couple of stitches. I fold a couple of sterile pads into a temporary dressing and press it against her head.

"Here, hold this while I get some tape."

I direct her hand to take over when Matt walks back in.

"Okay, what've we got?"

"Guys," Onyx calls from the rear. "Can you take it outside? We're gonna need some privacy and, Pearl, I could use your help."

"You good?" I softly ask Janey when I read her expression of mild panic.

Her face quickly steels in that stubborn expression I know well as she nods.

"Fine. Get out of here."

She heads for the bedroom and I follow Matt outside. Two other agents I recognize as John Punani and Adam

Byron are already going through the truck, while Gibson looks on from the back of one of the two black SUVs.

"Is medical coming?" is the first thing I ask Matt.

"No," he surprises me by stating. "At Branch's request, and I happen to agree. Clearly this isn't a one-man operation, so if word gets out the girl was found and her abductor taken down, it might force the rest of the rats into hiding.

"So, we'll make sure Gibson gets the medical attention he needs, and Onyx is the best person to judge the level and type of care the victim needs."

There's no doubt in my mind she's gonna need a lot of it.

"Now, wanna tell me how the guy ended up with a hole in his shoulder?" Matt probes.

I shrug. "I have no idea; I was aiming for his head."

Pearl

"What about Olson, did you find him?"

"Depends on what you mean. Do we have him? No, not yet, but Opal is looking at the back of his head while we speak. She's within ten feet of him at the back of a Greyhound bus."

"What the hell, Jacob. What if he gets away again?

All he has to do is go to the bathroom at one of the stops and he's out of her line of sight."

"Which is why I sent Mitch along to Wythesville. He's following the bus," my boss states calmly. *"We need to know where the kid is heading. We've confirmed it's not that unusual for these temporary staff transfers to take place between locations, and any such request has to be signed off on by the program director for each office, but that still doesn't necessarily tell us who's behind this. We can have Olson do the work for us without his knowledge."*

It makes sense, although it doesn't sit well with me. Even if it's just been luck so far, Jesper Olson has proven to be slick as an eel. I'd hate to have him slip through our fingers again.

But that's what Jacob is good at, focusing on the big picture while I tend to get tunnel vision about the job at hand.

"What about Gibson? Anything from Matt Driver yet?"

"It's not even been three hours since they got on the road. They're not even back in Lexington yet," he points out.

I check the clock on the dashboard and am surprised to find it's only one in the afternoon. It feels like a lifetime ago since we were crouched behind that damn trailer this morning, waiting for our chance. One I almost fucked up.

We'd all left at around the same time. One of the CARD agents was driving Onyx and the girl to Roanoke to be dropped off at a private clinic, arranged by Jacob.

Amelia's parents are to join her there, all under assumed names, in case they were being monitored.

Matt was transporting the prisoner and the third agent had hooked the trailer up to Gibson's truck and was right behind his boss driving back to their offices in Lexington.

"How's your head?"

My hand involuntarily probes at the bandage covering the three stitches I ended up with. Luckily, the ER waiting room at the hospital in Beckley, where Lee insisted on taking me after we picked up my SUV, was pretty much empty. I was in and out in a little less than an hour. We just got back on the road.

"My head is fine, but Lee won't let me drive."

I throw him a sideways glare. He ignores it, Much the same way he ignored my protests when he got behind the wheel of my Chevy Traverse.

"You can't see out of one eye," Lee points out dryly.

He's right, my face looks ridiculous with one eye swollen shut. He was given a few suspicious looks in the hospital. I even had one of the nurses ask if I needed help.

"I see you're getting along well. Which is great, because I want you to head home and get a good night's sleep, but tomorrow I'm going to need both of your help tracking down this Dr. Elenor Stern."

"Make sure to check your email later," Lee comments with a healthy dose of sarcasm. "I'll be sending over my time and hourly rate."

He shakes his head at Jacob's responding chuckle.

A silence falls over the vehicle after Jacob abruptly ends the call.

I stare out the side window, not really seeing the landscape whizzing by. In my head I'm replaying the pitiful scene in the trailer, with Raj and me trying to get Amelia in the tiny bath tub. God knows how long the girl had been left to lie in her own filth.

Raj had already done a rape kit before she asked me for help, but it wasn't until we were washing the poor thing in the small tub we noticed the abrasions between her legs. Good thing Matt locked that piece of shit in the back of his SUV already, or I would've ripped his dick right off.

"You okay? I can feel anger radiating off you."

I turn my head to look at him. For once I don't bother trying to hide my emotions.

"He raped her," I blurt out.

The only reaction is the flare of his nostrils and the tension in his jaw, but I have no doubt he feels it deep.

Maybe I could've been a bit less blunt—phrased it another way—but the truth is, rape is about as ugly as it gets. Wrapping it up in prettier words doesn't make the act any less brutal. It does, however, detract from the devastating impact on the victim.

"It's gonna be hard for her to come back from," I add. "She may not have physical scars, but I sometimes wonder if the invisible ones aren't harder to bear."

"She already had her share of those," he shares bitterly.

I put a hand on his arm. "For now, she's in the best hands possible. Onyx will make sure she's looked after."

Lee startles me as he suddenly slams his hand on the steering wheel.

"How many other kids like Amelia are out there? We've gotta stop these animals."

"We're working on it," I remind him.

Without warning he swerves my SUV onto the off-ramp for the next exit.

"Where are you going?"

When we're stopped for a traffic light at the top of the ramp, he finally turns his eyes on me.

"I don't want to go home and get a good night's rest. I have a little girl I already don't see enough of. I want to do whatever the fuck I can to make her world even a little bit safer."

"Hey, I'm with you so far. What are you suggesting?"

He grins at me, just as the light turns green.

TWENTY

LEE

"Fucking Knoxville?"

I glance at Janey who is just walking out of the bathroom, wrapped in only a towel.

"Yes," I confirm to Jacob.

"Christ, Remington. I gave you guys orders for a reason. Onyx mentioned Pearl took yesterday's events hard, that she seemed shaky. The plan was to give her a break, get her away from the heat of the case, and back into her comfort zone. I was counting on you to keep her from doing anything rash and to get her home."

Janey lifts an eyebrow when she catches what I'm sure is a pissed-off expression on my face. I'm fuming, but force myself to take in a deep breath before responding to Branch.

"First, let me remind you once again, I'm not on your payroll," I start, forcing calm in my voice. "Secondly, next time consider being straightforward...making your expectations clear. Or, hell, maybe try asking, instead of using manipulation and subterfuge to move human beings like chess pieces in some high-stakes game like a master puppeteer, hiding behind voice distortion equipment and technology. Trust goes both ways."

I take a deep breath and watch as Janey sinks down on the edge of the bed, a mix of surprise and concern on her face.

"Not that it would've made a difference," I add for Jacob. "Because, for the record, coming here was my idea."

In the silence that follows my rant, Janey mouths, *"Is that Jacob?"*

When I nod, she bulges her eyes. Well, technically one eye, since the other is still too swollen to open all the way, making her expression look more like an imitation of Popeye than conveying shock.

"So noted."

Not much as far as apologies go, but this is Jacob Branch...I'll take the curt acknowledgement he heard me.

"Where are you staying?"

Janey motions to her ears and I put the call on speaker so she can listen in.

"We got a room at the Days Inn on the east side of town."

Last night our original plan had been to get a hotel downtown, but that would've meant busy city streets and no easily accessible parking. We picked this place because it has rooms at street level with direct access to the parking lot. Janey's Traverse is parked right outside the sliding door.

She'd waited in the SUV while I checked us in—not wanting the kind of attention the state of her face would draw—and I'd been able to let her in through the room's sliding door.

I'd run out to pick up some food so we could eat dinner in the room. Then I put in a quick call to Yana before we ended up crashing shortly after. Both of us had been exhausted.

"*Good,*" Branch responds. "*Olson got off the bus at the Kirkwood Street bus terminal last night and got into a waiting green Hyundai Elantra. Opal and Mitch were able to follow it to a gated property on Green Valley Drive, a street up from the country club, which is just south of you. They've both been camped out down the street all night. It would probably not be a bad idea to touch base with them. See if you can pick one of them up. They'll need a rental and a room so they can move independently and divide their time.*"

"License plate for the Elantra?" Janey asks, already opening the laptop she left on the nightstand.

"*I already checked. It's registered to a Carla Amato, sixty-three and widowed. But she's listed at a downtown address, not the place on Green Valley Drive. I want to know who owns that house.*"

"I'll see if I can do a property search online," Janey suggests.

"While you do that, maybe I can check in at the front desk for an additional room."

"I'll leave you guys to it. Oh, and, Remington?" he adds. *"I'll make sure your Jeep is in your driveway when you guys get back."*

I'd almost forgotten it's still parked in Charleston.

"Appreciated," I thank him, but the line is dead.

Janey is already pecking away at her keyboard when I get up. I move into her space and with my finger under her chin, lift her head for a kiss.

"I'll get the room, check in on Opal and Mitch, and pick us up some breakfast on my way back. You need anything, call."

"I will," she mumbles, her focus back on the screen.

Slipping my phone in my pocket and snagging the keys from the top of the dresser, I head out to the lobby.

Green Valley Drive is in a quiet, mature neighborhood. The streets are fairly narrow, but the houses are set back a fair distance from the road and each other.

I have to drive up and down the road twice before I spot the 'for sale' sign Mitch told me to look for on the lawn. Their vehicle is halfway up the drive, mostly hidden behind a group of cedars. The place—across the street and two houses down from the gated address—looks vacant.

I park on the street, making sure to pull as far onto the grass as I can, and pretend to look at the house. I've only seen one car earlier, passing me on the road, but I check in both directions. Then I grab the coffees and bagels I picked up, get out, and casually walk up the driveway.

"Oh, thank God."

Opal reaches over the back of her seat to grab one of the coffees from my hands and takes a deep tug. I offer the second one to Mitch and drop the bag of bagels on the console between them.

"You never told us what you guys are doing here," Mitch wants to know. "Last time I talked to Jacob, you were supposed to be heading back to Lexington."

"Hey, I go where the story takes me."

I gather from Mitch's doubtful expression, he's not buying.

"Nice try," he mutters.

"It was Pearl, right?" Opal weighs in. "She doesn't trust us not to lose sight of Olson."

As much as that is probably true, at least in part, it's not why I turned the SUV around.

"Let's just say, after yesterday's events, we wanted to stay close to the action instead of sitting on the sidelines," I offer by way of explanation.

"That, I'll buy," Mitch concedes.

I change the subject. "Any movement?"

"Nothing," Opal informs me. "Mitch explored the back of the property and that eight-foot chain-link fence goes all the way around."

I play devil's advocate. "Shouldn't be that hard to scale for a young guy though."

"No," Mitch responds. "But he'd have trampled the

brush at the back of the fence, and I can guarantee you nobody went through there."

"Fair enough. So what are we doing? Who's coming? Because I should get back to Janey, I promised her breakfast."

Mitch snorts from the front seat.

"I see things have already progressed to the honey-do phase? That was fast."

I don't need to respond, Opal does it for me with a sharp jab to her man's shoulder.

"Leave him alone. I think it's sweet. Janey will never admit it, but she needs someone to look after her from time to time. She forgets to take care of herself when she gets..." She pauses, looking for a word. "Hyperfocused on work."

"I would've picked borderline obsessed, but we'll go with what you said," I concede.

Opal turns a bright smile on Mitch.

"See? He knows her so well already."

Pearl

"She says he's been placed in a foster home where they have two younger girls."

Lee looks as relieved as I am. I had my blinders on and was gung ho to go after Olson, but Lee made me wait until he made sure Ricky would be looked after. I may have been pissed at the delay at the time, but I'm so fucking grateful he did that now.

"Better for him," I comment.

"Much better." He jerks his chin at my laptop. "Any luck?"

Ownership to the property hadn't been hard to pull up. Gourmand Enterprises. It sounds like some kind of catering company or maybe something to do with event organization, but I haven't been able to pull up anything to confirm that. No website, no advertising, no accreditations.

"Nothing," I admit grudgingly. "Jacob suggested passing the name on to Matt. See if the name means anything to the Gibson kid."

"Call him instead," Lee suggests. "Maybe he's got something new for us."

"Good idea. What about you? Anything?"

He's been looking for Dr. Elenor Stern.

"I found reference to three doctors in the United States by the name of Eleanor Stern, all spelled with an A. One has a doctorate in botany and appears to be a bit of a phenom on TikTok. The other is a veterinarian in Florida. And the third one I found an obituary for in a newspaper in Wisconsin, she was a pediatrician and died early last year."

"Try the American Medical Association or the American Psychiatric Association," I suggest. "And try only by first name too. The spelling is unique. Stern might be her married name and you'd be surprised how often women forget or just don't bother to update accounts or memberships."

"Good point," he mumbles, fingers already tapping his keyboard.

I shoot a quick text to Matt Driver with the address and name of the owner before following up with a phone call. He must be busy because it goes straight to his voicemail. I'm barely done leaving him a quick explanation of what it is I'm looking for when he calls me back.

"Got your message," he informs me when I answer. "I just got off the phone with Branch. I had some information, but he told me to get directly in touch with you."

That's interesting. Usually, Jacob prefers passing on any information from outside sources. I'm wondering if Lee's dress down this morning is the reason for the change in his MO.

"I was just leaving you a message, checking if maybe you could ask Gibson if he is familiar with that name or address I sent. But I'm more interested in your information."

"I'll check with him. He's been quite talkative, which is what I'm calling about." Matt chuckles. "Apparently you made quite an impression."

"Would've left a permanent one, given the chance," I bite off.

"You and me both. I've got three kids, I'd like nothing more than to wipe scum like this off the face of the earth, but all I can do is catch them, question them, and set the system in motion. We were at him all night and again this morning. He finally gave up some information I think you might want."

I hear the ping of a message and glance at my screen to see it's from Matt.

"What is it?"

"Gibson's log-in name and password."

"For?"

"Pure Allies Youth Counseling Services."

"You're shitting me."

"I wouldn't. Anyway, I thought I'd pass it on. I'll let you know if that name and address you sent triggers more information."

I'm only half listening to him, mumbling a quick, "Bye," before typing the name he gave me into my search bar.

Pure Allies.

I don't believe in coincidences. I'd bet my laptop Gibson just gave us the link we've been looking for to GLAN Industries. The same mysterious company involved in the child exploitation ring operating from the Youth Center in Lanark, which funneled money through a bank account in the Cayman Islands in the name of *Pure Caribbean.*

No, that can't be a coincidence.

"What did he have to say?" Lee wants to know, but I'm focusing on my screen, my mind racing as my eyes catch on one term.

Pro bono.

It's at the top of one of the first hits that popped up on my Google search. A Facebook post in a community group in Crested Butte, Colorado, from a mother looking for *pro-bono* therapy for her son. Another parent mentions Pure Allies.

"Janey?" he has to prompt me.

"I need you to call Vera back. Find out from her what the name of that pro-bono online therapy group is."

Pure Allies doesn't appear to have a website they operate through, but I find reference to an application you can download to your computer or phone.

I log out of my laptop and sign back in on the other side of the secure partition I installed on my hard drive. It protects the important side of my hard drive, in case the app I want to download collects information once installed.

Once there I connect to an external source, which is the first in a sequence of servers, computers, cell phones, and even Smart TVs, I am able to access through back doors I've installed. If anyone out there is trying to track me, they'll have a hard time finding me.

Lee is talking on the phone in the background as I connect all the links in the chain. Once I'm comfortable my trail is sufficiently obscured, I find the Pure Allies application again and start the download.

"Janey?"

I swivel around and watch Lee walk up to the table.

"You'll never guess, she says it's called Pure Allies Youth Counseling."

I grin, turn back, and point at my screen.

"Bingo."

He leans over my shoulder, peering at my computer where a logo with the same name is on display.

"*Son of a bitch.*"

He pulls over a chair and sits down beside me.

"Do you think it's linked to—"

"Pure Caribbean and GLAN Industries? You bet I do."

It doesn't surprise me he'd come to the same conclusion. Investigating is his bread and butter too.

"Where did you find it?" Lee asks.

A message appears indicating the upload is complete and the moment I click 'OK,' a login screen pops up. I pull up the message from Matt and copy the username and password.

"Matt. Gibson coughed up the name and his sign-in information."

For a few seconds—feeling like hours—we watch impatiently as a blue wheel spins on the screen while it loads.

"Fuck me," he mutters. "Yesterday when he said he'd only met his shrink online, it had us both wondering."

"Turns out we were right on the money, and I'm convinced Amelia was signed up with Pure Allies as well," I share.

Finally, a very basic dashboard opens up, displaying a calendar, two option buttons for 'Voice' or 'Text,' and below those a window captioned, 'Recent Messages.'

The first message is time-stamped at eleven forty-two today. It reads,

You missed your call-in yesterday.

Get back to me ASAP.

We have a customer.

At the top of the message the sender's name is listed.

Dr. Elenor Stern.

TWENTY-ONE

PEARL

"Are you sure?"

I glance over at Kate, who's sitting across from me.

"It's a risk," she persists. "What if she figures out you're not Gibson?"

"That's why I'm reading back every message first," I tell her. "To get into the role, get a feel for the language he uses. I have to try, it's the only connection to Elenor Stern we have."

The app appears to automatically store a historic record of all text interactions, but no recordings of any voice communications. Only a log with date, time, and duration of voice calls.

The good news is that it looks like in recent months the bulk of communication between Dr. Stern and Gibson was via text. Only three calls are listed since the beginning of this year.

"I know you're right," Kate concedes. "And I trust you, but just promise you'll be careful."

"I'm always careful."

Kate snorts as she stands up and leans over the table.

"Janey—sister of my heart—I love your confidence, I do, but sometimes confidence can get in the way of caution."

"Kate—pain in my ass—I appreciate your concern, I do, but I have every precaution in place. No one's going to get the drop on me."

She squints at me, pointing a finger at my face.

"Sure about that?"

I press my lips together and stare her down.

The reminder shakes me more than I'm ready to admit. There hadn't been a question in my mind I'd be able to overpower Gibson with ease. What I hadn't been prepared for was equipment failure or simple misfortune.

In an orderly world, neither a malfunctioning bear spray nor an accidental boot in my face should have been a factor. Except they were. If not for Lee's quick reactions, the outcome could've been disastrous.

Sobering, to say the least. I'd overestimated my control over the situation and the only smart thing I'd done was hand Lee my gun.

Trust Kate to poke a finger in the sore spot. She knows me too well.

"I'll be extra careful," I volunteer.

Maybe I can build an added layer of security to prevent tracking, and it might also be a good idea to sign into the account while on the move. That is, on the off chance someone is able to trace the data source to my cell phone.

"That's all I ask." She straightens up and moves to the door. "I should get going. I'm sure Mitch is ready for a break. Where did you say Lee went?"

"He's running a few errands. He should be back soon."

Kate knocked at the door maybe fifteen minutes after he left through the sliding doors. We both were running low on clean clothes, and he suggested picking up a few basic things for each of us at a mall, fifteen minutes north of here.

I still can't believe I agreed to let him pick out underwear and socks for me. The alternative had been to go with him, but aside from the fact my face would probably still draw unwanted attention, the whole act of shopping together for those things seemed almost more intimate.

I'm not about to share the particulars of Lee's shopping excursion with Kate though. She'd find it far too entertaining, and I'm not in the mood for the ribbing I'd receive. I've got work to do.

"Okay, stay in touch," she tells me as she heads out the door.

"You too," I toss after her.

So far nothing's been happening at the address on Green Valley Drive. The green Elantra is apparently still parked at the top of the driveway, and there's been no sight of either Olson or the woman.

Which reminds me, I should check with Jacob to see if he's come up with anything else on Carla Amato. I also haven't heard from Matt yet if Gourmand Enterprises rang a bell with Gibson.

We've accumulated plenty of puzzle pieces but the big challenge is finding out how they all connect. We could have a team of ten operatives and still not enough manpower to properly investigate every lead.

So far, all we know for sure is Olson and Gibson know each other and both appear to be working for a well-organized operation. It appears Pure Allies Counseling is used for perhaps some type of selection process and plays a major role, but the only sure connection is Dr. Elenor Stern. The prescriptions and the messages on Gibson's account are irrefutable. What is unsure, however, is whether she's the only therapist donating their time who is part of the scheme, and who those other therapists even are.

We suspect Pure Allies may be connected to GLAN Industries, but don't have confirmation to corroborate that, and we also don't know how Gourmand Enterprises might fit in.

That's a lot of open questions, and the biggest one is who or what is GLAN Industries. The organization seems to have a vested interest in an odd mix of research, and both for-profit, and not-for-profit companies. Clearly, it has access to substantial capital but, despite that, is able to keep an unbelievably low profile.

We don't even know how large the scope of this operation is. What we've stumbled on this time could merely be the tip of the iceberg. We need to be smart how and where we focus our energies.

At this point, finding Dr. Stern is key. She's our one clear lead, but if she's the one coordinating Olson and Gibson's efforts, she absolutely cannot suspect we are on to those two. Which is why it's important to keep track of Jesper and make her believe Paul Gibson is still in the game as well.

Too many damn loose ends.

First things first; call Jacob.

"Pearl, I was just about to call you." He barges right in. *"I thought you might want to know there is no existing mortgage on the Green Valley Drive property. Looks like it was bought outright."*

Interesting.

"Anything else on Gourmand Enterprises?" I ask.

"Other than Carla Amato receives a bi-weekly pay deposit in her bank account from them, not much concrete yet. Her pay is a modest amount of $3,500 per two weeks."

A quick mental calculation brings that to about eighty thousand per year, which is more than the average annual family income nationwide. Jacob would call that modest, but lots of Americans would be ecstatic over that kind of money.

"Not a bad income for a woman alone."

"Perhaps, if she were a caretaker or housekeeper for the property," he suggests.

"We need to find a way to talk to her," I point out. "Or better yet, get inside that house."

"Gas leak in the neighborhood, that'd do the trick," he proposes.

"Can't be Lee or me. Olson has seen us both."

"Mitch can do it."

"He's gonna need to look legit," I point out.

"Leave that to me."

Before he has a chance to hang up on me, I quickly get him up to speed on my plan to connect with Elenor Stern through the app. It's basically a repeat of my conversation with Kate, with Jacob voicing concern and me allaying those.

"Go for it," he finally concedes. *"But I want a full briefing tomorrow night at eight. Make sure Remington is there as well as Mitch and Opal, even if they dial in."*

"Will do."

"Will do what?" Lee asks, coming in through the sliding door.

The phone at my ear has already gone dead.

"Jacob wants everyone in on a case briefing 8:oo p.m. tomorrow. And what on earth is that?"

I point at the mountain of shopping bags he drops on the bed. I see Kohl's, Target, Old Navy, and a few grocery bags. He turns his head to the bed and takes in the pile.

"You mean this? I thought you knew I was picking up a few things."

"Eight bags for some underwear, socks, and a couple of snacks?"

He shrugs and returns his eyes to me with a grin.

"What can I say? I like shopping."

Lee

I'm pretty proud of my purchases, but Janey is doubled over laughing.

I'm thinking that's not a good sign.

Okay, I may have gone a little overboard with the black stiletto booties, black pleather leggings, and white linen men's shirt, but I was trying to cram a couple of fantasies all into one.

In my defense, I also bought a pair of cargo pants similar to the ones she's wearing, a couple of plain T-shirts, and enough socks and underwear to last a week. Nothing fancy, nothing frilly—but serviceable.

Shopping's my jam. It's how I relax. Often I don't even buy anything, but there's just something about aimlessly wandering through a store that seems to ease my churning mind. Even Yana, at only six, shares that trait and loves going to the mall with her daddy when I go to visit.

Still, I'll take Janey's ridicule every damn day if it means I get to hear her laugh.

It's a first, and it's memorable.

First of all, she laughs like a girl—bright and melodious—which is a total surprise since her speaking voice is almost raspy with little to no inflection. Except of course when she's pissed.

In addition, Janey lost in laughter is a sight to behold. In fact, I think I could look at her forever.

"You're staring," she observes.

"I can't help it, you're so damn beautiful. You should laugh more."

Her hand flies up to her face and I'm not sure if she's trying to cover her black eye or hide completely, but I'm guessing from the pleased curve on her mouth she liked hearing it.

"Then you should go shopping for me more often," she snickers behind her hand. "Your choices are pretty funny."

"Why? What's wrong with what I bought?"

"Lee, you bought me stilettos and pleather pants."

"And the dress shirt, don't forget that," I point out.

"Yes, well, the shirt was a good choice, but those leggings and boots...they're gonna make me look like *Catwoman*."

Precisely.

That's the look I was going for. Or maybe a cross between *Catwoman* and the chick from *Kill Bill*.

"I almost bought the matching corset they had."

That has her laughing again, which I'm finding does more for my libido than the fantasy of her decked out in faux leather.

I try to convey as much with the kiss I lay on her after toppling her on the clothes-covered bed. Apparently, laughter got her blood pumping too, because she meets me with equal passion.

Jesus, the woman can kiss.

We go from zero to sixty. I'm in a hurry to get her naked and yank up her shirt, while she tries to shove my jeans down my ass without bothering to unzip first.

Neither of us is very successful, which is probably a good thing, since just then a knock sounds at the door.

I roll off the bed and pull up my jeans, which Janey managed to force halfway down my ass, as I make my way to the door. I quickly check on her to make sure she's decent before I open it. Mitch is leaning against the door-post, looking a bit rough but wearing an amused smirk.

"Sorry to interrupt," he announces, brushing past me. "But I just got off the phone with Jacob. I'm gonna crash shortly, but he wanted me to check in with you for tomorrow morning."

I must've missed something. "What happens tomorrow morning?"

"Didn't Janey tell you?"

"I was just about to, when you knocked," she says, her poker face back in place as she sits down behind her computer.

"Maybe someone could fill me in?" I prompt.

"Mitch is going to dress as a Knoxville Utilities Board employee and try to get entry to the Green Valley Drive house," Janey shares.

"Yeah, but he wants you as backup," Mitch tells her. "He's having a KUB van—at least one that looks like it—dropped off here at the hotel tomorrow morning. He says we'll find a uniform and some electronic gadgets inside. He wants you in the back of the van keeping an eye on the outside of the house while I'm inside."

I'd love to be the hero and offer myself up in her stead but, aside from the fact I probably don't have the appro-priate skillset, even suggesting it wouldn't go over well. If

I want to pursue anything serious with this woman, I'm going to have to check my alpha tendencies.

This is what she does—who she is—and her job comes with major risks. Mine brings its own challenges and risks, and she'll have to deal with those as well.

"You'll get used to it," Mitch mumbles, reading my thoughts before turning to Janey. "Van should be here between seven thirty and eight. I want to wait until after nine before we head out there. Most folks should be at work by then."

"How does Branch manage to get hold of a Knoxville Utilities van and uniforms at such short notice?" I'm curious to know.

"He's Jacob Branch." Janey shrugs. "Trust me, we've asked ourselves similar questions all the time. He gets stuff done."

"He does. Anyway, I'm gonna get some sleep, see you tomorrow."

As soon as he closes the door behind him, Janey announces, "If I'm going to be busy tomorrow, I may have to send that message tonight."

She indicates her computer, where I see she still has the Pure Allies app up on the screen.

"What did Jacob say?"

She mentioned she'd check in with him to float the idea of impersonating Gibson.

"He's fine with it," she explains. "I'm trying to come up with a plausible excuse why he would've missed a scheduled appointment and is responding to her message so late."

"Phone out of juice?"

"He had a generator. Besides, that wouldn't have taken him days to resolve."

True enough.

"What if he dropped it? Wrecked it?" I suggest. "He would've had to go into town—Beckley or somewhere—to get it replaced."

Janey is playing devil's advocate again. "He could've done that yesterday."

"Unless he didn't feel like he could safely leave the girl so soon again."

"Why?"

They say the closer you stay to the truth, the more believable the lie.

"Because she wasn't really waking up from the drugs. He was afraid to give her more."

This time she flashes me a bright smile.

"That'll work."

TWENTY-TWO

LEE

"Fuck, Janey."

I look down to see her elegant neck extended as she arcs backward between my legs to suck one of my balls into the warm heat of her mouth. I'm grateful for the firm grip her hand has at the base of my cock or I might go off early.

Never mind it's only been a few minutes since she surprised me in the shower. It was her exploring hands and mouth traveling down my body before she slid around, her back to my front, and went down to her knees, that already had me halfway there.

She's magnificent, her skin glistening as the water sluices down from her upturned breasts, small, but perfect. When I see her free hand disappear between her legs, I can't take any more.

Bending down, I pluck her off the shower floor, spin

her around, and lift her with my hands under her ass. Her legs automatically wrap around my waist as I brace her back against the wall and drive my dick into her tight pussy.

She immediately drops her head back against the tile wall, and I latch my mouth on to the soft skin of her neck as I power inside her. My legs soon start shaking with the effort to hold back my release, and when I finally hear her call my name—sweetest sound ever—I give in and let it rush through my body.

I sink down on the shower floor and try to catch my breath, still cradling her in my arms.

"Thank you," she mumbles, her face in my neck.

"I think you've got that backward, honey, I should be thanking you."

She lifts her head and leans back, a serious expression on her face as she looks me in the eyes.

"No." She gives her head a little shake. "You gave me back something that was taken from me before I even knew how precious it was. That's what I'm grateful for."

I lift a hand to cup her face and lower my forehead to hers.

"In that case, it was my absolute pleasure."

I'm about to kiss her when I hear the ping of an alert.

"Is that your phone?" I ask her when she scrambles off my lap at the sound.

"My computer. It's her," she announces as she wraps herself in a towel and darts into the bedroom.

Last night we waited until well after midnight for a reaction to Janey's—or should I say Paul Gibson's—

response to Elenor Stern's inquiry. Not that we sat idle, I continued my search for the woman, while Janey tried to find the source for the app. As time went on and we didn't hear anything back, the worry perhaps something in the carefully composed message she'd sent had alerted Elenor, grew.

It had been probably closer to one when I finally convinced Janey to come to bed, where I did my best to distract her. Reasonably successfully, if I say so myself, because she eventually fell asleep draped over me. She'd still been sleeping when I snuck out of bed this morning and hit the shower.

Grabbing a towel of my own, I follow her into the room.

"It *is* her," Janey says triumphantly. "And she bit, hook, line, and sinker."

She shifts her laptop slightly, making it easier for me to read.

I told you to be more careful with dosing. This one is petite.
Clean her up and get her ready for transport in a day or two.
More details when I hear from the customer.

"This one?" I point out.

"I know, I caught that too. This wasn't Gibson's first rodeo. Jacob says he'd found some other names of kids who went missing after going on a quest. I'm gonna send Jacob a screenshot of this and ask him to find out from Evolution Quest whether any kids went missing from a trip Gibson was assigned to."

"You should ask him to check in with Driver too, we haven't heard from him, have we?"

She shakes her head. "No, doing it right now."

Janey still seems to be buzzing when she gets dressed after sending the message to Branch, with a request for him to touch base with Matt.

"You should probably eat something first," I suggest when it looks like she's getting ready to leave.

I'd bought a bunch of protein shakes, fruit, granola bars, and some other quick-grab food yesterday.

"I don't think I could eat right now," she shares. "I'll grab something for on the way."

She snags a banana, curls a hand around my neck in passing to give me a sweet kiss, and darts out the door.

Once again, I'm tempted to go after her, but hold back. Practice makes perfect. I grab a protein shake instead, pop another pod in the coffee maker, and sit down at the table with my laptop.

I've done a search on the AMA website for any psychiatrists with Elenor—without the A—Stern, with zero result. Then I tried by just putting in the first name, with the same outcome. So, this morning I'll do the same search once again, but this time the last name Stern. I'm pretty sure that'll produce something. Hopefully not a substantial list, but I should be able to whittle it down to something manageable once I eliminate all men.

Twenty minutes later, a name jumps off the page at me: Nora Winwood-Stern. A fifty-six-year-old psychiatrist with a home address in Oak Ridge, which is about thirty minutes from here.

My gut tells me this is her.

A little more research turns up the number for a clinic in Oak Ridge where she is listed as Dr. Nora Stern, so I give the number a call.

"Scarboro Mental Health Services, how may I direct your call?"

"Is Dr. Stern available?"

My question is met with a brief pause before the chirpy voice is back.

"Are you a former patient?"

Former? Does that mean she's no longer practicing, or just no longer practicing at the clinic.

"Actually, no, I'm a journalist. I was hoping to ask Dr. Stern a few questions for an article I'm doing on an online counseling service she is affiliated with."

"Are you sure you're talking about our Dr. Stern?"

"Positive."

"Well, that's very strange. For one thing, Dr. Stern hasn't been with us for almost four years and, this has to be off the record, mind you..." she lowers her voice. "I don't think she'd be able to answer any questions. Early onset Alzheimer's. Philip—that's her husband—insisted on looking after her at home, but I heard he'd moved her to an assisted living facility."

Definitely not the discreet receptionist you'd expect at a mental health clinic, but today I'm not complaining. It feels like I'm on the right track here.

"Just to confirm, if you don't mind; we're talking about Dr. Nora Winwood-Stern, correct?"

"Yes, but I'm surprised you were given that name, she actually hasn't used it since she divorced her first husband. Philip Wainscott is her second husband. She never took his last name, though, and had reverted to using her birth name; Elenor Stern."

The hair on the back of my neck stands on end.

"Did you say Elenor?"

Pearl

"Yes?"

The voice over the intercom is female.

"Utilities, ma'am. We have reports of a gas leak in the neighborhood, I'm gonna need to check your lines."

"My lines?"

"Yes, ma'am. Your gas lines, any gas appliances, water heater and the like."

There's a brief pause and I'm starting to get worried she's not going to let us in, because then we're fucked. If this was a real call and she refused, the police department would be called in for assistance, which is clearly not an option for us. Or, it's possible she's checking with Knoxville Utilities to confirm the gas leak.

Shit, either way the cover is blown and Olson, and whoever else is in the house, would be on high alert.

Finally, the intercom crackles to life again.

"Will it take long?"

I blow out the breath I've been holding while Mitch answers her.

"I'll be in and out like a flash, ma'am."

"All right, then. We're having a problem with the gate though. Someone's supposed to come fix it sometime today so you'll have to enter the code yourself. It's 1739. Just follow the driveway around to the back."

For good measure he smiles and salutes the security camera mounted on the gate post. Then I see him leaning out the window from my perch in the rear of the van, punching the numbers on a keypad under the small speaker. The ornamental gates swing open and he starts up the drive.

"Phew. That was close," he comments.

I can hear him in stereo, with one naked ear, and through the communications earbud in the other.

We found a case with electronic gadgetry in the van. The communications equipment, some button-sized audio bugs, a pair of clear glasses for Mitch to wear with a small camera mounted in the frame, and a tablet for me to follow and record the video feed.

I duck low in the shadows as we approach the house. I turn my attention to the small screen and try to visualize the inside layout of the large, modern Tudor. The house was built in an L-shape, with sharply peaked rooflines and dormers. I'm guessing five, maybe six bedrooms.

I knew it was a big house from the satellite images, but from the street you can't really appreciate the size because of the heavy tree cover.

As instructed, Mitch follows the driveway around the three-car garage to the rear of the property. He pulls into one of two parking slots at the back of the garage marked with a sign that says, 'Deliveries.'

A short, graying woman I recognize from her license picture steps out of a door to our left and motions to Mitch, who gets out of the van and walks around to the rear, opening the back doors.

"Are we good?" he asks in a whisper as he grabs a utility belt and straps it on.

I give him a thumbs-up.

Then he grabs his toolbox, slams the doors shut, and follows the woman inside.

"Is it dangerous?"

"Sorry?" I hear Mitch ask.

"The gas leak: should we be worried?" the woman I know to be Carla Amato asks. *"I'm supposed to be getting the house ready for an important event and if there's a problem, I need to tell the owner."*

"When's the event?"

"It starts on Friday, but the first guest may be arriving as soon as tonight."

Boy, Mitch is smooth. Barely in the door and already he's getting useful information.

"It's not likely dangerous, ma'am. It appears to be a

pressure issue in the lines. This is mostly just routine. Like I said, I shouldn't be long."

The camera pans around what looks like a combination mudroom/laundry room, momentarily focusing on a pair of dirty hiking boots tucked under a bench. I quickly mark the time signature down for easy retrieval.

"Is this a gas dryer or does it run on electricity?" I hear his voice.

"I'm not sure, I think electric."

On the screen, I catch a brief glimpse of the narrow space behind the appliance as Mitch appears to check. The machine is plugged into an outlet.

"Looks like it," he confirms.

Then he follows the woman into a massive kitchen, where she points out an industrial-sized range sporting six burners, a grill on either side, and two side-by-side ovens. I may not be the appropriate person to judge since I'm not really much of a cook, but that thing would be more at home in the kitchen of a restaurant. It seems overkill in a regular house.

Mitch spends some time turning on the burners, grills, and ovens one by one.

"Don't you need to look behind it?" Carla, who's been following his every move, asks.

"No. If there were a leak or any interruption of the pressure in your lines, the flames would've flickered." He turns on a big one in front again. *"See? Yours show a nice steady flame."*

I have no idea if what he says is right, but the woman seems to accept it as truth.

"I should check your water heater and furnace next. Where can I find those?"

She leads him into a hallway that appears to run all the way to the front of the house. She opens a door tucked under the stairs and flicks on a light switch.

"You're going to have to find your own way, I don't go down there," she announces as she steps aside.

Unlikely Olson is hiding down there or she wouldn't have let Mitch go down alone.

The space is unfinished and looks fairly new, like the rest of the house, but the ceilings are low. I can tell Mitch has to duck under pipes and beams. The light of the overhead bulb only reaches so far, and he has to turn on a flashlight to find the water heater and furnace against the back wall. To the right of the furnace, I spot two, stacked, plastic bins.

"Mitch," I draw his attention.

"I see them," he mumbles, moving in that direction.

He opens the lid of the top bin, revealing strands of white Christmas lights. Underneath is a handful of thick, half-burned candles, and half a dozen Halloween masks. Tucked in a corner is a rolled-up piece of paper. Mitch quickly unrolls it to reveal a sketch of a room layout with windows, doors, and a fireplace marked, and what look to be six round tables arranged around the room. On the bottom are some small scribbles I can't quite make out.

"Important?" I ask.

"Don't know."

I watch him roll it up and tuck it in his tool bag. Then he replaces the lid and carefully lifts the top one down to get to the next bin. This one appears to contain mostly paperwork and my interest is immediately piqued.

"Is everything okay down there?" Carla's voice calls down.

Fuck.

"Yep. Just checking one last thing and I'll be up," Mitch calls back.

"Take what you can," I hiss in his ear.

Reaching in the bin he grabs a handful of papers, shoving them in his bag. Then he uncovers a simple ring-bound notepad and takes that too. He's about to slide the lid back on when I spot a folded card sticking up. It has some kind of ornate design on the front.

"Wait. What's that? Is that a brochure or something?"

I watch as he picks out the card and holds it up. The image is some kind of pen sketch, it looks like maybe some kind of cornucopia, I can't quite make it out, but I can read the words underneath.

PURE DELIGHTS
DINNER AND AUCTION

"DEFINITELY TAKE THAT."

TWENTY-THREE

PEARL

"On the range hood in the kitchen, underneath the fireplace mantel in the living room, and in the main foyer there's a large landscape painting. I was able to tuck one under the edge of the frame."

These listening bugs use a cell phone signal to transmit, making it possible to tap into the audio from anywhere. I have no idea how Jacob got his hands on these, but they're a vast improvement on the old ones that used radio frequency and had a limited range of transmission.

While Mitch drives us away from the house, I pull up the audio feed on my computer.

"No sign of Olson though. I wish I could've gone upstairs," Mitch comments. "I swear I heard movement up there."

I'd been watching and listening as he asked Carla

Amato about any more gas fireplaces on the upper level, but she claimed there weren't any. She'd seemed to become progressively more nervous as she showed Mitch around the house and appeared rushed to finally show him out.

"That was probably him. Give me a minute and we should be able to listen in," I tell him.

"Let me just find a quiet spot and get these decals off the van."

He turns into a quiet side street and pulls over to the curb. While he takes the magnetic panels off the doors outside and tosses them in the back, I climb into the front seat with my laptop.

"...she didn't say when, just to have the place ready and set up for Friday and that we'll have that one extra guest."

The feed is coming in from the kitchen, I hear the sound of a faucet running.

Behind me the back doors of the van slam shut, just as I hear Jesper Olson's voice.

"When is Paul supposed to be here?"

My heart rate speeds up.

"Tomorrow or Thursday."

The water turns off and then I hear the clang of metal on metal. Maybe a water kettle set on the stove?

"So what am I supposed to do in the meantime?"

The driver's side door opens, startling me, and I almost miss Carla's response when Mitch settles in behind the wheel, no longer wearing the KUB coveralls.

"...help me get the rooms ready. There's plenty to do.

She wants you to keep a low profile. She didn't seem too happy with you."

"The kid was fine when I went back into camp first. She was supposed to be right behind me. How was I gonna guess she'd get herself lost?"

"Look, I don't even want to know. I just take orders and do my job. Now, why don't you make yourself useful and take the girl's breakfast upstairs? Make sure she eats."

It takes only a second to register but Mitch beats me to it.

"Did she say girl?"

All I can do is nod.

He slams his fist on the steering wheel.

"All this time I was in that house and they were holding a girl in there?"

I'm sick to my stomach, but my mind is already spinning.

"We're gonna need help."

"LET'S NOT JUMP THE GUN, AND WHERE THE HELL IS Remington?"

Jacob sounds agitated.

Lee hadn't been there when Mitch and I got back to the hotel. He'd left a note saying he was looking into something and would check in later.

Mitch told Kate to follow us back. There's nothing to gain by surveillance now we have ears inside. It doesn't sound like Olson is going anywhere soon, and at some point, someone may notice the strange vehicle parked behind the bushes across the street.

Besides, we really will need all-hands-on-deck on this one. Although, by the sound of it, our boss isn't eager to rally the troops. Those troops being Mitch's former CARD team.

"Jacob, with all due respect, we're gonna need manpower and planning to tackle this on such short notice," Mitch takes him on. "There's a girl being held in that house right now. Hell, we don't even know if there will be more, or when those so-called guests are supposed to arrive. And God knows what happens when it becomes clear Gibson and the girl won't show up there by Thursday, they're bound to know something is up. They'll scatter like the wind and there aren't enough of us to keep track of everyone."

"I don't care about everyone. I care about the head of the snake. It's clear Stern is pulling the strings here. It's her I want. We bring in CARD or any other law enforcement agency, and they'll start asking questions and throwing their weight around in a way that won't escape notice. She will slip from our grasp then."

Jacob isn't always calm and collected, but I've never heard him as animated and heated before. My eyes dart to Kate, who shoots me a look across the room. She hears it too and decides to call him on it.

"Jacob, is there something you're not telling us? You seem...agitated."

Any response he might have had is pre-empted by an old-fashioned ringtone coming from my laptop.

"Is that..."

"Oh fuck," I mumble when I look at my screen. "She's calling."

"Who is? Stern?" Jacob snaps. *"Whatever you do, don't answer."*

No shit, don't answer. I almost roll my eyes, even as my heart is in my throat.

"I know, but not answering will make her suspicious."

"You can message her in five minutes, telling her you were outside and missed her call," Mitch suggests.

"Right, but what if she tells me to call her back? What do I do then?"

"I'm calling Matt, we'll have to get the kid to work with us."

Except, we won't have any control over what Gibson might say to tip her off. On the flip side, if we don't get his voice on the line if she asks, the game would be up anyway. Six of one, half a dozen of the other. It's a risk we're going to have to take.

My laptop pings and I see a notification pop up.

"She left a voice message."

"Well, let's hear it," Jacob urges.

"Paul. Where are you? Call me back."

THEY SAY THE MEMORY OF SMELL IS THE STRONGEST, which is probably why even at just the first sound of that voice, the scent of damp, musty air fills my nostrils. It's suddenly dark and I'm tied to a bed.

Even after decades, that voice is my nightmare come to life.

"Janey?"

It's Kate, she's kneeling in front of me. I can see the shock I'm feeling displayed on her face.

She recognizes it too.

Lee

"Philip Wainscott?"

The man standing in front of me looks like a stiff wind could knock him over. Looking at least two decades older than his wife, you'd think he'd be the one in a nursing home.

Only one Philip Wainscott in Oak Ridge, and to my surprise still at the same address his wife listed at the AMA when she was still married to her first husband.

"The one and only. Who's asking?"

He may look frail, but his sharp voice and keen eyes tell me he won't be a pushover.

I hope the truth—or as close thereto as the situation warrants—will be enough.

"My name is Lee Remington, I'm an investigative reporter. I'm doing a story on specialized counseling services for troubled youth, and I came across Dr. Elenor Stern's name. Your wife?"

The old man nods. "Yes, that's my wife, but clearly we don't share the same last name so that doesn't explain how you end up on my doorstep looking for me."

Definitely not a pushover.

"It was actually the office assistant or receptionist who answered the phone at the Scarboro clinic who suggested I speak with you."

"Is that a fact? I'm not quite sure how I'll be able to help if you are doing a story on counseling services, but I have a feeling it'll be the most entertainment I'll get today. Why don't you come in and explain? My Cerberus won't be back until lunchtime, so we have forty-five minutes."

He steps back inside and I follow as he shuffles down a dark hallway and into a study. The messy desk is stacked with old newspapers and publications, and the two walls on either side are covered with six-foot-high overflowing bookcases, showing an eclectic mix of at least ten years' worth of *National Geographic* magazines, medical textbooks, old *New Yorker* publications, a well-used copy of a familiar encyclopedia, and lots of other odds and ends.

He plops down on a creaky chair behind the desk and pulls a key from his shirt pocket, fitting it in the bottom drawer.

"Well, sit down. You can join me."

He pulls out a bottle of bourbon and a couple of tumblers from the drawer.

It's just past eleven in the morning, a little early for

bourbon, but I'm willing to sacrifice if it helps me get the answers I'm looking for. I accept the glass, and take a sip.

"Nice, isn't it? I have to keep it hidden from my gatekeeper; she'd confiscate it in a heartbeat.

"Now, why don't you tell me why you're really here," he challenges me. "Because my wife didn't work exclusively with troubled youth. She provided services to anyone in need, so I seriously doubt her name would've been mentioned in relation to any kind of specialized counseling."

The old coot is sharper than he looks, and I'm going to have to decide on the spot whether I trust him enough to tell him more.

I decide to gamble with the brutal truth.

"And yet your wife's name came up as connected with Pure Allies, it's an online counseling service for teens. Her name also appeared as the prescribing physician on a collection of bottles with medication used to keep an abducted young girl drugged while she was being groomed for sexual exploitation."

I'm afraid I've pushed honesty too far when his face drains of what little color he had left, and his hand clutches at his chest.

I'm already halfway out of my chair when he motions for me to sit back down.

"I ain't dying yet," he manages in a hoarse voice before he sits forward and pins me with piercing, watery brown eyes. "Never, in her entire life, has my Elenor brought harm to a living being. Not ever!" he adds in a raised voice. "Young man, if I weren't spitting nails right now, I'd be laughing at how far off the mark you are."

"Mr. Wainscott, I'm not here to accuse your wife," I try to calm him. "From what I understand, she's had some health issues and wouldn't have been able to write those scripts herself, but someone did...using her name. This same person is also impersonating her as an online therapist, preying on vulnerable kids."

"Certainly you don't think I..."

He can't even bring himself to finish that sentence.

"No. I don't, but I'm hoping you—"

A door slams shut at the front of the house, triggering the old man into action. He scoots his seat back, and quickly shoves the bottle and his glass into the bottom drawer.

"Quick, give me yours."

I toss back what's left and hand him the glass.

"You'd best get going before Beth barges in here," he warns me.

"Beth?"

"Beth Sweet...my Cerberus. She's a ballbuster. Looked after my Elenor before she moved to the care facility, and now I can't get rid of her. She shows up every afternoon."

As if on cue, the door opens and a woman pokes her head in. Manners instilled by my mother have me jump to my feet.

"Oh, you have company," she says in a gentle voice. "It's time for your lunch and your medication."

I can't see this woman—slightly plump, with gray hair,

and a wide-eyed smile—being a ballbuster, but I know damn well not to take anything at face value.

"I was actually just leaving," I volunteer, digging a card from my pocket and handing it to Philip Wainscott. "Whenever you have a minute, I'd love to finish our conversation."

A shiver runs down my back as I make my way to Janey's SUV I left parked along the curb.

When I pull away a moment later, I cast one last glance at the house, just in time to see a curtain fall back into place.

TWENTY-FOUR

PEARL

If not for Jacob's snapped, businesslike voice keeping me grounded, I might've curled up in a ball on the floor.

Of everything ever done to me, it's ironic the most paralyzing memory is that soft, soothing voice. Almost hypnotizing. The woman behind it one of the vilest, most inhumane creatures I've ever encountered. Worse than my mother, or any of the nameless, faceless men she encouraged to live out their depraved fantasies on my younger body.

I have to focus on the fact I'm no longer a defenseless child.

The woman was one of three people who were supposed to have perished in the fire that burned down Transition House and took with it all its dark secrets twenty-some years ago. Three people.

First Josh Kendrick resurfaced as the director of a youth

center in Lanark last year. Kate was undercover investigating a missing teen and recognized him, despite the passing of decades, the different name, and his altered appearance.

His voice had betrayed him too.

And now *Dr. Elsbeth Sladky*, back from the dead. What a coincidence.

"Pearl! I asked if you were ready," Jacob barks.

Or is it?

"Did you know?" I ask him.

In the small pause that follows, I'm trying to wrap my head around the possibility our boss has known more than he shared with us.

"We don't have time for this. Matt is on standby for your call, now patch the kid in."

Right. We still have to respond to the voice message. The plan is for me to run the voice call between Gibson and the therapist through my computer so we can listen in, and I can record and intervene if the guy goes off script. He's already been instructed to blame any kind of irregularities she may comment to on a bad connection.

I make the call to the number Matt told us to call in on.

"Hello?"

Gibson sounds nervous. Shaky. I hope he's shitting his damn pants. *Miserable excuse for a human being.*

"I'm about to patch you through, so get your act together," I snap. "She catches on something is off, it's your ass in a cell with Bubba."

To get him to cooperate, Matt ended up promising

Gibson he'd make sure he wouldn't be turned into some-one's bitch inside. That prospect apparently scared him more than anything. *Good.*

"Jesus, Pearl," Mitch mumbles, hiding a grin.

"Put the call through, Pearl," Jacob prompts.

There's a suspended silence in the room, the only sound... the line ringing on the other side.

"It's about time," is the first thing the woman snarls.

My skin breaks out in goosebumps.

"Sorry, Doc. Generator keeps crapping out and it took some time to get it going again."

Gibson plays his role as agreed, and I let out a breath I hadn't realized I'd been holding.

"Well, it won't matter anymore, tomorrow morning I want you to bring the girl in."

"Tomorrow?"

"Yes. Our newest customer wants a chance to test the wares before the others get here, and I'm going to need some time with her before that. He's flying in on Thursday. The rest of them are arriving Friday afternoon, as planned."

"Okay."

I glance up when I hear a sharp inhale of air to notice Mitch looking like he's about to explode. Kate notices too and puts a restraining hand on his shoulder.

"Is someone with you?"

The question has me tense up.

"No, no one. I mean, other than the girl, but she's sleeping. It's probably just a bad connection."

"You didn't drug her again, did you? Only restraints from now on."

Phew. She seems to buy it.

"I haven't since last time."

"Good. Now, one thing, I don't want you bringing the trailer here. It draws too much attention."

"Where do you want me to leave it?"

"Where it is. You can pick it up after the auction. And before I forget, the gate code is one seven three nine. Carla was supposed to get it fixed sometime this week."

I find Mitch's eyes on me and nod. He's probably thinking the same thing I am. With Matt listening in on the other side and Dr. Stern or Sladky, or whatever the hell she calls herself, laying everything out in the open, there's no un-involving the federal agents, no matter how much Jacob would like to.

"One seven three nine, got it."

"Oh, and, Paul? Plan to be there around one and don't make me wait. Any delays you let me know, understand? Right away."

"Yeah, all right."

She ends the call and for a moment no one says anything. Then I hear Matt's voice on the other line that is still open to my computer.

"Pearl? Did you get everything?"

I glance at my screen and catch the duration stamp on the recording I took.

"Two minutes and twelve seconds recording. Yes. I got it."

*"Good. And, Branch? If you're listening, and before

you do anything, we need to talk. I'll call you on a separate line."

Then he too hangs up.

"Take forty-five minutes, people. Eat, nap, go for a walk, do whatever you need to do to process and get your heads in the game. We'll reconvene at one forty-five," Jacob orders. *"And, Pearl? Find out where the fuck Remington went off to."*

The moment he signs off I turn to Kate, who looks exhausted. Not a surprise since she was parked on Green Valley Drive all night.

"Did you catch that?"

"What?" she asks, running a hand through her hair.

"He wasn't surprised," Mitch answers for me. "Jacob," he clarifies when she looks at him confused. "He didn't seem surprised when you recognized Sladky's voice."

"Why would he recognize her voice?" Kate probes.

"I don't know if he would or not, but he knows who Elsbeth Sladky is," I point out. "What her role was at Transition House. Yet he didn't seem surprised that Sladky and Elenor Stern are one and the same person."

"You know how he is," Kate dismisses. "All business, all the time."

"Maybe, but don't you find it a little too coincidental two people who were supposed to have died in the fire turn out to have been alive? It makes me wonder if he knew they'd survived, and if so, how? Haven't you ever wondered what his story is? It's obvious what drives us, but what about him?"

I know I've planted a seed when I see the shocked expression on her face.

We've all wondered about Jacob Branch, the mysterious voice on the phone, who seems to know everyone and has the ability to make things happen at the drop of a hat. But who is he really? What makes him tick?

I leave Kate to ponder for herself and grab my phone, turning it back on. I go to dial Lee to find out where he is, when I notice several missed phone calls from him.

He answers me on the first ring.

"I'm parked down the road from Elenor Stern's house in Oak Ridge."

"Wait, what?"

"Dr. Nora Winwood-Stern. That was her first husband's name. Elenor Stern is her birth name she reverted to after she divorced his ass. I spoke to husband number two, Philip Wainscott. Elenor Stern has Alzheimer's and is in a care facility."

"We already know Dr. Stern's real identity. We just heard her on a call. It's—"

I'm about to fill him in when I hear the shattering of glass.

Lee

That moving curtain could've been Philip, keeping an eye on me.

It could've, but something tells me it was the woman he calls his Cerberus. The gatekeeper to hell.

There was something off about her. She was a little... too smooth and too perfectly in character. She looked like a slightly younger version of Mrs. Claus. It didn't mesh with the way the old man portrayed her. Unless he'd been joking, which he may have been in part, but there'd been real tension emanating from him when she poked her head in.

The other thing that doesn't sit well with me is the fact she was his wife's caregiver first. I wish I'd had the chance to ask Philip how that came about, and how she ended up staying on to look after him.

I'm already turning onto the road to take me back to Knoxville when I make a right instead of a left, back toward the neighborhood I just left behind.

It's not often my journalist's instincts let me down and right now they're telling me there's something not right. My last abrupt change of plans had brought us to Knoxville and, as it turns out, that had been the right call to make.

A sudden sense of urgency has me floor it until I pull onto his street. I drive past the house and notice the light-gray sports sedan I saw sitting in the driveway when I left is still there.

An Audi S4 Prestige. Nice car, expensive too, and way out of character for a fifty-some or sixty-year-old housekeeper. In fact, now that I think about it, the woman herself had looked 'expensive,' almost doll-like. Smooth, newly peeled skin—or whatever the fuck it is women get done to their face—the lips a little too plump, and those wide eyes, as if someone had taped them open.

Or someone had extensive plastic surgery.

I quickly loop around the block and pull into the parking lot of a United Church just down the street. I'm able to drive all the way around the building and there I find a spot where I can back the SUV in behind some landscaping. Not much of the vehicle should be visible for anyone driving by, but from this angle I have a great view of Wainscott's driveway and the front door.

I think it's time to call Janey.

Over the next ten or fifteen minutes I try her several times but keep getting dumped straight into her mailbox. Next, I give Jacob a try. His phone rings seven times before it goes to voicemail. I'm starting to wonder if something is going on and am about to dial Mitch when Janey calls me back.

I quickly update her on my discoveries and she just starts to tell me something about Elenor Stern's identity when I catch sight of someone stepping out from behind the church in my peripheral vision. Before my mind registers what is happening, the passenger side window shatters, raining glass all over me.

I think it's instinct that has me duck down but with the steering wheel in the way, I end up with my head wedged against the door.

Somewhere in the distance I swear I can hear Janey yelling my name, but it's like I'm underwater. Even breathing seems difficult. I try to reach for the door handle just inches away but my arm isn't working.

That's when I realize I'm shot.

Pearl

"Lee, dammit! What's happening? Lee!"

All I hear is gurgling.

I feel panic clawing at me as I look to Mitch and then Kate for help.

"I heard glass shatter and—" I shake off the paralysis and force myself to focus. "I think he was shot. He said he was in Oak Ridge, parked down the street from Elenor Stern's house. Wait," I catch myself, thinking hard on the other name he gave. "Her husband's name is Philip... uhh...Wainscott. That was it, Wainscott."

"Give me the phone, Janey," Mitch orders, holding out his hand. "Get on your computer, find me that address." Then I hear him say to Kate, "Get on the horn with Matt, if he doesn't answer, call Punani. Tell them to get hold of law enforcement in Oak Ridge right now."

My hands shake so hard I mistype the husband's name the first time. I force myself to tune out everything else and focus only on the task at hand. Then it suddenly occurs to me; Lee was driving my vehicle. I have tracking on my SUV.

I access the program, pull up the list of license plate numbers and click on my own. A street map pops up showing a single, blinking red dot. I switch the view to satellite and zoom in. It looks like a parking lot, and when I hover my cursor over the building a name pops up. I click on it to pull up the information.

"He's in the parking lot of the United Church, one nineteen East Magnolia Street," I call out.

Next, I open a new screen, type in Philip Wainscott, Elenor Stern, and East Magnolia Street. The street number pops up right away; one fourteen.

Then I grab my bag and rush to the sliding door, only to realize I have no vehicle.

"Here," Mitch shoves my phone back in my hand. "I can hear him breathing, keep talking to him. I'll drive."

"Kate," he calls out as I open the door and step outside. "Call me with updates."

With my phone pressed to my ear, I run beside Mitch to his vehicle parked a few spots down. All I hear is his shallow, rattling breath, as I get in the passenger seat, and Mitch peels out of the parking lot.

"Hang on, Lee, hold on, honey. We're on our way. Keep breathing, for your little girl; she needs her daddy. And for me, I need you too. You're the only man I've ever trusted. I'd be..."

When the words get stuck in my throat, Mitch reaches over and gives my knee a squeeze.

"Keep going, Janey. He hears you."

"Please, keep breathing. I've never counted on anyone

in my life, but I'm counting on you, Lee. Please hang in there."

As Mitch drives us to Oak Ridge, I never stop rambling, barely aware of the stuff coming out of my mouth. But my words aren't nearly as important as my message is.

TWENTY-FIVE

PEARL

The moment Mitch pulls in behind a police cruiser, I am out the door and running.

The entire street was blocked off by emergency vehicles when we drove up. A cop directing traffic tried to wave us past, but Mitch rolled down his window and did some fast-talking. I don't know what he said, I was too busy listening to the first responders I could still hear over the open line.

I'd heard them arrive, the sirens first, and then running footsteps approaching, and a woman's voice trying to get Lee to respond. Then came the click of a car door opening, followed by rustling. The same woman's voice—closer now—started listing injuries to whoever else was there.

"Gunshot wound to the bicep, looks to be through and through." Then there'd been a pause when all I heard

was more rustling. *Shit, looks like the bullet entered the rib cage under his arm. It hit his lung. I need a chest seal."*

I'd sat there frozen, listening helplessly while Mitch raced us to the scene, but I'm not helpless now. I'm running like my life depends on it, aiming for the ambulance still parked next to the church. He's in there, I heard them remove him onto a backboard and from there onto a gurney. But I couldn't hear him struggle for breath anymore.

"Hey! Stop! Miss! You can't—"

A cop tries to stop me from approaching the ambulance but I easily evade him. I'll let Mitch handle him as well, and I rush for the rig, pulling open the back door.

I vaguely register the EMT hovering over the stretcher, but I'm focused on the man lying on it. His chest is bare—they must've cut off his shirt—save for the cords hooking him up to a beeping monitor, and he has an oxygen mask covering his face.

"You can't come in here," the woman states, right before plunging a needle in his chest.

"I'm his wife," I find myself lying.

She doesn't respond, but removes the needle, leaving a catheter in place she tapes down.

"Is he okay?"

My voice sounds thin and desperate, even to my own ears.

"Your husband has an injury to his chest and air started collecting in his chest cavity..."

"Pneumothorax," I offer.

She darts me a quick look before returning her eyes to the monitors.

"Yes, I had to decompress. Sorry you had to see that," she mumbles.

A guy pokes his head through a panel separating the cab from the back of the rig.

"Are we ready to roll?"

"I think so. His stats are leveling," the woman answers. Then she turns back to me. "Coming?"

I don't have to be asked twice and climb up.

"I'll meet you there," Mitch says.

I hadn't noticed he'd been right behind me.

"I'm Gwen. I need you to sit right there." She points at a bench on the opposite side of the gurney.

No sooner am I seated when the ambulance pulls away, lights and sirens rolling. Gwen sits down on a stool next to Lee's head and grabs a clipboard and a pen.

"What's your name?"

"I'm Janey."

"And your husband is?"

"Lee Remington."

"Any health problems? Generally speaking?"

Geeze, I don't know of any, but that doesn't necessarily mean anything. We haven't actually had a chance to share a ton of personal information, having been kind of busy with this case. I should've anticipated questions though. I'm sure she'll be asking about insurance information next, and I don't even know if he has that either.

"He's pretty healthy overall," I end up telling her. Then anxiety has me add, "Is he going to be okay?"

She throws me a sympathetic look that doesn't exactly alleviate my anxiety.

"He has a gunshot wound through his right upper arm. The good news is, it looks to have gone right through, so it's likely just soft tissue damage that should heal. The bad news is that same bullet reentered his body through the rib cage and punctured a lung." She lifts her arm and points out where the shot went into his chest. "I'm not gonna lie, he wasn't looking good when we got here, and it was confirmed when I put him on the monitor. But you saw me just relieve the pressure inside his chest and he's looking better now."

A deep groan sounds from the gurney as Lee blinks and tries to lift his head. Gwen puts a firm hand on his shoulder, keeping him down.

"Stay still, my friend. There's a bullet still lodged inside of you somewhere and, until the surgeon can get in there, we don't know what damage it's done."

"Janey."

His voice is little more than a sigh, but I don't have trouble recognizing my name.

I reach out and grab his ankle—the only part of him I can reach.

"Right here."

His eyes don't track too well but find me anyway. Then he says something else, but I can't make it out.

"What was that?"

Agitated, he reaches up with his left hand and lifts the mask from his face.

"Housekeeper...shot me. Beth...Sweet...is Elenor," he carefully enunciates.

I can tell it takes a lot out of him.

"Don't talk," I urge him. "It can wait."

He shakes his head and groans again. "No...husband in...danger. Check."

"Philip Wainscott?"

I already have my phone out and am dialing Mitch when Lee manages, "Yes."

Gwen brushes his hand aside and readjusts the mask on his face.

It's clear Mitch didn't check his screen before answering when he barks, "Talk to me," in my ear.

"It's Janey. Where are you?"

"Still by the church, cops are holding me up. How's Lee?"

When I glance over, his mask is back on but his eyes are still fixed on me as I relay the information to Mitch.

"He's hanging in there and was able to give some info. Someone needs to check on Philip Wainscott, just down the road at one fourteen. Elenor Stern's husband. Keep an eye out for Beth Sweet, she's the housekeeper. Lee thinks she's impersonating Elenor Stern. And she's the shooter."

"One fourteen and Beth Sweet," Mitch repeats. "Got it. Look after him. I'll be in touch."

When I lower my phone and end the call, Lee nods ever so slightly before he closes his eyes.

"Wow," Gwen comments. "Are you guys cops or something?"

I catch her curious look and shrug.

"Or something."

———

I don't do sitting idle well and I hate small spaces.

Which is why, instead of sitting in the too-small, over-crowded waiting room, I've been pacing the hallways and the lobby.

When we arrived at the hospital, Lee was immediately wheeled to the OR. His brief moment of lucidity seemed to have taken its toll on him and the remainder of the trip to the hospital he was out of it. I had only a second to press a kiss to his pale lips before they took him into the surgical wing.

That was two hours ago.

I've had texts from Jacob and Kate asking how Lee was doing, and the truth is, I don't know. No one has come to talk to me yet. Even Raj sent me a message, although she seemed more concerned with my well-being, but that's Raj for you, she's the mother hen to us all.

The only person I haven't heard from yet is Mitch.

"Pearl!"

I turn around to watch the man in question stalking toward me, but I don't like the grim look on his face.

"Any news?" he asks before I can ask him the same.

"Still waiting. You?"

He ignores my question and asks another one.

"How are you holding up?"

"I'm okay." I'm not, but it doesn't help anyone if I turn

into a basket case. "Now, what is it you don't want to tell me?"

He drops his head, mumbles "*fuck*," and stares at the toes of his boots. "The old man's gone."

"What do you mean *gone*?"

"We were too late, Janey. Cops found him in his study, single gunshot wound to the head. No sign of the housekeeper."

Oh no.

"Mrs. Remington?" sounds behind me.

It doesn't register until Mitch leans in and whispers, "I think he means you."

I swing around to a young man in blue scrubs wearing a kind smile.

"Lee?"

"Your husband made it through surgery well, Mrs. Remington." He holds out his hand. "I'm Dr. Hegel, trauma surgeon. Your husband is a very lucky man. Aside from the injury to the right lung I was able to repair, there was no substantial damage done. It was..."

He continues to explain but I no longer hear anything as relief turns my knees to jelly. I feel Mitch's arm around my waist, keeping me standing. I take in a deep breath and force myself to listen.

"...moved to ICU but if you'd like, you can briefly see him in recovery now. I'll show you the way."

All I can do is nod, but when the doctor motions for me to follow him, I turn to Mitch.

"She's gonna get away, Mitch. I can't let her get away."

"First things first; go see Lee, honey. I'll wait. I've got some calls to make anyway."

I'm so torn.

With every fiber of my being I want to see Lee is okay with my own eyes, but I also need to be out there tracking down Elsbeth Sladky, aka Beth Sweet, aka Elenor Stern.

The bitch has haunted my dreams for long enough. For all those years she was nothing but a ghost; a dark memory I had no defense against. But I can overcome flesh and blood. I want that chance.

"Sure?" I confirm with Mitch.

"Positive. I promise I'll be here."

It costs me to turn and follow the doctor, but when I walk into a room and see Lee watching from one of the beds as I approach, I know I made the right choice.

He's attached to softly beeping machines and bags of fluid with wires and lines. His rib cage is wrapped in bandages, which continue halfway down his right arm. But the mask is gone from his face, replaced with only a cannula under his nose, and his color is markedly better.

"Janey."

He lifts his left hand off the sheets covering the lower half of his body and turns his palm up. Recognizing the invitation, I cover it with mine, feeling his long fingers wrap tightly around me.

"Hey," I manage, my voice raspy. "You're awake."

A nurse walks up and checks the monitors.

"Yeah. Close call," he whispers, and then coughs with the effort.

"Don't talk," I urge him.

"Actually, the coughing is encouraged," the nurse assures me. "It helps clear remaining fluids from the lungs."

I wait for her to move away before I lean over the bed, putting my mouth close to his ear.

"You scared me," I confess.

The fingers of his hand squeeze mine.

"Sorry."

I nod sharply and swallow hard to escape the sudden sting of tears which threaten to fall.

"I heard you," he whispers. "On the phone, I'd dropped it somewhere but I could hear you talking to me." He's interrupted by another bout of coughing. "I held on to your voice like a lifeline, Janey."

He lifts my hand to his mouth and presses a kiss to my knuckles. For a moment he lets his lips linger before he returns my hand to the bed.

Then he takes the conversation in a direction I'd hoped to avoid.

"Wainscott?" he asks tentatively, as if he already senses the outcome isn't going to be good.

I give my head a little shake. "I'm sorry. They found him dead. Headshot. No sign of the housekeeper."

His eyes close briefly.

"She drives a light gray Audi S4 Prestige. Sports sedan." More coughing. "Gray hair, around sixty, average height."

"Light blue eyes and soft voice."

He looks surprised when I finished the description for him.

"I heard her voice," I explain. "Elenor Stern's. It's Elsbeth Sladky, the former—"

"I know who she is," he interrupts, resulting in another fit of coughing that has the nurse return to his bedside.

"All right, you need some rest," she declares firmly, looking at Lee, but the message is intended for me. "Say your goodbyes, you can have another visit with your wife when we move you to the ICU."

Lee pulls on my hand when the nurse moves to a bed on the other side of the room. I lean forward.

"Wife?"

I smirk. "Don't worry, it was just a ploy to get into the ambulance," I assure him.

"I don't mind."

There's an intensity behind his soft words I'm not sure I'm ready for. Not here, and not now. I straighten up and intend to take my hand back but he holds on tight.

"Go get her, Janey," he whispers.

I shake my head. "I don't want to leave you."

"I'll be fine. Go get her, Tiger. You need that more. Be careful though, I need you to come back to me in one piece."

I lean in again, touch his face with my free hand, and bend close to brush my lips over his.

"I will. She's taken enough pieces of me as it is, she won't get any more." I give him one more gentle kiss. "I care about you."

"Feeling's mutual," I hear him murmur as I turn for the door.

I'm not sure what prompted me to add those as my last words, but somehow, they make it a little easier to walk away from him.

If I've learned anything in these past weeks, it's that you can't always control life's curveballs.

I stop at the nurses' station to leave my number in case of an emergency.

As promised, Mitch is still waiting for me in the lobby, talking on his phone by the tall windows beside the front entrance.

"And?" he asks, tucking his phone in his pocket when I walk up.

"He's awake and talking."

"Good to hear."

"Yeah. He wants me to go after her."

Mitch puts a hand on my shoulder and ducks down to look me in the eyes.

"And what do you want?" he asks in a gentle voice.

"I want to get that girl out of the house, I want to finally get my hands on Jesper Olson, but what I want most of all is to rid the world of Elsbeth Sladky."

"Figured as much," he comments with a lopsided grin. "I'm parked right outside. I'll get you up to speed on the way."

Then he straightens up and starts heading for the doors.

I follow close on his heels.

TWENTY-SIX

*P*EARL

"Matt's team is arriving sometime tonight. They'll be bringing Gibson and his truck."

"Hear him out," Kate stops me on a whisper, before I can voice an objection.

It was already dark by the time we walked into the hotel room in Knoxville, finding Kate in the middle of discussing strategy in a conference call with Jacob and Raj. It doesn't look like she's had a chance to catch up on any sleep.

Jacob was just bringing us up to speed when he dropped the bombshell. Apparently, Gibson is to be part of the plan. I'm not sure I'm on board with that, but I'll hear him out.

"Gibson isn't expected at the house until sometime after noon tomorrow, so we'll have tonight and tomorrow morning to prep him."

"Prep him for what?" I can't stop myself from asking.

"*Getting us inside,*" Branch clarifies. "*I've been monitoring the audio feed, and a couple of hours after you and Mitch left for Oak Ridge, I overheard a conversation between Carla and Olson in the kitchen. She was relaying an earlier call from 'Doc' and mentioned something happening that caused a change of plans. Apparently instead of coming in tomorrow, they're now expecting Sladky to arrive sometime tonight.*"

"So why not go in tonight? Why do we need Gibson to get us inside? We have the code."

"*First of all, because Carla may be easy to pull a fast one on, but Elsbeth Sladky isn't. She'll be hypervigilant after what happened today. My guess is she'll want to collect the proceeds of this auction before she disappears from the radar again. We can't screw up this chance.*"

Again, it sounds like Jacob has personal knowledge of Sladky, information I file away for exploration later.

"*Gibson will be able to get us all the way inside the house, since no one will question his presence. That gives us the element of surprise. His truck will be like the Trojan horse.*"

"According to Matt, the bed of the truck has a cover," Raj takes over. "We can have a team hiding in there, waiting for a signal."

"You're forgetting one important component we're missing," I point out, accepting the bottle of water Mitch hands me. "The girl."

I tip the bottle back and take a deep tug when Jacob's answer has me spraying it out.

"We've got that covered. Matt is putting in a call for a female agent to pose as the girl."

"Like hell he is," I burst out. "If anyone goes in, it's me."

"Janey..." Raj pleads, probably appealing to my voice of reason.

But I feel perfectly reasonable. If anyone goes in it should be me.

"No," I tell her. "This is mine."

"Look," Kate tries. "Emotions are running high today. Maybe it's not such a good—"

I glare at her and shake my head. I feel like a fucking mastiff with a bone, and I'm not about to let anyone take it away from me.

"You don't look a thing like Amelia," Mitch points out.

"Bullshit. I have a similar build, you just need to get me a brown, long-haired wig and a ball cap to hide my Asian features. I can fake it long enough to get inside." Then I add for Jacob's benefit. "You're the one who forced me to go undercover at Evolution Quest and I did all right."

"You did," he concedes. *"But hear me, Pearl, we need someone with their head in the game. Who won't lose sight of the plan when things get hot."*

"I won't. And trust me, Jacob, I want this to work more than you do."

Part of me wants him to disagree so I'll have an opening to pry deeper, but he ignores it.

"We're going to need a distraction inside the house to

draw attention away from what happens outside, giving the rest of the team a chance to get inside before someone catches on. That means you'll have to be patient and wait for the right time."

"I can do it."

I'm encouraged by the fact he seems to be considering it, but apparently my assurance is still not enough for him.

"This morning you heard her voice on tape and it paralyzed you. What makes you so sure that won't happen again?"

"Because this time I'm prepared."

The truth is, she doesn't scare me. Not anymore. Not after I already faced the biggest fear of my life this afternoon. There's nothing she can do or say that would scare me more than the prospect of losing Lee.

"Very well."

We are instructed to eat and get some rest before the CARD team arrives later tonight. I briefly contemplate calling the hospital to check on Lee, but we only left Oak Ridge a little over an hour ago, and the nurse promised to call if there was any change.

It's probably better anyway to keep my focus on the job at hand. With any luck, I'll be able to check in on him in person by this time tomorrow.

I hope.

"Oh, I almost forgot to mention," Mitch announces as he walks in, a couple of paper bags with the dinner he picked us up in his hands. "Oak Ridge cops have Lee's phone, should he ask. Matt's already been in touch with them to let them know the shooting is part of an ongoing federal investigation, but, so far, local PD insists on holding on to any evidence."

Mitch slides my order of lo mein across the table and sits down with his own dinner. Kate opted in favor of a few hours of sleep over food.

Mention of Lee's phone reminds me of his daughter, and I suddenly wonder if perhaps I should try and dig up a number for her mother. I'm not really sure what the right thing to do would be, so I voice the thought to Mitch.

"At this point, I think I'd let him make that call. He may not want to unduly worry them. At least that's how I'd feel if I were lying in a hospital bed and had to decide whether or not to inform my daughter." He chuckles at himself. "She'd be pissed to find out later, but I'd rather take that than have her worry about something she can't do anything about anyway."

"Right," I mumble, feeling stupid for even having brought it up.

What he says makes sense, but I wouldn't really know since I've never really had anyone in my life worry about me, other than perhaps my teammates. Let alone a six-year-old girl.

I don't know anything about kids. Maybe I'm not cut out for relationships, and I'm definitely not cut out for children. This thing between Lee and me, it may not be a good...

"Stop thinking," Mitch says with his mouth full. "I know what you're doing; you're talking yourself out of a good thing—maybe the best thing that's ever happened to you—because you're running scared."

"That's ridiculous," I scoff.

Then I focus my attention on my lo mein, shoving a bite in my mouth, but that doesn't stop Mitch from taunting me with the last word.

"Is it?"

WHEN MITCH LEAVES TO JOIN KATE IN THEIR ROOM to grab some shut-eye after dinner, I open up my laptop.

I'm too restless to even try and lie down right now.

The first thing I do is check my email and my eye catches on one from an old customer I designed an online security system for. It came in late this afternoon when I was still at the hospital. Attached are a couple of screen-shots of error alerts he can't decipher.

I start reading the accompanying note when my phone pings with a message. It's from Jacob, and immediately my focus is back on the case.

She just arrived at the house. Turn on audio feed.

I don't question how he would have that information. Jacob has his ways.

It takes me a second to open the app, but then I hear her voice right away. Although Jacob undoubtedly is already recording this, I make sure to tape the audio as well.

"...*put my car in the garage and carry my bags up to my room.*"

There's a clinking sound of keys changing hands and a door closing. The feed is from the kitchen so I'm guessing whoever she handed her keys off to went out the back door.

"*Can I make you something to eat?*" I hear the house-keeper ask.

"*No, I ate, and besides, I have a few calls to make I need some privacy for. I'll be in the living room. Tell the boy not to disturb me.*"

The *boy* she's referring to must be Jesper Olson.

Footsteps move away from the microphone and I quickly switch audio to the feed from the bug Mitch stuck under the mantel over the fireplace. I pick up the click of the door closing and soft footfalls on the carpet.

"*It's me, we have a problem.*" There's a brief pause before she speaks again. "*The old man had a visitor today. You'll never guess who—Remington. Yes, the same one.... How am I supposed to know how he found me?... Oh, I agree, it's not a coincidence. First, he shows up back in Lanark, and now happens to be in Tennessee?... I know what's at stake. I'm not an idiot.*"

This time she's silent a little longer, presumably listening to the person on the other end.

"*We can't take that kind of risk and besides, that's no longer an option... Why? Because I eliminated the problem.*

Both of them. I didn't have a choice. In case you forgot, we have the auction this week. There's too much riding on it...I'll make sure all operations are shut down here...Yes, I know it means no one left behind. I'll take care of it... I'll let you know.

Holy shit.

I hear footsteps and then a door opening.

"Carla, lock up? I'm going upstairs."

I'm so focused on the audio feed, I jump a foot in the air when my phone starts ringing. It's Jacob.

"Who was she talking to?" I barge right in.

"Whoever it is, she doesn't want the others in the house knowing about it," Jacob responds calmly.

Too calmly.

"You know, don't you?" I suggest.

"I have my suspicions," he confirms to my surprise. *"But it doesn't change anything."*

"What do you mean?"

"Tomorrow goes ahead as planned."

"But if we take her down, we might never know who—"

"Let me worry about that. You worry about taking care of Sladky. You heard the woman; she doesn't intend to leave anything or anyone behind. We need to make sure she's not given the chance."

"I don't intend to let her slip through my fingers," I state firmly.

"No matter what? Are you ready for whatever that means?"

"Absolutely. Are you doubting me?"

"I'm not. But I wanted to make sure you weren't doubting yourself."

I open my mouth, ready with knee-jerk assurances, but stop myself.

Am I doubting myself?

I did let that punk Gibson get the better of me. And just tonight, I was definitely doubting my capacity for relationships.

Yet, when it comes to Elsbeth Sladky, there is not a doubt in my mind I'll be able to do whatever it takes to stop her.

"No matter what," I'm able to confirm with confidence.

"Excellent. Now get some rest, Janey. That's an order."

It's not until I crawl in bed after a quick shower that it hits me.

That was the first time I've heard him call me by my real name.

TWENTY-SEVEN

LEE

"Mr. Remington?"

I turn my head to the door to see James, one of the nurses, walk in.

"Delivery for you."

He holds up a cell phone and an envelope.

My phone is probably still on the floor of Janey's SUV, unless the police collected it. I haven't really given it much thought until now. It's been a restless and uncomfortable night. I've done little more than doze off and on.

That, plus whatever medication they've had me on, made it hard to keep a straight thought at all.

Still, I can only think of one person who'd send me a phone.

"Leave it on your nightstand?"

"I'll take it. Thanks."

I wait until he's gone before I open the envelope.

Guess I was wrong; the note is not from Jacob Branch.

Mitch told me the cops have your phone, and I was worried you wouldn't have any way to talk to your daughter.
Funny the things the mind focuses on when sleep won't come.
I hope to see you tonight
J.

JANEY.

Wait...if she hopes to see me tonight, does that mean she expects this to be over? Have they tracked the Sladky woman down?

All of a sudden, I feel disconnected—out of the loop—and I wish I could just hear her voice.

I pick up the phone and open the contacts, smiling at the fact she apparently not just pre-entered the numbers for each member of the GEM team, but managed to find the number for Lola, Yana's mom. I wouldn't put it past her to have hacked into my account for that.

But it's Janey's number I pull up first. I'm not about to disrupt her day with a phone call, but send a quick message instead.

You've got this, Tiger

With the phone still clutched in my hand, I close my eyes and rest my head back.

Pearl

I'm still smiling at Lee's message when I climb into the passenger seat.

Despite Jacob's orders last night, I couldn't get to sleep. The thought of Lee alone in the hospital plagued me. Not wanting to wake anyone else, I ended up taking an Uber to the nearest Walmart, where I picked up a replacement phone for Lee. Just in the nick of time too, since the store was set to close at eleven.

By the time I got back to the hotel, the CARD team had arrived. We spent the next hour and a half prepping Paul Gibson, who, by the end of it, looked like he was ready to burst into tears.

Then first thing this morning, before we were scheduled to meet for a final run-through of the plans, I arranged for the phone to be delivered to the hospital.

I glance over at Gibson, whose hands are clutched so

tight around the steering wheel, his knuckles are turning white.

"Relax," I snarl. "One look at you like this and she'll know something is up."

"Don't bite his head off," Raj's voice crackles in my ear. *"Save it for after. Right now, you need him on his game, not crapping his pants."*

Since we needed all-hands-on-deck, Raj is in charge of communications remotely. Mitch and Matt Rivers are in the back of the truck, hidden under the cover. Another two CARD agents are hunkered down at the fence bordering the back of the yard, waiting for their signal, and a third is up the street, prepared to come through the front gate once I create the distraction. Finally, Kate—a bona fide sharpshooter—should be in position by now in a tree on the neighboring property, with a clear view of the front of the house.

We were able to review the video feed Mitch took, going through the house yesterday morning, to give everyone a good idea of the layout. I'm feeling confident about the team, the one glaring exception being the punk behind the wheel of the truck.

"Everyone in position?" Raj calls out.

A confirming, *"Check,"* follows in three different voices.

"Hear that, Pearl? You're a go."

"We're up, let's go," I tell Gibson, who is the only one not wired up.

We're parked behind an empty warehouse about a five-minute drive from the target location. Gibson chauffeurs like a senior out for a Sunday drive, clearly nervous, but I hold back any comments. Instead, I flip down my visor to make sure this damn wig is on straight and to tug the bill of my ball cap down lower over my eyes.

Then I fasten the same handcuffs Paul had chained Amelia with on my wrists in front of me. Matt tinkered with them so only one side actually locks in, the other slides free easily.

When we turn onto Green Valley Drive, I slump down farther in my seat and update the team.

"One minute to destination."

Gibson pulls into the driveway and stops at the gate.

"Nice and slow," I mumble, keeping my head down as he starts lowering the window.

I listen to the four beeps on the keypad, but nothing happens.

"It's not working," he hisses under his breath.

"One seven three nine," I whisper. "Try again."

Four more beeps, but this time it's followed by the gates opening.

I almost jump at the sound of a voice over the intercom.

"Paul?"

It's Carla.

"Yeah. It's me."

"Good, come around the back."

I blow out a deep breath when the truck starts moving.

"Remember, pull up within a foot of the back wall," I remind him.

The idea is it'll create a narrow alley out of sight of any of the security cameras we were able to detect. Mitch and Matt will be able to hole up there until I give them the signal.

One last time I go over the steps in my mind, before Gibson parks the truck.

My stomach is in knots when he opens his door and gets out. Then he reaches in and grabs the chain attached to my handcuffs. As planned, I climb over the center console and get out of the truck on his side.

Keeping my head down so my cap and the long curtains of hair hide most of my face, I shuffle demurely behind him as he moves around the truck to the back door. It requires a ton of willpower not to look up and assess what kind of situation I'm walking into.

My hope is all three players are assembled in the kitchen, away from the entrance to the hallway, because that's the direction I plan to bolt. Placing myself between them and the stairway. What I absolutely don't want, is for any of them to be able to get to the girl upstairs, potentially using her to create a hostage situation. Mitch and Matt will come in through the mudroom, closing off any escape route.

When we step over the threshold the first voice I hear is Carla's.

"Are you sick?"

"Stomach bug or something," Gibson thankfully responds quickly.

"And the girl?"

I feel my hair being lifted and quickly turn my head

the other way, before pressing myself against Gibson's back. As much as it disgusts me to get this close to the guy, it's a way to keep her from seeing my face before I'm ready.

Raj had pointed out it would be natural for a victim to choose the safety of the assailant she knows over an unfamiliar threat.

"She's fine."

I shuffle along as Gibson follows Carla into the kitchen.

"Yo, man," I hear Olson.

That's two of the three in the kitchen, but I haven't heard Sladky yet.

From my vantage point behind the kid's back, I can only see part of the kitchen through the curtain of hair.

"Doc..."

"Paul, good to see you. Right on time."

It's one thing to hear her voice through the audio over my laptop, but hearing it in the same space, with my own ears, sends a cold chill through my blood. I force myself to look around as best I can with my limited view.

There she is, I see her legs, ankles crossed. She's sitting on one of the kitchen chairs at the table which, if I remember correctly, is to the left of the hallway entrance. I'd rather have her near the sink with the other two, but I can't do anything about that.

"Amelia? Show yourself, honey," she coos. "Show me how perfect you are."

The moment I see her get to her feet; I move.

With both hands in the small of his back I shove Gibson out of the way, sending him stumbling to my left.

"Now!" I yell to signal the others, as I veer to my right where I know the hallway to be.

I pull my hand free from the cuffs and reach for the small of my back where I tucked my weapon, wrapping my fingers around the grip as I pull it free.

Adrenaline-fueled and blinded by the stupid wig, I don't see the kitchen chair tossed in my direction, and it knocks my legs out from under me and I hit the floor hard. I lose my grip on the gun, which goes sailing along the wooden floors.

Scrambling to my feet, I rip the wig off my head just in time to see Elsbeth Sladky dart into the hallway. She moves surprisingly fast.

As I hear Mitch and Matt enter the kitchen and chaos ensues behind me, I run after the woman, who is already heading upstairs.

I'm younger and fitter, but not fast enough to catch her before she ducks into a room, slamming the door behind her. I've already lost the element of surprise, but I'm determined not to give her enough time to regroup and kick open the door.

The girl she's holding as a shield in front of her is probably not much older than Amelia. Her underdeveloped body is clearly malnourished and her face is blank. No reaction at all to the woman holding a pair of scissors pressed up against her neck.

This girl is already broken and doesn't put up a struggle as Sladky backs them up toward the balcony.

I have no weapons—my gun is somewhere on the kitchen floor downstairs—but my mind is already calculating distance and speed.

"Well, would you look at that? Surprise, surprise," Sladky singsongs mockingly. "If it isn't my precious little Janey."

The woman looks nothing like the one I remember, except for her eyes, and her voice. I fight against the almost physical response I have to hearing her call me by that name.

Conditioning.

"I see you remember me," she sneers with a satisfied smile.

Refusing to let her intimidate me, I take a tentative step forward to show her she doesn't have the same effect on me. Immediately she presses the tip of the scissors harder into the girl's skin. With her other hand, she reaches behind her and manages to open the door to the balcony.

"What's her name?" I speak for the first time, working to keep my voice casual.

"Does it matter? She's chattel, of little value as she came, but we turned her into something precious, something coveted. Didn't we, sweet Sasha?"

I look down at the girl and notice her face may be blank, but her eyes are sharp. On me. Maybe not broken yet.

I try for another small step but she matches by stepping back out on the balcony.

"I have a shot," I hear Kate in my ear.

"No."

It's too risky for the girl, and besides, Sladky is mine.

"No closer, little Janey, or this little birdie will fly," the woman warns when I ease another step forward.

From the hallway comes the sound of footsteps rushing up the stairs. I knew they'd eventually follow me up here. As soon as I see Sladky's eyes slide over my shoulder to the door, I know it's the momentary distraction I need. As I tuck my shoulder down to rush her, I yell at Sasha to drop down.

At the last second, she manages to twist out of the way, giving me the space I need to ram my shoulder into Sladky's sternum, causing her to lose her balance. Using her involuntary motion, I twist away from her grappling hands, hook a leg behind hers, and pull them right out from under her.

The momentum topples her over the railing.

There is no scream, just the wet thud of a body hitting the pavement below.

I lean over the railing and look down, giving into a strong need to know for sure. After all, the woman was supposed to have died two decades ago, but turned out to be very much alive.

Her limbs are angled awkwardly and a puddle of blood is spreading under her head. Somehow, though, her eyes are still open, staring up at me, and her mouth is moving as if trying to say something.

"Are you okay?"

I jump at the heavy hand on my shoulder and voice in

my ear. I whip my head around to find Mitch's hazel eyes on me.

I don't know, am I?

Turning back to the body below, I note her eyes are now closed, her mouth slack and unmoving. Phil Dresden, one of the CARD agents, is kneeling beside her, checking for a pulse.

It's not until he looks up at me and shakes his head, indicating Elsbeth Sladky is really gone this time, that I answer Mitch.

"Yeah, I'm good."

TWENTY-EIGHT

LEE

There is nothing as undignified as a grown-ass man walking up and down hospital hallways, clinging to an IV pole, with his butt hanging out of a gaping, too-short, hospital gown.

Nothing.

However, I was told the sooner I was up and about, the sooner I'd be heading home. So I got up and went about, despite being a rough four yards of fabric short of being decently covered.

I'm only on my second shuffling loop of the ward I was moved to this morning, and am already pretty winded, when I notice Janey coming down the hallway toward me.

"Tell me you got her," I comment when she's within earshot.

She waits to answer until she's right in front of me.

"Yeah, I got her."

She tilts her head back and she's not nearly as pleased-looking as I expected.

"You're walking around, I'm surprised."

To be honest, so am I. Breathing hurts like a son of a bitch, but I guess that's to be expected.

"It's my stamina that's taken a hit. My legs are fine."

Her eyes move slowly down my body.

"Mmm, you don't say."

"Woman," I growl. "There's not enough material in this ridiculous gown to cover the tent you're causing."

"Maybe we should get you back to your room then," she suggests.

"Don't get any ideas," I manage, but I don't have enough breath left to finish my joke.

I'm slow as a turtle getting back to my room, and I have no shame left as I flash her my ass, crawling back in bed. The nurse put the head of the bed up since it's supposed to make breathing easier, but I'm still gasping like a fish out of water.

I sit back, closing my eyes for a moment while I catch my breath.

"Janey?"

"I'm here."

She takes my hand in hers and I blink my eyes open, meeting her gaze.

"What happened?"

"You were trying for a marathon instead of sticking to a casual stroll."

I grin at her sassy response. It's also evasive as hell,

because I have no doubt she knows that wasn't what I was asking about.

"Nice try. Talk to me."

When her eyes start drifting off, I squeeze her hand.

"I killed her."

She says it bluntly, almost like a challenge.

"Good. Did you expect me to be shocked?" The look on her face says enough. "Tell me what happened," I prompt her.

I listen without commenting as she fills me in on everything I've missed. We're interrupted only once when a nurse comes in to check my blood pressure, but Janey continues as soon as she leaves.

"It's going in the books as a successful raid by the CARD team," she explains. "Two young girls rescued, three perpetrators taken into custody, and the ringleader dead as the result of an unfortunate fall trying to escape via the balcony."

"GEM was never there?"

"Correct. Jacob wants to keep our involvement completely under wraps."

"Smart," I comment, drawing a curious look from Janey.

"Why do you say that?"

"Because I don't think Elsbeth Sladky is the end of the line. Whoever is behind GLAN Industries is still out there. I have a feeling that's who Jacob's ultimate target is."

"There *is* someone still out there," she confirms. "Last night Jacob and I overheard Sladky on the phone with that person. She mentioned shutting down operations and didn't intend to leave anyone behind. We didn't get anything from the number she dialed, it was likely a burner phone."

I shake my head. I don't think I've ever encountered anyone so ruthless and inherently evil as that woman.

"The world is a better place without her, Janey."

She cracks a little smile. "I know. But, Lee, there's something else you should know. They were discussing you. Yours was obviously a familiar name to them. Sladky thought you were dead, but it wouldn't take much for whoever is still out there to find out you're still alive."

"So I'll be careful."

It's not like I haven't been careful already. We decided back when Yana was born, she would have Lola's last name so there's no obvious connection to me.

"That would be good, because I've decided it's kind of nice having you around," she shares with a smirk.

"Is that a fact? Then how about you come here and show me with a kiss?"

"You're injured."

"Not where it matters," I counter, giving her hand a little tug.

She gets to her feet and leans over, planting a chaste peck at the corner of my mouth. But when she tries to pull away, I hook a hand behind her neck and capture her mouth, kissing her properly.

Unfortunately, I have to come up for air too soon.

"It's gonna be a long couple of weeks," I mumble

against her lips. "The doctor tells me no vigorous exercise for a while."

She chuckles as she sits back down. "You survived getting shot, you'll survive a little restraint too."

"Not much choice. He says I'll be here until at least after the weekend," I grumble.

"Were you at least able to talk to your daughter?"

"I was. I talked to Lola first to let her know what happened, and we decided to keep the fact I'm in the hospital from Yana for now. At least until I can see her face-to-face."

"And how is she doing?"

I know the fact I have a kid freaks her out a little, which makes me appreciate her concern even more.

"She's okay. Her mother says she's doing much better now her meds have been adjusted."

"Good. That's good."

"I'm hoping maybe next time I go see her you can come with me."

She laughs uneasily. "Oh, I don't know. I'm not very good with kids."

"That's bullshit. I've seen you with Ricky and even the other kids, they gravitate to you," I counter.

"Only because they don't have much to compare me to."

"You undersell yourself," I point out. "Kids aren't really that complicated. They tend to take things at face value. All you have to do is be yourself."

"I don't know how to be anyone else."

"Which is exactly how I know Yana is gonna love you," I assure her.

I'm not sure she's going to take my word for it, but she'll find out soon enough if I have anything to say about it. For now, I'll leave it be.

"Well, we know I'll be out of commission for a bit, but what about you? What's next? Back home?"

Not having her close by is going to seriously suck, but I can't expect her to hold my hand. The work she does is important and I don't want to take away from it. If it's already hard for me not to be actively doing something, I know it would be hell for Janey.

"No, actually. What went down on Green Valley Drive today is not public knowledge yet and won't be for another few days. The most even the neighbors would've seen would be a few delivery vans coming and going. Nothing out of the ordinary."

"They want it to look like the auction is going ahead as planned," I venture a guess. "A sting to go after those customers."

"Yeah. Among some other things, the CARD team recovered Sladky's phone, which she used to connect with them. Because Matt wants to limit the number of people who know about it—given that we don't really know who these customers are or what kind of reach they might have—he's asked us to assist as outside support."

"So you're going to stick around," I conclude, wearing a smug grin.

"Of course. I'm not going to pass up a chance to help bring down a few more dangerous pedophiles."

I raise one eyebrow. "That's it? That's the only reason?"

"Or the opportunity to bring you home from the hospital," she concedes with a smirk.

"Much better."

Pearl

Funny, part of me never wants to see the inside of that house again, and another part would love to be there right now.

Instead, I'm back in my hotel room, monitoring and recording communications, while Mitch and Kate are back in the field, assisting the CARD team in taking down the last of the sick perverts showing up for the auction.

The first one to arrive yesterday turned out to be a former child-actor who flew in from LAX and was picked up by Mitch posing as a limo driver. Kate was waiting at the house, impersonating Beth Sweet, the name Sladky had used in her communications with him.

Hers wasn't an easy task, since she needed to get the men to admit, on tape, to the reason they were there, without raising suspicions.

So far, the actor turned out to be the most gullible. Eager to sample the wares as promised, he'd willingly transferred the deposit Kate requested and hung himself when he readily discussed his preference for "underage pussy," a term he volunteered himself.

Today had been trickier, with the arrivals scheduled within a few hours of each other. It didn't leave Kate a lot of time to get what she needed from them, but they just managed to get the third guy out the door before Mitch showed up with this last customer.

The earlier two were a cardiac surgeon from Florida, and the CEO of a large cosmetics company. This last guy is the son of a newspaper tycoon, a cocky little bastard with several rape claims filed against him over the years, all of which were miraculously retracted before he could be officially charged.

No doubt daddy's billions came in handy, but I don't think any amount of money could buy him out of this one.

"...*You came highly recommended by a good friend and business acquaintance of my father's,*" the arrogant little ass pontificates. "*I hope you can deliver; I haven't found a supplier yet who can keep up with my exclusive tastes, and I require regular replacements of merchandise.*"

I swallow down the bile crawling up my throat as I listen to Kate's response.

"*And what might those exclusive tastes be?*" she prompts.

I don't know how she can do it, staying in character. I would've lost my shit already.

"*Absolutely no older than fourteen and preferably underdeveloped. No scars, marks, health issues. Long hair, straight teeth, and no taller than five two.*"

"*That's quite a specific list. And why the frequent replacements, if you don't mind me asking?*"

"*I expect perfection and that window is narrow once I have them properly initiated into the joys of bondage. They age quickly. Besides, my pleasure lies in the training.*"

I bet it does. *Sick, fucking fuck.* Kicking my chair back as I get up from the table, I start pacing the room. I can't listen to a second more.

"Take the fucker down," I snap in my headset.

"*With pleasure,*" Kate responds directly.

The next moment a high-pitched scream rings in my ears, right before I hear a door slam open and a rumble of footsteps.

"*Let him go, honey,*" I hear Mitch say in his calm voice. "*Matt's got it from here.*"

"*Pearl, you got that?*"

"For damn sure I did," I tell Matt.

EVEN SIX HOURS LATER, CURLED UP AGAINST LEE'S good side after filling him in, I still feel sick to my stomach.

He presses a kiss to my forehead.

"They'll get their asses handed to them—quite literally—in jail. Nothing lower than child predators, you know that."

I rub my cheek against his chest.

"I hope so. They deserve everything coming to them and then some."

"Right, and you've done your part to see that happens, but you've gotta let it go now. Focus on the girls you were able to get out of there, and think of what Shamyra narrowly escaped. How are they doing anyway?"

"Amelia and her parents left the safe house in Roanoke last night. They're heading back home to pack up their belongings. They've decided to move to New Mexico, near Amelia's grandparents."

"The change of scenery will hopefully do her good," he suggests.

"I think so. Huntington holds far too many bad memories."

"And the other girl? Sasha? Anything more known on her?"

"Full name is Alexandra Babanin. She was adopted a year and a half ago by a family in Sioux City, Idaho, after spending most of her early childhood in an orphanage in Moldova. She'd been missing since the middle of April."

"*Christ*. Welcome to the good old US of A," Lee comments sourly.

"Onyx is flying into Knoxville today. She'll accompany the girl back to Idaho and make sure she has proper counseling in place."

"Everyone else heading home?"

"Mitch and Kate head back to Kentucky tomorrow."

"But you're staying."

I already told him as much, but I guess even tall, handsome, successful guys like Lee need a little reassurance from time to time.

Tilting my head back a little, I look up at him, smiling.

"I'm staying. Matt helped me get my vehicle back from the police impound lot and it's currently at the shop to get a new passenger window, new driver's seat and mats, and a good detailing. I can drop off my loaner and pick it up tomorrow morning."

"Sorry I bled all over your SUV."

I place my palm on the middle of his chest where I can feel his heart beat strong.

"Don't be. It's a good reminder of what I almost lost."

He lifts his head and presses a gentle kiss on my lips.

"Don't plan on going anywhere, Janey. You good with that?"

"More than good."

"Okay, you lovebirds..." An older nurse walks in, placing her hands on her hips as she stops beside the bed. "Visiting hours were done twenty minutes ago."

I scramble off the bed, slightly mortified at having been caught.

"He can be all yours again after eight tomorrow morning," she adds for my sake, a twinkle in her eyes.

Then she walks out again, and I quickly give him another kiss before I rush out after her.

"Janey?"

I duck my head back in the room. "Yeah?"

"When you come tomorrow, we should talk about living arrangements."

"Living arrangements?" I echo, my voice a little too-high pitched.

Lee grins from his bed.

"I'm gonna be out of commission for at least a few

weeks. It'll be tough looking after me when you live near Louisville and I'm in Lexington."

"Who says I'll be the one looking after you?" I taunt him.

"That's fine, if you'd prefer not to. The cops dropped off my old phone. I'm sure I have a few saved numbers in there I can call on for help."

I bristle at the suggestion.

"Like hell you will," I snap, and stomp out of his room.

I swear I can hear him laugh down the hall.

Bastard.

TWENTY-NINE

LEE

"We're here."

I startle awake at Janey's voice.

I'm a little disoriented though, I expected to be parked in my driveway, but instead we're in front of a house I don't recognize in the middle of nowhere.

It wasn't long into our three-hour drive home I fell asleep. I've slept more in the past almost week than I did in the month prior. Fatigue seems to be my new normal, and from what I'm told it could linger for months.

But I didn't know confusion was part of that picture, because I'm positive Janey said we were heading to Lexington.

"I thought we were going to my place?"

Janey looks a little sheepish.

"You assumed. All I said is we're heading toward Lexington, which we were at the time."

"Janey, where are we?"

The house is a two-story, with three dormers over a full-width front porch and backs on to the forest. We're in the hills somewhere.

"Not far from Williamstown and about fifteen minutes from Mitch and Kate's place."

"You mean Opal?"

I know Opal's real first name is Kate, I've heard Mitch mumble it more than once, but I've never commented on it. I'm starting to understand Jacob's reasons for assigning his team alternate identities. Even more so now it's becoming clear he's always known—or at least must have suspected—the predators running the former Transition House survived the fire.

Only one remaining now though.

"Yes, Opal, but I figure since we'll virtually be neighbors for at least the next few weeks, you may as well know her real name. It's Kate Jones."

I nod before returning my gaze out the window at the unfamiliar surroundings.

"So what is this place and why are we here?"

"Kate knows the owners. They had to relocate to Bangor, Maine, for the husband's job. They're not sure yet whether they want to sell this place or hang on to it, so they're trying it as a short-term rental while they decide."

"You're renting it?"

She shrugs.

"It made sense. From my apartment it's an hour and twenty minutes if I need to go into our office in Hebron, which would take me only about half that from here. For any medical emergencies the hospital in Williamstown is just a fifteen-minute drive. Also, seemed like a nice place for you to recuperate. Nicer than being housebound in the city. Here, you have lots of fresh air, great views, and a few nice hiking trails up the hill at the back of the property."

As much as I like my house, I wasn't looking forward to being cooped up in there for any length of time. It certainly doesn't have these views or the fresh air.

"I also thought—since this place is fairly private—your daughter maybe could visit you here," she continues to ramble nervously. "Florence is only half an hour from here. I hope this is okay."

It means a fuck of a lot she's even taken that into consideration, given her admitted apprehension around meeting Yana. She's really thought this through.

I reach for a lock of her hair and gently pull her toward me, kissing her pretty mouth.

"More than okay. It's pretty damn close to perfect."

I'm rewarded with a bright smile, and the next moment she's out of the SUV, coming around to the passenger side to open my door. It's on my lips to tell her I can look after myself, but I think better of it. If I ever have a hope in hell of Janey allowing me to take care of her, I'll have to lead by example.

"I'll get the bags in a bit," she announces, heading up the porch steps and punching in a code on the keypad.

When we walk in, she points out a study to the right of the door.

"There's a Murphy bed we can set up in here if the stairs prove to be too much for you," she suggests.

"The stairs will be fine," I grumble.

There's no way in hell I'm sleeping down here if she's sleeping upstairs. If I have to crawl my way up there, I won't spend another night without her in my arms.

The open living space is sparsely furnished, making it feel much larger in here than it looked from outside. A dining table and four chairs are to the left of the entryway, and beyond that is the kitchen with one of those eat-on islands with stools. A large, glass sliding wall makes the living room at the back of the house nice and bright. I can see the view of the hill all the way from the front door.

Someone put some bucks into renovating this place.

"Nice," I comment.

"I think so too," Janey agrees. "The pictures Kate sent me didn't exaggerate."

She walks ahead into the kitchen and opens the fridge. It looks well-stocked.

"She told me she'd get us a few things," she scoffs. "There's enough food to last us a month." Then she turns to me. "Can I get you something to drink before I go grab our things?"

"I'd kill for a good cup of coffee. That stuff they serve at the hospital is glorified dishwater. But I can get it myself," I add.

I don't want her to feel like I need to be waited on hand and foot. I'm not helpless.

"How about today you let me look after you and tomorrow you can find your own way around."

"Fair enough," I concede and move toward the well-aged canvas sectional.

I pick a spot facing the view, while still leaving me able to make eye contact with Janey finding her way around the kitchen.

Nice. Really nice.

I lay my head back and let my body relax. No city sounds, sirens in the distance, or cars driving by. I've always considered myself a city boy—feeling the need to be close to the action—but I have to admit, I'm liking how peaceful this feels.

"Coffee should be done in a minute." I twist my head to look at Janey. "Oh, and before I run out to grab our things, are you okay with Pad Thai for dinner? I was thinking that's pretty quick and easy."

"Sounds perfect. I didn't know you could cook. It'll be the first decent, home-cooked meal I've had since the fish we fried at the lake," I tell her. "But my mother made sure I'm no slouch in the kitchen either."

"Good." She grins back at me. "Then tomorrow, if you feel up to it, dinner is on you."

When she walks out of sight and I hear the front door open, I pull out my phone and look up Vera's number.

"I was wondering if I'd hear from you," she says, answering the call. "I just saw Ricky yesterday."

"I would've called sooner, but I was in a bit of an accident and was laid up for a while."

"Oh no, are you okay?"

"I'm fine now. How is the boy?"

"Doing better now that his father's been arrested."

"Good, I hope it helps the kid sleep better."

"I'm sure it will."

"Say, do you think it's possible for me to get the number for his foster parents? I'd like to give them a call, maybe talk to the boy if that's okay with them."

"I should probably give you the number for his case-worker. She'll want to vet you first."

That makes sense.

"Of course, or you can give her mine. Whatever works."

"I'll do that then."

Behind me I hear Janey walking in the door again.

"How are things at Evolution Quest?"

She snorts. "For now, we've been shut down pending a full FBI investigation. All staff have been temporarily laid off."

"Shit, I'm so sorry about that, Vera."

"Don't be. I'm still sick to my stomach at the thought we referred those kids to a ring of pedophiles. Hell, I worked alongside some of them."

The news about the raid in Knoxville had become public, so it doesn't surprise me it would've been brought to her attention. The *Charleston Gazette* had run the story, and Pure Allies—the online counseling service— had been mentioned by name. Luckily, Evolution Quest's possible involvement was left out, but it doesn't come as a shock the FBI is turning over every rock.

"Not knowingly."

"Maybe not, but we clearly need to improve our screening process."

I'm not going to argue with that. Unfortunately, bad guys tend to find ways around those eventually.

"Look, as soon as the company is back up and running, I'll write that article I promised. Make sure you get some positive press. I hope you don't give up," I add. "It's a good program you guys run. I've seen the positive change it made for Ricky in just a few days."

"That's nice of you to say."

"It's the truth."

She promises to get in touch with Ricky's caseworker and ends the call.

When I turn to Janey, she's walking toward me with a couple of coffee mugs. It's piping hot, but that doesn't stop me from taking my first good hit of caffeine in days.

"How is he?" she asks, taking a seat beside me.

"From the sounds of it, better with his father in custody."

She turns pensive as she stares out the windows.

"Yeah, but who's going to look after him now?"

As someone whose experience being in the system was even worse than the situation she was taken from, her concern is understandable.

I reach over and give her knee a squeeze.

"We will, even if it is from a distance."

Janey

"Did you hear?"

"Hear what?"

Lee is stretched out on the couch pointing at the TV when I walk in. A local news anchor is talking about road closures, but I see a familiar name flash on the news scroll at the bottom of the screen.

Judge will allow cameras in courtroom during Congressman Melnyk's trial set to start tomorrow.

"Good. The world should know what a perverted dirtbag he is. He deserves to be taken apart in front of an audience."

"Agreed. I'm there for it. Bring on the popcorn."

"I'll pick some up next time I'm out."

He grabs my hand as I pass by him on my way to the kitchen, tugging me down on the couch beside him.

"Glad you're home," he mumbles, leaning over for a kiss. "How was work?"

I grin. I've noticed he's getting bored. Good thing we head into Lexington at the end of the week for a follow-up with his own physician. I know he's eager to get the okay to return to work.

"We heard from Matt Driver today," I inform him. "He says he's not been able to crack Olson, but Carla Amato took a deal. In exchange for reduced charges, she directed the FBI to an address in Bowling Green, where they found two more missing kids being held in an old barn at the back of a farm property."

"Jesus."

"One of the stable hands ran when the FBI rolled up to the main house. They found him floating in the creek an hour later, a gunshot wound to the head. They figure it was self-inflicted."

"Coward."

"Yeah. Do you want to hear an interesting bit of information Matt passed on? One of the stabled horses the guy was in charge of is named Pure Delight."

Lee shoots up straight. "That's not a coincidence."

"Nope. Jacob almost bit my head off when, after Matt ended the call, I offered to dig into the horse's background. Said to drop it, he'd take care of it himself, and told us to go home."

"Territorial," Lee suggests.

"Definitely. Even Onyx, who rarely lets anything Jacob says bother her, seemed a bit taken aback by his strong reaction."

"So..." Lee drawls, playing with my fingers. "Does that mean you're done for the day?"

"Unless I have to cook, or did you already have something in mind for dinner?"

He grins and gets to his feet, pulling me up with him.

"I've got dinner covered. Go put on something comfortable and a pair of hiking boots, I've got something I wanna show you."

"What?"

I'm not good with surprises. They're rarely good.

"Trust me?"

I voice my frustration with a grunt. He doesn't play fair bringing trust into it. Instead of answering, I turn on my heel and head up the stairs.

Five minutes later when I finish tying my boots, he is waiting by the sliding doors, a backpack hanging off one shoulder.

"Ready?"

When I reach him, he takes my hand and leads me outside.

The trail we're on is one I haven't been on before. It's pretty steep and it doesn't take long before Lee needs to stop to catch his breath.

"How much farther is it?"

"Not much, just give me a minute."

He lets his backpack slide on the ground and rests his hands on his knees. I pick it up and sling it over my shoulder.

"Holy shit, what do you have in here?"

"Dinner, and I'm supposed to carry that." He points at the pack.

"I've got it, lead the way."

The spot he brings me to is a large, flat rock at the top of the trail, overlooking the rental house in the valley below. It really is a beautiful location. I walk up to the edge and let my eyes wander over the landscape, lit up gold by the sun sinking lower in the sky behind me.

"This place is beautiful," I comment, turning back to Lee to see him pouring wine into a couple of plastic tumblers.

"I didn't want to risk glass in case I fell on my face."

"Probably smart," I mumble, a bit stunned as he hands me a glass. "Is there a special reason we're up here?"

"There is, but I suggest you take a fortifying sip of your wine before I tell you. Come sit."

I'm not sure I like the sound of that, but I sit down beside him on the edge of the rock and take a sip.

"I contacted the owners yesterday."

"You did?"

I'm surprised he had their contact information, but he may have gotten that from Kate. Who didn't tell me a thing when I got the information from her just this morning.

"They intend to sell the house."

"Oh." I try not to let on this is not news to me.

"Actually, it was the news I'd hoped to hear. I like this house; I can see this as a place to come home to."

"You want to buy it?"

"Why not? Like you said, Mitch and Kate are close, Yana is just thirty or so minutes away, it's off the beaten track, so a safe place for her to visit, and to top it off, the GEM office is an easy commute."

I'm trying to process what some of what he says implies, but it's probably safer if I just ask.

"What are you saying, exactly?"

"I'm saying, *if* this is a place where you could see yourself living as well—now, or at some point in the not-so-distant future, I hope—I would like to put in an offer on this house. What do you think?"

I toss back the rest of my wine, set my glass down, and

get up and wedge myself between his knees. Then I put my hands on his shoulders and look him in the eye.

"I think that might be a little awkward, since I really don't want to end up in a bidding war with you."

After the initial shock wears off his face, he cracks out that award-winning smile of his.

"Guess that means we have to share," he concludes.

"Well, we haven't killed each other yet."

His arms wrap around my hips, pulling me close.

"I just love it when you get all sweet and mushy on me," he teases. "But I think I may need to pour you another glass of wine."

"Why is that?"

"Because I invited Lola, Mike, and Yana to come down here this weekend."

I don't wait for him; I twist out of his hold and go after the bottle myself.

"Janey?"

I turn my head and glare at him.

"Have I told you I love you?"

No. You. Have. Not.

THIRTY

PEARL

This is ridiculous.

I'm not scared of men twice my size, but the prospect of meeting a certain six-year-old girl has me shaking in my boots.

I can't for the life of me remember the things I liked at that age. I've been roaming around the grocery store for over half an hour now, looking for inspiration.

Lee must be wondering if I got lost. Before we left Lexington, I did tell him I was stopping at the grocery store in Williamstown to pick up a few things.

He had his doctor's appointment this morning and was eager to get back after receiving the go-ahead to cautiously resume normal activities. It's a pretty safe guess why he was in a hurry. We did stop by his house so he could pick up a few things, along with his Jeep. He'll need his wheels.

The short-term rental agreement I signed on the house was for six weeks, just to be on the safe side. We're only two weeks into it but neither of us are in any hurry to return to our own respective places. This house feels right.

We've talked about it in the past few days—the possibility of buying the place—which led to a discussion around finances. His and mine. That was a little awkward and uncomfortable. Lee turns out to be in decent financial shape, has minimal mortgage left on his house, no major outstanding debts, and some investments for his retirement. The awkwardness came when I shared my balance sheet.

Even back when I was stripping, I began to invest a little in the stock market and had some lucky breaks. I used some of that money as launch capital when I started my cybersecurity business and that turned out to be a good investment. I did okay, made far more than I had a need for, and invested most of that surplus as well.

The bottom line is, at this point I could stop working altogether and exist comfortably, with still plenty left over should I live to be a hundred years old.

Money doesn't mean much to me, other than simply a tool to ensure security and control. I have no desire for extravagant things, I don't have a lifestyle that requires a lot, but I like knowing it's there if I need it.

So I mentioned buying the house would barely make a dent in my bank account, and that's when I could feel Lee shut down.

It worried me, and I actually approached Raj for

advice, relaying Lee's and my conversation. She said for some men their self-worth is hung up in their ability to provide for those they care about, to the point they feel emasculated when they aren't able to.

I could see Lee being a man like that so, on Raj's advice, I left the subject alone, giving him time to come to terms with my bank account on his own.

I'm standing in the baking aisle, debating whether Yana would prefer chocolate or vanilla cake—since I figured a little girl would surely love cake—when my phone rings.

It's Lee.

"Should I be worried you panicked and are making a run for it?" he jokes. But not really.

I can hear the genuine worry in his voice.

"You've got the panic part right," I admit. "But I'm still at the grocery store. I've decided I want to make a cake, but I don't know what Yana likes. Should I get chocolate, vanilla with sprinkles, or plain? Does she like strawberries? I could do a strawberry shortcake. She doesn't have allergies, does she?"

His deep chuckle is oddly reassuring.

"Take a breath. Yana is easy, eats almost anything, and will be thrilled with any kind of cake. However, strawberry shortcake is one of her favorites."

I let out a relieved breath.

"Oh good. What about drinks? Does she like juice? Or is she allowed soda?"

"Janey, stop stressing," he grumbles. "We have

enough in the house. Get the stuff for the cake if you must, but then get your ass home."

In the end I still have three bags of groceries when I walk in the door. Lee catches sight of me and shakes his head, but he still walks up, takes the bags from my hands, and carries them to the kitchen.

"She's here for the day, Janey, not a week or even the weekend," he comments when he starts emptying the contents on the counter.

"Then it'll keep for the next time," I reply as I put the groceries away.

I'm putting the strawberries and heavy cream in the fridge, and am just backing out when I feel Lee's arms slip around me from behind. He shoves his face in my neck.

"You're going a little crazy, you know that, right?" he mumbles.

"I'm nervous, okay?" I turn in his arms so we're face-to-face. "A lot is riding on her liking me. She's the most important person in your life and if we end up here, living together, and she doesn't care for me, it would be very uncomfortable for you."

"First of all," he starts, brushing my hair out of my eyes. "Yana is not the only important person in my life; you are too. And on the off chance you guys don't hit it off, it would be something we can work on. Secondly, there is no *if* we end up living together here, since we already are."

"For now," I counter.

"Right. We never did finish that conversation, did

we?" he guesses accurately. "Why don't we grab a drink, head out on the back deck, and hash this out."

Armed with a glass of wine, I follow him outside. I'm not normally much of a drinker—in a rare social setting I might have an even rarer glass of something—but here I seem to have settled in this new habit of sharing a single drink with Lee out on the deck at the end of the day. It creates an enjoyable transition from workday to down-time. Something I didn't have before, which is why my workday really never ended and I had trouble with the concept of relaxing.

Lee taught me that in the short time we've been together; a life/work balance.

Still, I'm a little apprehensive at the conversation ahead when I sit down in the chair next to his.

"I won't lie," he dives right in, "I was a little thrown finding out your net worth is about twenty times mine." He shrugs. "I'm a guy, I like to think I'm needed, and with you already being so damn competent and beautiful—and apparently independently wealthy as well—I wasn't sure what I had to offer."

When I open my mouth to protest, he holds up his hand to stop me.

"I know—stupid—you don't have to tell me, but I've had a few days to get my head straight. The thing is, I actually like this equal partnership, where being together is a choice and doesn't become a necessity for either one of us."

"I've been thinking too," I admit. "If both of us sell our current properties, we could buy this place outright. We wouldn't have to put a monetary value on that, but simply look at it as each of us trading one home for another. What each of us brings to the table doesn't have to be a dollar figure, but rather an equal emotional stake."

He plucks my glass from my hand and sets it on the railing, before he grabs my hand and pulls me out of my chair and onto his lap.

His arms wrap around me, one hand making its way under my shirt to cup my breast.

"I like the way you think," he mumbles by my ear. "Now, with that out of the way, what else can I do to relax you?"

His other hand slips down the front of my pants and under the edge of my panties, which I know he'll find damp. For someone for whom sex was one of life's unfavorable by-products before meeting Lee, I've sure missed it these past couple of weeks.

"You're doing it," I whisper, twisting my neck so he can reach my lips.

His tongue slides into my mouth just as the heel of his hand presses against my clit and his long fingers start fucking me.

Out in the open and exposed to the elements, I've never quite felt so fully alive, and I suddenly need to share all of me.

The words feel strange on my lips but right in my heart.

"I love you."

Lee

"Babe, what the hell are you doing up at five in the morning?"

Janey turns her head, a streak of flour on her cheek.

"Baking strawberry shortcake, what does it look like I'm doing?" she snaps.

Clearly the effects of last night's efforts did not tide over to the morning. After a languid night of lovemaking that had us pass up on dinner, Janey had been a pile of Jell-O in my arms. This morning she appears to be wound tight.

"They won't be here until eleven or so," I volunteer. "There's plenty of time."

"Time? Are you kidding? There was so much I was supposed to have done last night, but you kept distracting me."

All I do is raise my eyebrows. I recognize a rant when I hear one, and I'm learning it's easier to let it run itself out.

"I have the whole house yet to clean. Then I was going to set out an age-appropriate treasure hunt on one of the trails in the back, I thought she might enjoy. And I'm still gonna need time to get cleaned up and find something to wear."

She returns her efforts to the batter she's beating like her life depends on it.

I could point out to her how ridiculous her to-do list is, and despite that I'd still be happy to help her accomplish all of it, but actions may speak louder than words right now.

I duck into the pantry and grab the apron left behind by the owners from its hook and put it on. Then I move over to the sink where I wash my hands.

"What are you doing?" she asks, looking over.

I notice the corner of her mouth jerking as her attention is captured by my naked ass poking out the back.

"Helping. What can I do?"

She shakes her head, stifling a grin. Then she dives into the fridge and comes up with the strawberries, handing them to me.

"Clean those."

"I can do that."

I dig up a colander from one of the drawers and turn on the faucet to rinse them, when I notice Janey still looking at me.

"Thank you."

"For what?"

"For indulging my freak-out," she clarifies.

"Totally self-serving," I admit.

"How is that?"

"I figure if I give you a hand now, we'll be done sooner. I may have some time left to get you relaxed before Yana gets here."

Unfortunately, I never get the chance.

Not only is Janey a perfectionist in everything she does—which meant she felt the need to go over everything I contributed until it was to her satisfaction—but it only just turned ten when the doorbell rings.

I can literally see Janey's hands shaking as she straightens a throw pillow on the couch for the umpteenth time. I could take a moment to reassure her again, but figure it's better to rip the Band-Aid off.

"Daddy!" Yana's voice shrieks before I have the door half open.

I barely have time to brace before my little whirlwind leaps into my arms. I wince with the impact, but there's no way in hell I'm gonna let go of my girl.

"Careful. Remember, Daddy got hurt," Lola cautions in the background.

"Hey, Baby-girl. I missed you."

My daughter leans back in my arms and scrutinizes me. "You don't look hurt."

"That's because it's mostly better."

I let her slide down until she's back on her feet and turn to Lola and Mike, giving her a quick hug and him a firm handshake.

"Nice place," Mike comments.

"A bit off the beaten path though," Lola adds.

"It is nice and quiet," I tell Mike before turning to his wife. "And best of all, it's safe and secluded. Why don't you come in?"

Yana had already ducked past me into the house, and I find her face-to-face with Janey in the hallway.

"Who are you?"

"I'm...uh..." Janey stammers.

"Yana, this is Janey."

"Oh, are you Daddy's girlfriend? He told me about you."

I'd brought up the subject last time I talked to her on the phone. I figured I'd give her a heads-up.

Janey's eyes flit over to me.

"I guess I am," she tells Yana, holding out her hand.

"Excellent," my precocious daughter declares. She grabs the offered hand and instead of shaking it, pulls Janey toward the open sliding doors. "Daddy says there are deer in the yard. Can you show me?"

I told her we saw *a* deer last week and a skittish one at that, but in Yana's mind every deer is like Bambi.

"Wow, this is quite the place," Lola observes as she looks around. "Not a lot of furniture though."

"I'm sure it'll fill up once Janey and I move our respective households in here. We more than likely will have to cull." I walk into the kitchen. "Can I get you guys a coffee?"

"Please," Mike says. "I never had a chance to grab my second cup this morning, Yana was in a rush to get out of the house. Bouncing off the walls with excitement," he explains before adding, "That's why we're a little early."

"I'll have a coffee too," Lola pipes up. "So, you guys are going to live here? Together?"

"That's the plan."

I grab a few mugs from the cupboard and wait for the comment I know will come. Lola has a tendency to mother me, although it's really our daughter she's looking out for. Of course, my life isn't really her business, but I appreciate it comes from a place of caring.

"That's rather sudden, isn't it?" she predictably follows with.

"Not really our business, honey."

It's Mike—a burly, laid-back guy—who, as usual, tries to keep his wife in check as best he can. One of the reasons why these two work well together, and she and I would never have lasted.

"I'm just saying, it's a big move that may have an impact on our daughter as well."

"Pot meet kettle," Mike counters when I hand him his coffee. "Need I remind you, the two of you were barely broken up when you and I met and moved in together only three weeks later?"

I'm grinning when I hand an eye-rolling Lola her mug.

"Touché," I tell her. "Have I told you I like your husband?"

She huffs and perches a hip on one of the stools at the island, noticing the strawberry shortcake Janey meticulously assembled under the large glass dome she found.

"Yana's gonna love that."

"Janey made it for her. And Lola? Be nice to her, she's been busting her butt trying to make this perfect for Yana, and she barely got any sleep, she's so nervous she might do something wrong."

As I'd hoped it might, her expression softens.

"That's really sweet."

"Yeah, it is."

"Mom!" my daughter yells, storming into the house. "Guess what? The deer is hiding and probably won't come out until it gets cool when the sun goes down, but Janey showed me tracks. And she says there could be a black bear farther in the woods. We may go for a hike later and look for bear tracks. Isn't that great?"

I have my doubts about how *great* her mom thinks it is but my daughter clearly does.

She adds, "There is even a big tree I can climb."

Janey walks in behind her, smiling a little at Yana's enthusiasm.

Yeah, I was right not to worry. I figured those two would hit it off.

"So you like it here, huh?"

Yana nods.

We're sitting on the deck, waiting for the sun to go down behind the hill and the deer to come out, before I drive her home.

The kid is exhausted after exploring the woods all afternoon. Of course, she loved the treasure hunt, swung like a monkey from the old tree, and was like a little sponge, soaking up everything Janey taught her.

We just finished the hamburgers we cooked on the grill and Janey is grabbing us each a second piece of the strawberry shortcake. We had the first piece for lunch.

"When can I come back?" she asks.

"If we're around, any time you like," Janey, who comes walking out with cake, answers her.

"Next time can I spend the night?"

"Sure, as long as it's okay with your mom."

I send Janey a grateful smile. I feel lucky the woman I love is comfortable including my daughter in our life.

"Daddy, look," Yana hisses, pointing toward the tree line.

A deer walks tentatively into the clearing, followed by a small, gangly fawn.

"It's Bambi."

"Sure is, Baby-girl."

EPILOGUE

LEE

"I'd like to offer you a position."

I listen to Jacob as I look around the table.

Janey came home last night, sharing that Jacob had requested I sit in on a meeting at the office today. It's not a surprise this meeting coincided with the release of my follow-up article on Congressman Melnyk, who is now a permanent resident at Big Sandy, a high-security federal prison. I'm sure Jacob knew I wasn't going to consider any other job until I'd finished that story.

I catch Janey's eyes before I answer him.

"I appreciate the offer, but I like what I do," I start. "That said, I realize our objectives run parallel a lot of the time, and in such cases I'd be happy to work with GEM. But...on a consultancy basis. And for a fee, of course," I add, making Onyx snicker.

"Be easier if you were on the payroll," Branch grumbles.

I bet it would, but I'd like to maintain some autonomy, especially since I'm no closer to finding any documentation on who Jacob Branch actually is. The man is a ghost.

"I told you he wouldn't go for it," Onyx contributes with a smirk. "Good thing I drew up that consultancy agreement as well."

"Fine. Have him sign that and the nondisclosure agreement."

She slides a folder across the table to me. Inside is what looks like a fairly standard NDA. I skim over the legal jargon and sign with the pen Mitch hands me.

The next form is a contract, listing a very generous flat-rate dollar amount on a per-case basis, details to be agreed upon at the onset of my involvement. I'm comfortable signing this as well, since I'm not locking myself in.

I hand the papers back to Onyx.

"Both are signed," she states for Jacob's benefit.

"Good. Now, what do you know about David Wheeler?"

All eyes are fixed my way so I safely assume that question was intended for me.

"Only heir to his father's multinational shipping corporation, which he sold as soon as it was in his name. He was a well-known philanthropist who focused on charities benefiting children and teenagers. I read an interview once in the *Wall Street Journal* where he was asked why he focused on those particular charities, and he said his own childhood had been detached and lonely. I know he was the main benefactor behind Transition House and he was reported to have died in the fire."

"Is that all?" he probes.

"No. I also know he was presumed to be Dr. Elsbeth Sladky's lover—he spent an unusual amount of time at Transition House—I believe him to have been the one who arranged for my mother's murder, and I don't think he's dead," I conclude.

"I share that opinion and would add one of my own; I suspect Wheeler is not only the partner we figured Sladky had, but is also the man behind GLAN Industries."

"Do you have anything to corroborate that?"

There's a brief pause before he responds.

"Not much. Mostly a gut feeling at this point," he admits. *"There's a lead I'd like to follow up on, which you may be able to help with."*

"Which is?"

"You know Wayne Dunne."

I'm about to ask how he would know that, but realize he'll just tell me his standard, cryptic, *"I have my ways."*

"He was my roommate in college."

"And he's also the grandson of Neville Dunne, who was one of the founding members of the Thoroughbred Guild of America. It's an exclusive membership by invitation only. I need an invitation."

This is about the horse; Pure Delight. That's the lead he's talking about.

"You want me to call Wayne out of the blue and get you an invitation to the club?"

"Not me—Onyx."

"I don't think so," she protests, clearly not aware of this plan. "What am I supposed to do at a horse club? You'd better have a very good reason for sending me in the field."

Jacob lets out a deep sigh. *"Right. Onyx, take me off speaker and find a quiet spot. The rest of you I'll brief later. Remington? I'm counting on you."*

Great.

PEARL

"This Wayne Dunne was your friend?" I ask when we get into Lee's Jeep.

We shared a ride, because we were supposed to visit Lee's lawyer in Lexington to officially pick up the keys for the house.

Once the decision to buy was made, we wanted to finalize as quickly as possible. We put in an offer on the house, which the owners immediately accepted, and we had both our properties up for sale the week after. Because we listed them slightly lower than comparable properties, and offered a quick closing, we ended up selling within a few days of each other.

We've been there for two months now, but I can't wait to get home and call it our own. Who knew I'd turn out to be so domestic? I even hung pictures I took of Yana helping Lee build a platform in that old tree for her to play on.

"Hardly. He was a roommate and a lousy one at that. Last time I saw him was maybe fifteen years ago."

"So how are you going to finagle an invitation from him?" I probe.

"That's a fucking great question, I have no idea," he grumbles.

He reaches over the console for my hand and laces his fingers with mine.

"I'd rather talk about how we're going to celebrate our new home together later."

I grin at him.

"Whatever ideas you have, they better be of the quickie variety, because I invited Lola and Mike to come over with Yana for a nice dinner."

"Tonight?"

I shrug. "I wanted Yana to be part of the celebration, and I wanted her mom and stepdad to be there to see her new room."

It was supposed to be a surprise for Yana tomorrow, when Lee was scheduled to pick her up for her first overnight at our place, but I thought it might be nice if all her parents were there.

Lee and I spent a couple of nights getting her bedroom painted and decorated. I can't wait to see her face.

I turn to find Lee's eyes on me. Then he lifts our hands and kisses my knuckles.

"Love you, Janey."

I grin.

I DART ONE LAST GLANCE OVER MY SHOULDER, MAKING sure everyone is still sleeping before I slip out the door and ease it shut.

The only light comes from the yellowed nightlight plugged into the wall outside the bathroom at the other end of the hallway. I tiptoe toward it, leaving the girls' dorm room behind. Passing by the only other door I pause for a moment, listening to make sure there are no sounds from inside. Then I rush ahead and duck into the bathroom.

I don't turn on the light, familiar enough with the layout after spending the past five years of my life in this hellhole. Despite the pitch dark I know there are three bathroom stalls to my left, a counter with three sinks on my right, and along the back wall six narrow lockers with a shower on either side. That's where I'm heading.

There's no one here—yet. I pick the shower stall on the left and duck behind the narrow privacy wall, just in case someone I'm not expecting walks in.

I feel rather than hear someone come in a few minutes later. Nothing more than a slight movement of air as the door to the hallway opens. I hold my breath and wait for the sound of a stall door opening but it doesn't come. The only warning I get is a slight rustle of clothing a fraction of a second before a familiar voice sounds only inches away.

"Raj?"

I release the air I'd been holding before answering.

"Right here."

Despite the darkness, our hands meet, grabbing on tightly.

"Are you ready?"

The million-dollar question.

I'm so torn about this. Who is going to look out for the others when I'm gone?

The plan is to make our way to Lexington and seek help there since we know we won't get any here in Lanark. But what if no one believes us? Or worse; what if we get caught before we make it? What will happen to the others then?

"As ready as I'll ever be," I whisper back, shoring up my courage.

"Good." My hand gets a squeeze. "We should get going before someone comes in here. I taped the latch on the kitchen door so we should be able to get out easily."

I nod, realizing right away it won't be visible.

We're supposed to slip out the back and hide in the dumpster right outside the kitchen door which is scheduled to be picked up every Thursday morning before seven, about four hours from now.

"Now or never," I confirm, feeling a little tug on my hand.

I follow closely, holding on tight as we make our way out of the bathroom and sneak toward the stairs. We both know to avoid the third step down because it creaks, but still wait for a moment at the bottom of the stairs to make sure nothing is moving in the house.

The tile floor of the kitchen is cold under my bare feet. We agreed to leave everything behind, including our shoes. We didn't want to risk dropping or banging something and someone hearing. So bare feet and hands-free it is.

As we inch toward the back door my heart is pounding so hard, it makes my chest hurt. So close now.

When we stop, I hear a soft, "Shit."

"What?" I whisper back.

"The door is lock—"

Suddenly the bright overhead lights come on and a voice has my blood freeze in my veins.

"Did you really think we'd let you just walk out of here?"

I DIDN'T RESIST.

I hadn't resisted since he dragged me out of the house and threatened to make life hell for the girls if I didn't comply. Sacrificing myself was the only way I could think of to look after them.

The fire I had in my heart died a long time ago, and all I'd done since was exist. From one breath to the next, from meal to meal, with as only highlight the drugs that allowed me to disappear.

It may have been weeks, or months, or years, but when the car stopped in front of Transition House, it sparked a flame that boiled my blood.

I'd been too late for the girls—they were gone, and all I could do was hope they'd be okay—but I could still save myself, and make sure what happened to us can't happen to others.

I STARTLE AWAKE WHEN THE CURTAIN AROUND MY BED IS pushed back, and a nurse walks up to my bed.

"Good morning, soldier. I'm afraid we'll have to change those dressings again today."

I have to shake my head to clear the remnants of those years' old memories. They've been haunting my dreams since I woke up in the military hospital in Germany with no recollection of how I got there.

Perhaps this was my wake-up call.

My second chance to make good on a promise I made almost a decade ago.

ONYX

"Beverage? Ma'am?"

I turn to find a young kid, little more than a teenager, offering me a tray with a selection of drinks. I smile and select a flute I'm sure holds champagne. I don't plan on drinking it—not when on the job—but having a glass in my hand will ward off being offered every few minutes. I need to be on my game and could do without frequent interruptions.

The Thoroughbred Charities of America fundraiser is quite the elaborate event. Looking around the hotel's ballroom, I spot a good number of designer outfits among the well-dressed guests as I try to locate the guy I'm supposed to meet. Unfortunately I have no idea what he looks like.

Hamish Adrian.

Damn Jacob Branch for throwing me to the wolves. I don't have much experience with covert operations and definitely feel out of my element here. I'm normally in charge of coordination and communications but, in his infinite wisdom, Jacob has decided I should go undercover as a wealthy Pakistani socialite, looking to invest her money in thoroughbred horses.

My contact is a former Canadian horse trainer who is looking to establish himself in the US. I wasn't given a physical description for Mr. Adrian, but was assured he would recognize me.

"Ms. Baqri? Onyx?"

The rich baritone has me swing around.

First thing I notice are his dark eyes, aimed at me. My skin breaks out in goosebumps under his intense scrutiny. My eyes drift, taking in the rest of his appearance, but quickly focus back on his eyes.

"That's me. You must be Mr. Adrian?"

I struggle to keep my voice even, shaken by the tight and marred skin creating the appearance of a mask. It's clear some graft work has been done, but the damage from extensive burns is still visible on a large portion of his face and neck. His head is shaved, almost making the scars stand out more.

"Hamish," he corrects me.

Then he extends his right hand, which is missing two fingers and—like the skin on his face—looks badly scarred. I notice he is studying me closely, and I get the sense I'm being tested. Holding his eyes, I take his offered hand without blinking.

Silently I curse my boss for the minimal information he provided. All I was told is that this man is going to lend my cover story credibility.

"Hamish," I echo, tilting my head as I let go of his hand. "I don't detect a Scottish accent."

"There isn't one. I was named for my great-grandfather, a farrier from Dundee who came across after world war I and settled in Canada. I'm a third-generation Canadian."

I suppress a smile at the hint of pride in his voice.

"Horses are in the blood, then?" I observe.

"You might say that." He gestures toward an empty table furthest from the podium. "Let's have a seat."

I lead the way, all too aware of the deep plunging back of my gown. Not my pick—I would've chosen something a bit more modest—but Jacob insisted if I wanted to pull off the cover of rich socialite, I should start by dressing like one.

He picked the gown.

A sleek, satin, champagne-colored tank dress, hugging my pronounced curves. The color is perfect against my brown skin, but the tight fit would be better suited to someone younger, and definitely skinnier than I am.

"So, how do you know Jacob?" I ask when he takes a seat beside me.

"Shared interests. We go way back."

A rather evasive response, leaving me even more curious. Especially since I'm always in the market for anything I can find out about my boss, who is no more than a voice on the phone to me.

I'm about to push for more information, when a server walks up with a tray of drinks. I pass, but Hamish selects a Glencairn glass which undoubtedly holds bourbon.

The waiter seems mesmerized at the sight of his mangled hand.

"Thank you," I quickly tell the young man, who startles and rushes away from the table.

Hamish either doesn't notice the awkward moment, or he's accustomed to stares and chooses to ignore them.

"So, I understand you have plans to step into the thoroughbred racing scene," Hamish comments.

I have no idea what Jacob told him about me, so I tread carefully, sticking close to my cover story.

"Yes. I hope to, but I'm discovering it's quite a challenging world to get into."

My objective is to obtain a membership to the Thoroughbred Guild of America. The membership is by invitation only, and so far, I haven't been extended one. Not for lack of trying, mind you.

"A polite way of saying it's an old-boy's club," Hamish points out, sitting back in his chair as he unapologetically scrutinizes me. "From where I'm sitting you have a few strikes against you right off the bat. You're the wrong gender, the wrong color, you're too young and too beautiful, and no one knows you."

He seems to recognize my look of disbelief at his blunt observations, and continues before I can voice my displeasure.

"No sense beating around the bush, you should know what you're up against." He takes a sip of his bourbon. "The good news is, I can help you."

He may be right, but his calm arrogance rubs me the wrong way.

"And how do you propose to do that?"

Credit to him, he barely reacts to my snide tone.

"Even though I was sidelined the past couple of years, and have recently moved here, I know this business," he states calmly. "I'm willing to introduce you to it."

"What the gain for you?"

His grin is a bit lopsided, but it transforms the left side of his face.

"Like I said, I'm new to town, and even though I have a decent reputation in the industry, those who've heard of me only know me by name. I need to re-establish myself in this community. Build up trust, but people aren't that receptive to a face like mine. Having a beautiful woman by my side will make me more approachable. So you'll be helping me as much as I'll be helping you, and trust me, it won't be a hardship."

I'm guessing whatever caused his injuries was the reason for the hiatus from the racing world, and possibly for his choice to rebuild his career here. I can see how connecting with me—or at least my cover identity—might be beneficial to him, but I'm not that sure how he'll be able to help me out.

So...I want to have a little chat with Jacob before I take him up on his offer.

"Excuse me for a minute, please?" I get out of my seat and slip out from behind the table, throwing him an apologetic smile. "I have to find the ladies room."

I smile and nod at people I pass as I find my way out of the ballroom. Once in the hallway, I bypass the bathroom and find a quiet corner in the lobby.

"I wasn't expecting you yet," Jacob announces when he answers my call.

"I don't see why not," I retort. "Since I you clearly left some information out."

"Like what?"

"Well, it might be helpful to know how much—if anything—you told him about my assignment, since he offered to help me out." I'm annoyed and I don't bother hiding it. "Considering I don't know how much he knows, I'm not quite sure what he's offering to help me out with."

Apparently, I raised my voice, an elderly woman passing through the lobby glances at me suspiciously.

"I haven't told him much. Not because I don't trust him, because I do, but this is your assignment. It's your call how far you want to let him in. I suggest you play it by ear."

Next I hear a click.

Wonderful. He hung up.

Now I'm pissed off.

Is he testing me or something?

Aggravated, I duck into the bathroom to splash some cold water on my face, before returning to the ballroom.

Hamish Adrian is sitting exactly where I left him.

"Okay," I concede, stopping next to him.

He tilts his head back to look at me.

"Okay...what?"

"I'd like to take you up on your offer of help."

He flashes me that lopsided grin before getting to his feet. Even though I'm not a small woman at five foot nine, I notice Hamish Adrian still has a good six inches on me.

"Excellent. We can begin by getting a little closer to the action."

He places a hand in the small of my back and guides me nearer to the stage where the charity auction is about to start.

I KICK MY SHOES OFF THE SECOND THE DOOR TO THE suite clicks shut behind me.

Much better. I rarely wear heels and I've been on my feet most of the night. Hamish was relentless, dragging me along from one group to the next as he worked the room. Networking, he called it.

During the course of the night, I not only made a few tentative contacts, but was able to learn a little more about my enigmatic guide as well. There are some people who seemed familiar with his name, despite his disappearance from the scene five years ago. In talking to some people, I discovered Hamish was seriously injured in a tragic stable fire at a training facility north of Toronto. Whenever someone brought it up, Hamish would swiftly redirect the conversation.

Clearly he's not comfortable discussing what happened and I'm not going to push it. I barely know the man. Besides, I can do a little snooping on my own. I'm sure I'll be able to find information online. I have to do background searches on some of the industry people I met tonight anyway.

However, it'll have to wait until tomorrow, I don't know how long I'll be able to keep my eyes open.

In the bathroom I pull the pins from my hair, which had been twisted in an intricate updo for the occasion. Letting it fall down my back, I briskly massage my scalp with my fingertips, groaning at the release of tension. Next I zip out of my dress and change into a shirt and yoga pants.

Padding barefoot into the sitting room, I flick on a

light near the courtesy bar, and pick up the remote. Maybe a little TV while I wait for the inevitable phone call.

I'm about to lie back on the couch when a knock sounds at my door. Grabbing my phone, I walk up and squint through the peephole into the hallway.

Hamish is standing outside.

"Is something wrong?" I ask, opening the door.

"I forgot to mention something I overheard earlier," he shares as his eyes seem to take in my appearance. "I'm sorry. I gave you my number but never got yours, and I would've sought you out tomorrow morning, but I have to be on a flight at six thirty."

The man looks distinctly uncomfortable, tugging at the knot of his tie.

"It's fine. You didn't wake me up or anything, I'm still waiting for a phone call. What was it you forgot?"

"Apparently there's a private auction near Bowling Green in two weeks. The Gilded Bridle. It's thoroughbreds only, and exclusively by invitation, but I think I might be able to get us in. That is, if you're interested."

Absolutely I'm interested. You never know who I might encounter at an exclusive, private auction.

"I am."

"A winning bid at the Gilded Bridle will go a long way to getting your name out there."

And may open some doors which have stayed firmly shut thus far.

I'm going to need to talk to Jacob, I'm pretty sure my

expense account won't begin to cover even a starting bid in an auction like that.

"So noted," I tell him.

Then I open my contacts to the number he gave me earlier, and shoot off a text. A muffled ping sounds from his suit jacket.

"Now you have my number so you can get in touch."

He nods, the left side of his mouth twitching.

"I'll call you as soon as I have news."

"I appreciate that, and thanks again for tonight. It was very helpful."

He lifts his damaged hand to his head in a mock salute as he backs away from the door.

"Night, Onyx."

It's not until I turn on the TV, looking for a news channel, it occurs to me I never gave Hamish my room number. We said goodbyes in the lobby.

I have a sneaky suspicion where he might've gotten it, though.

Jacob Branch is my boss, and the owner of GEM, an organization dedicated to locating and recovering missing kids. Often these children are, or become, victims of sexual exploitation. Our mandate does not end with the retrieval or rescue of the children, but extends to tracking down the predators responsible, and ensuring they receive the justice they deserve.

I am one of three operatives. All women, each with their own set of skills.

I'm normally responsible for planning, communications, and after-care for victims. For some reason, on this case, I've been forced to the foreground, taking the lead in the field. Not my strength, but my boss is not a fool and I'm sure he has his reasons. He's just not sharing them.

"Jacob," I answer a moment later when my phone rings as if on cue.

"And?"

"Your friend was helpful," I admit reluctantly. "I made a few connections I'll check into when I get back to the office tomorrow."

Even though I'm only an hour or so from home, renting a suite in the hotel where the fundraiser took place fits my cover, but tomorrow morning I'm back to being myself.

For now, anyway.

"Message me the contacts and I can get started with some background research," Jacob offers.

I'm too tired to argue and send him the names.

"Got it."

"Jacob? Who is Hamish to you?"

My question is followed by silence and for a moment I think he's hung up on me again, but he surprises me.

"You could say we're brothers-in-arms." Then he adds, *"Catch up with you tomorrow."*

Before I have a chance to respond the line goes dead.

Figures.

ALSO BY FREYA BARKER

GEM Series

OPAL

PEARL

ONYX

High Mountain Trackers Series:

HIGH MEADOW

HIGH STAKES

HIGH GROUND

HIGH IMPACT

Arrow's Edge MC Series:

EDGE OF REASON

EDGE OF DARKNESS

EDGE OF TOMORROW

EDGE OF FEAR

EDGE OF REALITY

EDGE OF TRUST

PASS Series:

HIT & RUN

LIFE & LIMB

LOCK & LOAD

LOST & FOUND

On Call Series:

BURNING FOR AUTUMN

COVERING OLLIE

TRACKING TAHLULA

ABSOLVING BLUE

REVEALING ANNIE

DISSECTING MEREDITH

WATCHING TRIN

IGNITING VIC

Rock Point Series:

KEEPING 6

CABIN 12

HWY 550

10-CODE

Northern Lights Collection:

A CHANGE OF TIDE

A CHANGE OF VIEW

A CHANGE OF PACE

SnapShot Series:

SHUTTER SPEED

FREEZE FRAME

IDEAL IMAGE

Portland, ME, Series:

FROM DUST

CRUEL WATER

THROUGH FIRE

STILL AIR

LuLLaY (a Christmas novella)

Cedar Tree Series:

SLIM TO NONE

HUNDRED TO ONE

AGAINST ME

CLEAN LINES

UPPER HAND

LIKE ARROWS

HEAD START

Standalones:

WHEN HOPE ENDS

VICTIM OF CIRCUMSTANCE

BONUS KISSES

SECONDS

ABOUT THE AUTHOR

USA Today bestselling author Freya Barker loves writing about ordinary people with extraordinary stories.

Driven to make her books about 'real' people; she creates characters who are perhaps less than perfect, each struggling to find their own slice of happy, but just as deserving of romance, thrills and chills in their lives.

Recipient of the ReadFREE.ly 2019 Best Book We've Read All Year Award for "Covering Ollie, the 2015 RomCon "Reader's Choice" Award for Best First Book, "Slim To None", Finalist for the 2017 Kindle Book Award with "From Dust", and Finalist for the 2020 Kindle Book Award with "When Hope Ends", Freya spins story after story with an endless supply of bruised and dented characters, vying for attention!

www.freyabarker.com

Milton Keynes UK
Ingram Content Group UK Ltd.
UKHW020936030923
427961UK00012B/117